The Girls of Spring Hollow

NEW FAIRY MOON

by David Michael

Published by
Four Crows Landing

This is a work of fiction. All characters appearing in this work are fictitious. Any resemblance to real persons, living or dead, is purely coincidental. Most of the locations are made up too.

Designed by David Michael.

Cover artwork and layout by Don Michael, Jr.

Published by Four Crows Landing.

1.02-2012-05-16

for Serene

PART 1
THE HOLE IN THE FENCE

~ 1 ~

FAYE

MORNING

FAYE WOODS WOKE to a day of firsts. In addition to being the first day of June, this was her first morning after her first night in her new bed, in her first new house–that she remembered–after the two long days of her first move. Her first morning in six years waking in a room all her own. No Flub snoring in his little bed in the corner. Or worse, curled up on her legs because he got lonely in the dark or because he had to go in the middle of the night and her bed was closer than his.

This was also her first morning where she wasn't worried about other Flub surprises like cold, damp sheets. Not that Flub, five years old, had wet his sheets or anyone else's for more than a year, but Faye did not find that reassuring.

Faye pushed thoughts of Flub from her mind as she sat up and stretched.

If not for the smells of dirt and diesel smoke and the sounds of huge engines and jackhammers–because today was also the first day of repaving the street in front of the Woods' new-to-them home of Hawk Briar–the morning could not have been more perfect.

Faye shivered and pulled the sheet back to her chin. She had left open the French doors that led to the balcony over the front porch, so her first morning in her new bedroom was chilly from the still-cool morning air. Before the end of the week, cool mornings in Tulsa, Oklahoma, would be a fond memory. Until then, though, or until Mom caught her leaving the doors open, she would sleep every night with the balcony doors open. Because she had a *balcony*. How could she not leave the doors open? Even if leaving the doors open also let in the sounds and smell of the construction crew, she had a balcony. And she was going to use it.

To go from a small bedroom cramped with two beds, her desk, and a carpet of a color she could no longer remember owing to the layer of Flub's toys that always covered it, to her own room had been heaven enough. To be able–with Dad's help–to claim the upstairs bedroom with the balcony, though, had been the cherry on top of the dollop of whipped cream on top of the icing on the cake. The only way this morning could have been improved was if it were also her birthday. And if the construction crews would leave.

Faye scooted to the edge of her new, full-sized bed. This bed seemed huge after sleeping on a twin bed all her post-crib life. A big bed in a bedroom all her own–and a balcony. Maybe she had gone to sleep and woke a princess. A couple of years ago, that's exactly what she would have thought. Now, though, her new, white student desk, next to her new, white chest of drawers, was covered with pencil drawings of Yosai Nomuri, her manga character. Yosai Nomuri, ninja warrioress, was most emphatically *not* a princess.

Thoughts of Yosai Nomuri, and the cold of the hardwood floor against the soles of her bare feet pushed the last of the old princess fantasy from her mind and made her wish she had a pair of fuzzy, white slippers. She knew just the pair, as she had seen them at Target a few days before, when Mom had held the slippers up and offered to buy them for her, and she had foolishly said, "No, thanks. I don't need slippers."

She pulled her untucked top sheet with her as she walked to the open French doors. She saw herself in the white cheval mirror that stood against the wall. She refused to think that she looked like a princess–a disheveled, sleepy-eyed princess with blonde hair going every which way. Or that the sheet wrapped around her shoulders looked like a princess's shawl, even as it trailed behind her like a train. Her princess phase was long behind her. And most evidence of it had been successfully hidden in the huge attic of Hawk Briar, never to be seen again if Faye had anything to say about it.

The move into Hawk Briar had been accompanied by a total overhaul of her bedroom furniture. New bed, new chest of drawers, new student desk. Only the cheval mirror had been in her room at the old house. Faye suspected that Mom choosing white for all the new furniture was a subtle hint that Mom, at least, still thought Faye needed traditional "girlie" accouterments. One last hurrah of the princess phase. At least none of her new furniture was pink.

Faye pushed open the screen door and stepped out on to the balcony proper. She kept the sheet with her because the balcony faced west and was in the shadow of the roof. The morning sun had not yet seen the balcony where she stood and the air was even cooler out here. She had to pull her train of sheet out of the way of the screen door so it could close. Then she took in a deep breath as she admired the view. Her view.

Hawk Briar faced west across Outer Circle Drive, directly across the street from The Parsonage. All the houses in the Spring Hollow neighborhood had names like Hawk Briar or

The Parsonage or Jack Rabbit Run. At least the older houses did, the ones built around Spring Park and along Inner and Outer Spring Circle Drives. If the houses in the North Tract Addition had names, they were not carved in stone or painted on wood signs like the Circle Drive houses.

South and west of The Parsonage was the Spring Hill Church and South Cemetery. The real-estate agent had told them Spring Hill Church had been a Presbyterian church once, but was now just part of the neighborhood's charm and a registered historic site. The real-estate agent had added that there was only one plot remaining in the South Cemetery, and it was reserved for the woman who lived in The Parsonage, Mrs. Lipscomb.

North and west of The Parsonage was the North Park, another reason Hawk Briar had seemed like the perfect new home when Mom and Dad first brought Faye and Flub to see it. North Park did not have a pond with geese like Spring Park, but with its tall oaks and elms and other trees that Faye had no idea what they were, with its sunny green grass, scattered benches and picnic tables, North Park looked like no other city park Faye had seen. An iron fence that had become thick with a hedge of holly bushes surrounded the park. A wide double gate on the east fence always stood open, pushed against the fence and just as overgrown with the hedge as the rest of the fence. Another, smaller gate on the south side provided access to the cemetery behind the Parsonage. A dry streambed snaked across the western side of the park, with a small bridge made of native stone arched across it. The brightly colored playground equipment in the northeast corner was the only concession to the modern world.

The hill that rose behind The Parsonage and the North Park was covered with even more trees. Those trees created a small forest that masked the truth that the hill was an embankment where two highways crossed. The trees even muffled the sounds of the traffic on those highways.

Faye wrinkled her nose at a fresh whiff of diesel smoke. Too bad the trees couldn't muffle all the construction going on in front of the house.

The balcony Faye stood on was built over Hawk Briar's front porch, with wooden frame railings that matched the Tudoresque style of Hawk Briar's architecture. The floor of the balcony was a marbled white tile. Faye planned to have a set of chairs and a table on the balcony, though Mom had frowned and said nothing when Faye had announced that the night before. Maybe she could borrow the set from the back porch until Mom and Dad caved.

From the balcony Faye could see the street in front of her house. A man on a small tractor was drilling holes in the street with a jackhammer while a crew came behind him and pried up the pieces. A front loader and a dump truck waited to pick up and haul away the chunks of pavement.

The city had been repaving Inner Circle Drive when Faye and her family first visited Hawk Briar. Outer Circle Drive had had a lot of patches and rough spots then, but to Faye's eye those had added to the charm of the neighborhood almost as much as the eclectic mix of house architecture and the tall, old-growth trees. The well-used streets showed that Spring Hollow had history, and was not just another new development with cookie cutter houses and short trees held up with guide wires. If the Woods had not rushed their move, the family would have had to wait at least another two weeks. As it was, Dad had to park on the street a couple blocks away last night so he could use the car today.

The sound of a chainsaw revving overwhelmed the other sounds of machinery and drew Faye's attention to a group of men gathered by the east fence of North Park. One of the men held a chainsaw that belched smoke with each rev. Another held a pair of limb loppers. All three wore leather gloves. The man with the chainsaw revved it again, and Faye saw him start cutting into the thick holly hedge along the park's east fence.

Faye sighed. She had seen that the repaving included new sidewalks along both sides of the street, but she had been hoping that the holly bushes would not be trimmed back. The bushes were thick, extending nearly six feet and taking up almost the entire space between the fence and the curb, but they had been well-maintained. When she saw how far back the bushes were cut, Faye hoped they weren't just taking the bushes out entirely.

"Poop," she said as the two other men wearing thick gloves began pulling back the severed holly branches.

Faye heard the blue jays screeching just before she saw a small flock of the birds burst out of the bushes and fly overhead. The men by the bushes shouted in surprise and jerked back as white spots appeared on their sleeves and shoulders.

The men working on the bushes brushed the bird droppings off their sleeves. Faye couldn't hear what they were saying over the sound of the jackhammer, but she could see that the men working in the street were laughing at them.

"Few! Few!" She heard Flub through the screen door behind her. "Few! Few!"

She deigned to look over her shoulder at her little brother. "Don't call me– Hey! Stop jumping on my bed!"

"It's not like it bounces that good, anyway," Flub said. He landed on his butt, then pushed himself off her bed. He stepped up to the screen door, but didn't open it. "I want to go to the park, Few. Mom says you have to go with me."

"I doubt she said I have to go right now. I just got up. You just got up."

"But I want to go to the park, Few."

"Stop calling me Few. I should never have taught you to read."

"You didn't teach me how to read. Mom did."

"I was there when it happened, Flub. I share the blame."

"Don't call me Flub." He stood straight. "My name is Finn Reilly Woods. Eff arh double-you." He tapped himself on the chest as he recited each letter of his initials. "That doesn't spell Flub. It doesn't spell anything. Mom said so." He narrowed his eyes. "Does Mom know you're on the balcony? Can I come out? I want to watch the trucks."

"No. You can watch from the porch. And get out of my room."

"I'm telling Mom you're on the balcony."

"Go ahead. It's my room. It's my balcony."

"Few!" Flub said again, pointing the fingers of both hands at her as if they were two guns. "Few! Few!" His thumbs moved up and down with each "shot".

"I said, get out of my room." She turned and took a step toward the screen.

Flub shot her once more. "Few!" Then he spun and ran away. Or tried to. His socks slipped on the smooth wood floor and he stumbled. Before she could say anything, though, he righted himself and "skated" out of her room, pushing and sliding with his socked feet.

Faye turned to face the street again. The men with the chainsaw and hedge clippers had already cut a ten-foot stretch of hedge from the northeast corner. Where they had trimmed only a layer of green remained on top of naked, gray, twisted limbs. The hedge would grow back, but it would be at least a year before it looked as pretty as it had.

Someone moved on the porch of The Parsonage across the street, and Faye saw Mrs. Lipscomb there, also watching the men attack the hedge. Faye could not see Mrs. Lipscomb's face clearly, but she could *feel* the resigned frustration and irritation the old woman was directing at the men.

Mrs. Lipscomb turned and looked up at her, and Faye could *see* now, and feel, the intensity behind the woman's gray eyes. Because the intensity was focused on *her*, Faye Ellen Woods, called "Few" by her brat of a little brother. Faye managed a nod and a slight wave with one hand before looking away from the old woman. It took more effort than she expected, as if the old woman was trying to keep her from looking away, but she did it. She could feel Mrs. Lipscomb still staring at her, but Faye refused to look back. She focused on the men pruning the hedges.

A small face peered out of the shadows exposed in the heart of the hedge. A young man's face, or maybe a boy's, but smaller than a face should be.

The sound of a girl's voice, drew Faye's attention. She saw a girl about her age with shoulder length curly, dark hair, wearing a red and black plaid ruffle dress with black boots, and carrying a small cage with an animal in it. The girl came up the street from beyond the construction, walking across the yard of The Parsonage. The girl called out to Mrs. Lipscomb, then joined Mrs. Lipscomb on the porch.

When Faye turned back to the hedge, the little face had disappeared. She tried to find the face again, but there were only gray branches and a few torn bits of what might have been faded ribbon.

Below her, she heard the front door open and close as someone came out onto the porch. She stopped trying to find the face again and walked to the railing. She leaned over and looked down. Flub came into view and walked toward the curb.

"Flub!" she shouted. "Don't get too close to the street."

"Mom already told me," Flub said, stopping much closer to the street than Mom probably had in mind. A few of the men prying up broken slabs of pavement paused to wave at him, then waved at her when they noticed her. Flub waved back. Faye ignored them.

"You should watch from the porch," Faye said.

Flub didn't move.

Faye shook her head. Little brothers could be so irritating.

She had been excited when Mom told her she would be a big sister. Her excitement had dimmed a bit when she found out the new family member would be a brother and not the little sister she had wanted. She *still* wanted a little sister.

At least she no longer had to share a room with Flub. Now ... if she no longer had to share a *house* with Flub ...

A shadow passed over her, chilling the air even more and causing her to shiver again. She tugged the sheet tighter around her as the shadow continued into the yard. When the shadow passed over Flub, it was as if he disappeared. Faye could see only the shadow-grayed grass of the front yard.

She looked up at the sky, expecting to see a cloud or an airplane, but the blue-gold dome above her was clear. No clouds, and no airplanes.

When she looked down at Flub again, he was there, standing too near the edge of the yard as before, as if nothing had happened.

She felt Mrs. Lipscomb looking at her again, so Faye kept her eyes averted as she turned around to go back inside.

The screen door closed behind her as she noticed the pair of white, fuzzy slippers just under her bed. The red and white Target tag still connected the two slippers.

The shivering came back.

She had not put the slippers there. She did not own slippers.

She stood there until she decided that Mom must have bought her the slippers yesterday, at Target, and had sent them up to her room with Flub. Except she was not sure that believing Flub had placed the slippers so neatly in exactly the right spot was any less insane than thinking that the slippers had just appeared there after she had wished she had a pair.

~ 2 ~
BRENNA
MORNING

"READY, NORV?" Brenna asked the sleeping rat, picking up his cage and bringing his pink nose level with hers. Norv's whiskers twitched as he smelled her breath. He opened his ruby eyes for a second, then closed them again. "Wake up, sleepyhead, or you'll miss the walk over." Norv shifted in his bed of cedar shavings, his tiny muscles moving under his dark cream fur, but he did not open his eyes again. "Silly rat," she said, then blew him a kiss anyway.

She set Norv's cage back on her writing desk, then grabbed her black purse, the one with the square silver studs that matched her black boots, and loaded it with her cell phone that she should have put back on its charger last night–two bars of battery might be enough because she wasn't expecting any calls today–her keys to the house, and a packet of Norv's food pellets. Then, with her purse in one hand and Norv's cage in the other, she left her room.

The red plaid ruffles of her black skirt bounced as the soles of her boots clomped on the polished hardwood of the stairs. Mom would have a fit, if she were home. Possibly several fits. Because Mom never liked to get upset at just one thing. It

wasn't efficient. Brenna listed the clomping of the boots–
"You're making too much noise"–the possible scuffing of the
finish on the stair steps–"Those are steps are old growth oak,
irreplaceable"–and, to make it three complaints, because
designers hate even numbers of anything, she added wearing
her new dress–"You're just going to get it dirty. Your boots
too." But Mom wasn't home, so the only sounds were Brenna's
boots clomping on the steps.

The downstairs smelled wonderful from Eloísa's
preparations for dinner. Brenna had just had breakfast, and
lunch was hours away, but the aroma of onions and cumin and
chili powder and seared beef made her mouth water in
anticipation of dinner. Most of the week Mom insisted Eloísa
cook traditional southern food, because that was what Dad
liked, or, more often, some recipe based on bizarre ingredients
that the latest diet fad said burned more fat or contained fewer
carbohydrates, but on Wednesdays Brenna chose dinner. Which
meant, most of the time, she let Eloísa choose.

Whatever Eloísa had chosen, it smelled good to Brenna.
She breathed it in as she walked to the kitchen. Eloísa was using
a pair of tongs and a spatula to lift a large, seared roast out of
the skillet and into the slow cooker.

"Don't you bring El Rata into my kitchen," Eloísa said
without turning around.

Brenna stopped on the threshold of the kitchen, where the
hardwood floor of the dining room met the stone tiles of the
kitchen. "Fine," Brenna said. "But don't be surprised when
Norv gets you nothing for your birthday."

"I want no presents from El Rata." Eloísa placed the roast
into the slow cooker. "I want nothing from him at all." She put
down the tongs and the spatula and wiped her hands on a white
cloth towel that hung from her apron string. She turned to face

Brenna, a mock stern look on her face. "You are taking El Rata with you today? Good. Maybe I will get around to cleaning your room today. Mrs. Guin has been asking me why I have not done that lately."

Brenna bit her lip. "Umm," she said. "You don't have to do that ..."

Eloísa's left eyebrow went up and Brenna stopped talking. Eloísa had worked for the Guins for as long as Brenna could remember, for longer than Brenna had been alive. Eloísa was the maid and the cook. When Brenna had been a toddler, Eloísa had been her nanny. Brenna was as much a mystery to Mom as Mom was to Brenna, but Eloísa knew Brenna.

Eloísa smiled and slanted her head so she was looking at Brenna through her lashes. She said, "You have something you don't want me to find, little girl? Is that it?"

"No," Brenna said. "I mean, yes, but that's not the point. I just ... it just seems like I should ... clean my own room ... ?"

"You have found your diary again, maybe? And written new things?" Eloísa put her right hand over her heart. "You have my solemn oath, Miss Brenna Guin, when I find your diary, I will tell no one what I read in it."

Brenna smiled and laughed. "I did write a new poem."

"It is another of your *peáns* to 'dark Latin eyes'? If so, I may have other rooms to clean today. I already have Telemundo to help me pass the days. And Telemundo does not require that I squint and guess whether you've written another poem, or an unusual grocery list."

Brenna gave Eloísa an exaggerated look of shock. "A grocery list? Are you criticizing my poetry? Or my handwriting?"

Eloísa shrugged, still smiling. "Chocolate, chestnuts, mahogany? These are a boy's eyes? Or a cookie recipe? Maybe a decorating scheme?"

Brenna stuck out her tongue. "No," she said. "This one is about Norv—"

"El Rata? How can you write a poem about a rat?"

"He's cute." Brenna held up Norv's cage so Eloísa could get a better look. "See?" Norv's head came up. He looked at Brenna, then swiveled his neck to look at Eloísa.

Eloísa put her hands up as if shielding herself from Norv's gaze. "He is disgusting."

Norv twitched his whiskers, then turned his back on Eloísa and settled into his cedar shavings.

"You are going to The Parsonage?" Eloísa asked when Brenna lowered Norv's cage. "To see Mrs. Lipscomb?"

Brenna nodded. "Yes. I'll be back for lunch." She blew a kiss at Eloísa because she knew the woman would not let her get close while she carried Norv. Then she turned and clomped-flounced her way out of the house, swinging Norv's cage and her purse.

Brenna was glad Mom was working on location today. Telling Eloísa she was going to visit Mrs. Lipscomb was easy. Eloísa only nodded and asked when she would be getting back. With Mom home, though, nothing was easy. There would have been the complaints about Brenna's clomping and scuffing and wearing her new clothes, then the comments about how Brenna was always over at The Parsonage, helping Mrs. Lipscomb without being paid, and finally the wondering aloud how much longer Mrs. Lipscomb would be able to live in The Parsonage before she died or had to move to a retirement home and The Parsonage could be properly restored as befitted a historic landmark. All of this while Brenna stood there, ready to leave, trying to leave, trying not to hear while also trying to make the appropriate responses so Mom would not get upset at her for not listening and then forbid her to go.

Brenna walked along Inner Circle Drive widdershins. As

the crow flew, Mrs. Lipscomb lived only a block away. As the Brenna carrying the Norv had to walk, however, the distance was closer to three blocks. Her house, Spring Beach, faced due west, but there was no east-west spoke street connecting Inner Circle and Outer Circle, only diagonals. So she had to walk either clockwise north to New Spoke Drive or widdershins south to Sew Spoke Drive. Next week, she would have to take the New Spoke route to avoid the roadwork.

She remembered the three weeks that the work had been going on in front of Spring Beach. For as long as she could remember, Mom and Dad had complained about the state of the streets in Spring Hollow. Then, when the city had arrived to fix the problem for them and the rest of the residents, all she had heard were endless complaints about the noise and the smells and the decrease in lot size caused by the new sidewalks. The complaints had not stopped with the completion of work on Inner Circle Drive, though, as the smooth, new pavement had attracted more joggers and bikers and others who liked to exercise in a circle, not to mention more non-Spring Hollow residents coming to visit Spring Park. Which had prompted Mom to insist that Dad have a new fence built around the backyard. A taller fence, and one that enclosed the old path that led from the street to Spring Park.

Brenna wondered when Mom would start lobbying the housing association to put a gate across the 36th Street bridge that was the only remaining way into Spring Hollow. After all, what else were historic, colorful old neighborhoods for, if not for the wealthy and upwardly mobile to wall off and enjoy all by themselves? Just thinking about it made Brenna shake her head and sigh.

Norv, awake now that they were outside, stood on his hind legs, balancing against the swinging motion of the cage, looking around as they walked. He always enjoyed their walks through the neighborhood–as long as no dogs barked at them; he took that personally–and Mrs. Lipscomb did not mind when Brenna brought him over.

The smooth, new pavements of Inner Circle Drive and Sew Spoke Drive ended abruptly at Outer Circle Drive. Brenna heard and smelled the construction crew before she saw them. She crossed Outer Circle Drive and walked along the gap between the street and the hedge-encased iron fence that enclosed the Spring Hollow Cemetery.

The quiet of the cemetery seemed to dampen the sounds of the roadwork. Brenna went up on tiptoes as she walked to look at the grave markers. Most of the markers were simple marble or granite slabs. A few obelisks and statues were scattered amidst the markers, though, and even fewer mausoleums. The Spring Hollow Cemetery dated from before 1900, before Oklahoma was even a state, when Spring Hollow was still a small town located just a short train ride from the heart of downtown Tulsa. In one corner, some Native Americans graves were marked. The cemetery had been closed when the neighborhood was isolated by the crossing highway construction of the early 1960's. Only one lot remained open, and Mrs. Lipscomb had told Brenna more than once she was putting off using that as long as she could.

That was part of what Brenna liked about Mrs. Lipscomb. The woman accepted death–even her own death–as a natural, inevitable part of life. Mom, on the other hand, had thought it morbid when Brenna once said that she wished she could be buried in the Spring Hollow Cemetery.

Brenna walked across the front lawn of the Spring Hollow Church. Mrs. Lipscomb had told her that except for the occasional wedding, no services had been held in the church in more than thirty years. Even weddings had become less and less frequent as the upkeep on the church flagged, and as the housing association restricted the number of possible events.

The noise of the construction was just as loud here as it had been when in front of Spring Beach. Movement above and behind the workers drew Brenna's eye. She saw a girl about her own age standing on the balcony of Hawk Briar, also looking at the roadwork. The girl had long, straight blond hair and was wrapped in a sheet. The elevated position, the sun in the girl's hair and shining on the sheet made the girl look like a fairy-tale princess surveying her domain. Brenna laughed and shook her head. So the family who had bought Hawk Briar had finally moved in. The big house had been standing empty with a "Sold" sign out front for most of the last month. Mrs. Lipscomb had told Brenna that the family that bought the house had a girl her age. Now that she had seen the girl, though, Brenna no longer wondered if they might be friends. She had no patience for girls stuck in their princess phase.

Mrs. Lipscomb was on the porch of The Parsonage when Brenna arrived. The porch stretched across the entire front of the house. Wide, wooden supports held up the roof over the porch and a weathered wood railing enclosed the porch. Vine-like rose bushes twisted around the slats and banister of the porch railing and went round and round the supports. A large porch swing hung to the left of the front door. Three rattan chairs surrounded a matching round table to the right.

"Good morning," Brenna said as she mounted the wide concrete steps.

Though she usually sat at the table, today Mrs. Lipscomb stood at the north end of the porch. She held a rose stem in her left hand and a pair of hand pruners in her right, but she was not looking at the withered rose bloom. Instead, she was looking along the fence that separated North Park from the street She turned to look over her shoulder at Brenna. "Hello, Brenna," she said. Mrs. Lipscomb smiled, but Brenna saw something dark behind her eyes.

"Are we deadheading the roses today?" Brenna asked as she placed Norv's cage on the table beside an extra pair of pruners. She picked up the pruners and went to stand beside Mrs. Lipscomb. She heard the growl of a chainsaw before she saw the men cutting at the hedges along the fence. "That's horrible," she said as the men started pulling at the old holly bushes. "I thought putting in sidewalks would be a good idea. I never expected they would tear up such beautiful bushes, though."

"The bushes will recover," Mrs. Lipscomb said. As if to emphasize her point, she cut off the dead rose bloom with the hand pruners. The dead bloom fell to the porch among a collection of similarly pruned dead blooms around Mrs. Lipscomb's feet.

Brenna noticed that several men working on the bushes had white spots on their shoulders and their ball caps.

"You missed the show," Mrs. Lipscomb said. "A flock of jays took off and pooped on the men." She gestured at the men working on the hedge with her pruners.

"Gross," Brenna said, then laughed. "That's funny, though."

"Funny, yes," Mrs. Lipscomb said, glancing across the street. The tone of her voice did not sound amused, though, even as she said it again. "Definitely funny."

Brenna followed her gaze and saw that the girl still stood on the balcony of Hawk Briar. The girl was not looking at the roadwork now. She was looking at where the men had started cutting away the hedge. Brenna saw the front door of Hawk Briar open and a little boy burst out. He ran off the porch and into the yard and got close enough to the street that he was difficult to see.

Brenna picked out a rose bloom past its prime and selected a point just above the first set of five leaves on the stem to decapitate it. As the bloom fell, a shadow passed over the sun and a chill touched the back of her neck.

"That, though, was not funny," Mrs. Lipscomd said. "Not funny at all."

"What?" Brenna asked. "What happened?"

Mrs. Lipscomb did not respond. When Brenna looked up at her, Mrs. Lipscomb had her lips pressed together in a thin line. Mrs. Lipscomb did not meet her eye, though. The old woman only picked the next withered bloom and cut it off.

~ ~ ~

"I lived in Hawk Briar when I was a little girl," Mrs. Lipscomb said as she and Brenna continued deadheading the rose bushes. The jackhammer splitting the street made it hard to talk. They had to talk between staccato bursts. Mrs. Lipscomb was still on the porch, in the shade. Brenna stood on a stepladder positioned just in front of the porch so she could reach the spent blooms further up and deeper in. She had on a pair of Mrs. Lipscomb's leather gardening gloves. "We moved away," Mrs. Lipscomb went on, her voice different, "after ..."

Brenna looked up and saw Mrs. Lipscomb staring at a withered bloom, its once magenta petals dried and curled, resembling an old scab more than a flower. Mrs. Lipscomb did that sometimes. She would start one of her stories about Spring Hollow, then fade away.

"After what?" Brenna asked during the next lull of the jackhammer.

"After VJ Day," Mrs. Lipscomb went on, her voice still sounded distant. "That was 1945. Long before the highways were built. They had only just started surveying for the North Tract Addition then." Mrs. Lipscomb shook her head, blinked, and focused on the rose bloom again. "These rose bushes were already here, though. The first pastor's wife, the first to live in The Parsonage, anyway, she planted them. Her name was ... Mrs. Creech, I think. I never met her, of course, but I always thought her roses were the most beautiful I had ever seen. I wanted to watch them bloom every summer of my life. I hated moving away, but with the war over, my father's job was over too. We had to move back to ..." She stopped again. "Listen to me. Rattling on like that hammer out there."

"I like it when *you* rattle on," Brenna said. "You're less deafening."

Mrs. Lipscomb laughed, coughed, then laughed some more. "You say the nicest things. Anyway, when me and Bobbie–Mr. Lipscomb–moved back into the neighborhood in 1976, though, into this house, the bushes had almost been killed by years of overpruning and underwatering. It took Mr. Lipscomb and I nearly ten years to nurse them back to health."

"They look healthy now," Brenna said. She extracted her arm from a treacherous loop of branches. "You fed them before I got here, right? I think this bush here has its mouth open and ready to bite my arm off."

"Don't be silly, dear. They only eat little girls when there are no rats available."

"Hey! No feeding Norv to the rose bush. I thought you liked Norv."

Mrs. Lipscomb somehow looked both innocent and mischievous at the same time. "Only the best for my one-hundred-year-old rose bushes."

Brenna saw the girl and the boy from Hawk Briar walking along the street, coming toward the gate of North Park. "How about little boys?" Brenna said. "Are these rose bushes like the Spring Hag and have a taste for–?" She stopped as Mrs. Lipscomb's expression lost all amusement. She had never seen Mrs. Lipscomb look upset before. "What is it?"

"Don't joke about the Spring Hag," Mrs. Lipscomb said. "You don't know. You weren't– No. I'm sorry." She stopped and took a deep breath. "I'm sorry," she said again. "I didn't mean to snap at you. I'm just a cross old woman at times."

Brenna looked away from Mrs. Lipscomb, and saw the girl and the boy again. They were standing near the far corner of the North Park looking at the bushes or the fence. Whatever they were looking at, from this angle, Brenna could not see it, even when she leaned backward a bit. She had to lean forward again when the stepladder threatened to fall. As she watched, the little boy dropped to all fours and scooted through bush and fence into the park.

"I didn't know there was a hole in the fence," Brenna said.

~ 3 ~

FAYE

LATE MORNING

FLUB RAN AHEAD of Faye as they walked across their front yard, then across the front yard of Four Crows Landing next door. From there they could walk on the new sidewalk in front of Jack Rabbit Run and Broken Quartz to get around the construction. Flub paused to pet the heads of all the concrete rabbit statuary that decorated the landscaping of Jack Rabbit Run, taking long enough that Faye passed him and he had to run to catch up with her.

"Hold Finn's hand when you're crossing the street," Mom had said. "And don't let him get too close to the men tearing up the street."

Mom wanted Flub out from under foot while she unpacked the kitchen. Flub wanted to go the park. So, of course, Faye's first morning in Hawk Briar was taken away from her and given to Flub.

Faye did not mind. Too much. She wanted to see more of Spring Hollow.

Spring Hollow's houses had more variety than the single-story, white frame houses of their old neighborhood, which all looked almost identical. The houses of Spring

Hollow, by comparison, were quirky and looked as if they had been built to suit both the neighborhood and their particular lot.

None of the houses they walked past looked like Hawk Briar, or like any of the other houses of Outer Circle Drive. Four Crows Landing was a single-story ranch of native stone with charcoal trim. Jack Rabbit Run was a gingerbread house built of red brick. And Broken Quartz had the straight lines and hard angles of what people used to think houses of the future would look like. Faye loved all the houses.

As they walked, Outer Circle Drive went from being broken, to stripped, to freshly paved and stinking of new tar and boiled oil. When they were past the construction, they crossed to the west side of the street.

Faye wondered if it was still the west side of the street, because it had curved around some as they walked. It wasn't quite the northwest side yet. West by northwest, maybe.

The new sidewalk on this side of Outer Circle Drive ended and they had to walk across the yard of Mended Bow to get around a Bobcat digger excavating for the next section of sidewalk.

The men with the chainsaw and hedge trimmers had finished cutting back the hedge along the North Park fence. The hedge was now a scrawny, ugly shadow of what it had been before. There was no sign of the men now, and the severed limbs of the hedge were piled near the broken curb. Faye hoped that they were not planning to trim the hedges along the rest of the fence around North Park.

"Why did they make the gate so far away?" Flub asked.

Faye did not answer, just like she had not answered his questions about the statuary rabbits—"Wouldn't it be cool if they were real rabbits?"—the odd shape of Broken Quartz—"Why does that house look like a fire station?"–or any of the other questions he had asked one after the other as they walked.

The two of them picked their way between the severed trunks and roots of hedge and the piled branches toward the gate. Flub skipped ahead of her again, calling and waving to the men prizing up the broken pavement. Embarassed, Faye looked down and saw a short, straight branch, about a foot long with three sprigs of leaves sprouting from the narrow end. Faye stopped and bent over to pick up the branch. In her right hand, the branch looked like a wand of holly leaves. Or a conductor's baton. If a conductor's baton had sprouted three holly leaves.

Faye straightened and flicked the branch in a clockwise circle, then forward. Like a conductor before an orchestra, and not at all like a fairy princess granting a wish.

"Few!" Flub shouted. "A hole!"

"What?" Faye asked, looking for him. She saw Flub's shoes disappear through a gap in the hedge. "Flub! Don't–"

She decided to keep the branch as a souvenir of her first day in Spring Hollow, then stepped over to where Flub had disappeared.

"Wow!" Flub's voice came through the shadows of the hedge. A few seconds later, he added, "My name is Finn."

Standing four foot ten inches, Faye was a head taller than the hedge. She went up on tiptoes to see who Flub was talking to, but saw no one. She squatted and saw that four of the iron bars along the bottom of the fence had been bent outward, toward her, as if a small car had run into the fence from the other side. The bars had been bent enough that a large dog–or a little brother–could get through. Torn and faded strands of ribbon hung from the bars and from the thicker branches of the holly bush that had grown around the bars.

Faye thought she heard another voice, not Flub's. Then

Flub said, "Tag! You can't catch me!" She saw Flub run past the hole on the other side of the fence.

Faye eyed the bent bars and the hole they created. If a brat of a little brother could fit through, then maybe the brat's big sister could too. If she had no dignity.

This brat's big sister had dignity, and to spare. Faye stood. She peered over the hedge again, through the bars of the fence, looking for Flub. She still could not see him. Nor anyone else, she realized. From what she could see, the park was empty.

She heard Flub squeal a happy noise, then laugh. He was running around in the park. He was not trying to hide from her. Why couldn't she see him?

"Flub?" she called out. "Where are you?"

"I'm over here, silly Few."

"I can't see you, Flub. Where are you?"

Flub's head appeared out of the hole in the fence. "I'm right here. Come on. This park is even better than the other one." His head pulled back again and vanished.

Faye heard another voice, but could not make out the words. Flub's head appeared again. "Edward says you have to come through the hole in the fence."

"Who is Edward?" Faye asked, but Flub was gone before she had finished the question.

Faye looked over the hedge again and still saw nothing. She looked around. The open gate to the park was still at least a hundred feet away. More important, none of the men working on the street seemed to be paying her any attention, and there did not seem to be anyone else walking along the street.

Faye went down to her hands and knees and eyed the bent bars. She hoped they were pushed wide enough so she would not get scratched. The fit looked a bit snug. She noticed she still held the holly branch in her right hand. The white shorts she wore did not have pockets the branch would fit, so there was no other way to carry it. She looked at the bent bars again and wondered why she had been worried. And why she had not seen the hole before. The hole was more than wide enough for her to fit. She crawled through the hole in the fence into North Park.

Except this was not North Park.

She pushed back and until she was sitting on her feet. She looked around. The well-kept grass blew in the morning breeze as she expected, but the grass was longer than it should have been. The trees looked older, and their leaves were a deeper green. The breeze pushed the trees the same, like it did the grass, but with more respect. Where the playground equipment should have been, with its bright-colored slide and monkeybars and layer of wood chips, was a pile of weathered sandstone boulders. Finally, where there were benches in North Park, here were crude standing stones.

Two upright stones, carved from the same sandstone as the boulders, separated by just enough space that a person could walk between them were topped by a third stone of the same type. The standing stones were of various sizes, ranging from shorter than Faye up to maybe three times her height.

The iron fence still surrounded the park, but these untended holly bushes had grown to almost cover the fence. Beyond the fence to the west and north was not just a few trees planted by the city to cover the highway embankment. There was a forest. A *real* forest.

The only things that seemed the same were the gate on the south fence that led to the cemetery, and the small stone bridge. Even those, though, were different. Because the shadows beyond the cemetery gate defied the morning sun, and because the streambed in this park was not dry. Faye could hear the water rolling and bubbling over sand and small rocks.

She heard Flub laughing and saw him running through one of the standing stones, chasing another child. Something about the child, about this park that was North Park but was not North Park at all, *something* made the hairs on her arm stand up and made her want to crawl back through the hole in the fence and run back to Hawk Briar where Mom was organizing the new kitchen and Dad was upstairs catching up on his work email.

"Flub," she said. He did not seem to hear her. "Finn," she said, louder this time. "Finn, come here."

"Ah, Few," Flub said, but he stopped running and walked to her. "Mom said I could play in the park."

"I don't think this was the park she had in mind."

"This park is better, Few. Why do you have a wand?"

"What?" Faye looked at the holly branch in her hand. "It's not a wand. Who were you playing with–?"

"You should introduce me to this lovely young lady," said the boy who appeared beside Flub.

Faye pulled back, startled. She had not seen the boy approach, and he seemed too small to be speaking the way he spoke. Though he did not stand as tall as Flub's chest, he did not look like a child. He looked like a little man. A man shrunk to a height of less than two feet. He had dark-brown hair and skin only a few shades lighter. He wore no shirt and a pair of crude shorts that looked as if they had been fashioned from small animal skins. He wore moccasins of similar construction on his feet. Her eyes came back to his face, and she realized his was the face she had seen in the hedge.

"Edward, this is my sister, Few," Flub said.

"Lovely Few," said the little man, "I am Edward Pennyfeather, and I am pleased to make your acquaintance." He bowed deep, his right hand on his chest, his left hand moving with a flourish.

"My name's not Few," Faye said as the little man straightened.

"Then I beg your forgiveness, Miss Not Few," the little man said, bowing again just as deeply, "and I humbly request the honor of your true name, spoken by your own lovely lips." Still bowed, he cocked his head to one side and looked up at her, his eyes twinkling.

"Faye," she said, feeling her face grow warm from Edward's gaze. "Nice to meet you. Edward."

Edward straightened again, smiling. "The pleasure is all mine, I assure you, Miss Faye. And may I be the first to welcome you to North Park Other." With that, he turned and threw out both his arms, as if offering the whole park to her. "Frollic, cavort, gambol, to your heart's content." He spun back around, and the air sparkled around him. "And, please, feel free to visit as often as you like. It has been so long since we have had any visitors here in Spring Hollow Other." Edward stopped talking and seemed to be looking past Faye's shoulder, at the fence behind her. "And may I also say," he said, his eyes tensing but with his tone still bright and friendly, "what a fine pair of wings you have."

Faye twisted her neck to see behind her, but saw only the iron bars of the fence and the branches of holy twisting around them. "What?"

"Few's got wings!" Flub said. "Wings wings wings. Few's got wings!"

"What are you talking about?" Faye asked.

"Now, now, Finn Reilly Woods," Edward said, pronouncing Flub's name exactly the way Flub did, with just hint of a "wuh" as the first sound of "Reilly", "we will have no more of that. You and I were playing tag, yes? And you were, I believe, 'it'."

"Wings?" Faye asked.

"Tag!" Flub said, reaching out with his right hand.

Edward dodged, throwing himself backward, away from Flub. "You missed me, Finn Reilly Woods." The little man seemed to hover in the air for an instant, then he spun on the toe of his right foot and bounded away. "You must catch me!"

Faye watched the two of them run off, trying to fit both North Park Other, reached through a hole in the fence, to North Park, and a little man who called himself Edward Pennyfeather, into what she had learned of the world in eleven years. Neither North Park Other nor Edward Pennyfeather fit. Yet here she was and there Edward Pennyweather was and so what she had learned of the world in eleven years no longer seemed like quite so much.

She stood and turned around and looked over the hedge out at what should be Spring Hollow, the neighborhood where she lived, to see what Hawk Briar looked like from this side of the fence. The Other side. Except the holly hedge on this side had grown up to the full height of the iron fence. She was not tall enough.

Her eyes followed the iron bars and the holly branches that twisted around them up to the ornate points at the top.

The largest hawk she had ever seen—its body was as large as Edward—perched on the point of one of the bars, just above her head. The hawk had its back to her. Two white stripes marked the gray tail feathers of the hawk, and a touch of red down peeked through the mottled gray and white near the shoulder.

Faye caught her breath. She had never been so close to a wild bird before.

As if heard her intake of breath, the hawk's head rotated into profile, and one black eye looked at her. She expected the hawk to fly away immediately, but it remained, looking at her looking at it.

The hawk's head shifted again, and it no longer looked at Faye. The hawk had been relaxed before, waiting. Faye was not sure how she knew that, but as she watched, she felt the bird tense, sensing something. Then the hawk spread its wings and leaped. The bird glided out of sight beyond the fence.

The hawk gone, Faye looked at the fence again. With sharp holly leaves poking through, the fence looked unclimbable. Faye looked down the fence to her right, where the open gate would be into North Park. On this side, in North Park Other, the wide gates were closed, with a rusty chain and padlock securing them. Also, the holly bushes had grown to cover the gates as well. The only ways out of North Park Other seemed to be the gate to the cemetery and the hole in the fence she and Flub had come through.

Flub and Edward were still playing tag. Edward was "It" now, chasing Flub toward the gate to the cemetery. Faye had no doubt Edward could tag Flub whenever the little man wished, but Edward feigned missing and stumbling and running out of breath, laughing the whole time, in much the same way Dad used to play with both them in the backyard of their old house. Dad, though, had never seemed to be about to take off flying at any instant, and blades of grass bent under his steps. Edward danced and glided, almost leaping from one blade of grass to another as he moved.

Faye started to call out to Flub, to tell him to come back over to her. Not to get too far from the hole in the fence that seemed to be the only way back. But she took only a few steps into the park, then stopped. She said nothing.

Everything felt like a dream. Coming through a hole in the fence to find a very different park with a little man named

Edward Pennyfeather. Seeing a red-shouldered hawk big enough to carry off small dogs that had not been frightened by her or all the noise Flub had been making. How could it not be a dream?

"Um," said a girl's voice behind her. "You need to leave."

Faye turned around to see a girl her age standing after coming through the hole in the fence. The girl was squinting against the sunlight. Faye recognized the girl from earlier, when she had seen the girl going to The Parsonage. The pale skin of the girl's bare knees and her calf-high black boots both showed scuffs and dirt from crawling through the hole in the fence. The girl wiped her hands together, then shielded her eyes with her left hand to look at Faye, as if the sun were in her face.

"My name is Brenna," the girl said. Her green eyes shone in the shadow under her hand and seemed friendly, but her expression was worried. "Brenna Guin, and I'd love to meet you, but Mrs. Lipscomb says you need to leave the park."

"We just got here," Faye said.

"It's not safe," Brenna said. She looked as if she was about to say more, but she stopped and looked around. Her eyes grew wide. "Wow."

"What's not safe?" Faye asked.

Brenna's focus returned to Faye. "I don't know. I told Mrs. Lipscomb I saw you and your brother crawl through the ... the hole, and she got very upset. She sent me to tell you to leave. That the park isn't safe there ... here ... on the other side. You need to leave."

"You don't own the park, Brenna," said another girl's voice, behind Brenna.

Brenna jumped, startled, and stepped away from the hole in the fence. Faye and Brenna watched another girl, about the same age as both of them, crawl through the hole. This new girl had honey-colored skin and brown hair nearly as dark as Brenna's black, but wavy instead of curly, and her eyes were a rich chocolate color. As the girl stood, Faye saw the girl wore a teal tank top with a peace sign printed on it in tie-dye colors and blue denim Bermuda shorts. She had leather sandals on her feet.

The girl wiped her hands on her shorts as she said, "Just because you think you can make Spring Park private–and you can't, you know–doesn't mean you can tell people what parks they can play in." The girl was at least a head shorter than Brenna, but she positioned herself as if she would fight Brenna.

"This has nothing to do with Spring Park or my Dad's stupid fence," Brenna said.

The new girl was not listening, though, and the belligerence drained out of her posture. Like Brenna had before her, the new girl was looking around with her eyes wide and her mouth open. "What in the world ... ?"

"This isn't North Park," Brenna said, looking from Faye to the new girl as she spoke. "Mrs. Lipscomb says it's not safe and we shouldn't come here. We need to go."

Just as she had felt the tension come to the hawk before, Faye felt the new girl tense. The girl's nostrils flared as she breathed in with her nose. Then her eyes narrowed and her lips pulled back from her teeth.

Before Faye could ask the girl what was upsetting her, the girl shouted, "No! Get back!" Her voice was rough, guttural. Not at all like a girl. More like a growl and a bark. Then the girl was past Faye, running into the park before Faye had realized she was about to move.

Faye turned and watched the girl running straight to where Flub and Edward were playing by the gate to the cemetery.

"What are you doing?" Faye shouted. She dropped the holly branch and ran after the girl.

The gate to the cemetery was open now. Faye could see nothing of the graveyard beyond the gate, though, because a shadow filled the open space. More than a shadow. Something moved there but she could not see it. She could only make out the movement. She could feel the menace of the shadow, though, even from this far away. Flub was still there, near the gate, but she could not see Edward.

"Finn!" she shouted. "Finn!" She tried to run faster.

The new girl ran faster than Faye, her legs taking strides that seemed too long for a girl that size.

Faye watched as she ran, trying to figure out what the girl could possibly be trying to do. Flub turned around and saw Faye, then saw the girl running at him. His face went pale.

"Stay away from him!" Faye shouted. To her surprise, she heard the girl shouting the same thing.

The blackness of the open gate somehow moved into the park. It was not just a shadow now, but what it was Faye still could not see. She felt rather than saw the blackness reaching for Flub.

The new girl was still at least ten feet from Flub when she leaped, her arms stretching forward.

The girl's leap arched down, but she did not fall. Instead, her hands slapped the ground and pushed her body back up. Then her legs were under her and pushing and she leaped *over* Flub and came down on her feet between Flub and the darkness of the open gate. The girl had her feet wide and her hands out to each side. The darkness pulled back from the girl, into the gate. The gate swung with a squeal of long neglected iron hinges, then clanged shut.

Faye reached Flub and scooped him up into her arms. He was crying. He wrapped his arms around her neck. She felt the tears on his cheek when he put his face against her neck.

The girl still stood there, fingers curled into claws and she was breathing hard. A sound like growling came out of her throat.

"What do you think you're doing?" Faye asked, not even trying not to shout.

The girl's head turned and she looked at Faye from the corner of her eye. The center of her eyes looked more yellow now than brown. Her teeth were bared, making her canines more prominent. "Didn't you see that ... that ... thing?" the girl asked, her voice hoarse.

"You scared my brother half to death." Faye looked past the girl at the gate. The deep shadows she had seen before obscured her view of the cemetery, but these shadows held no menace. At least, no immediate menace.

"I was just ... trying to help ..." The girl stopped and turned around to face Faye. She was still panting from her run and that inexplicable leap, but her eyes had returned to their chocolate color and she was no longer baring her teeth. Her expression lost its fierceness and became quizzical. She looked at something just over Faye's right shoulder. "Why do you have wings?"

~ 4 ~
LUPE
LATE MORNING

LUPE WALKED ALONG the quiet neighborhood streets enjoying the cool of morning on her way to the North Park. The pleasant mornings would end soon, she knew. This time next week the morning temperatures could be over eighty-five degrees, and the afternoons would be unbearable. She did not want to miss any pleasant Tulsa summer days. Not that it was really summer yet. There were still three weeks to go before the first day of summer. Summer *vacation*, though, was three days under way. Five, if Lupe counted the two days of the weekend that had immediately followed the last day of school–which she did not. Weekends were available all year. Summer vacation, though, was a limited quantity, not to be wasted sitting around watching reruns on Cartoon Network. Or cleaning her room, as Grannie Litta had suggested.

Lupe had thought about going to Spring Park and feeding the ducks, and had brought a plastic bag of bread heels. As she walked, though, she had remembered–again, and it had peeved her just as much as it always did–that the Guin's, who lived in the house called Spring Beach, had finished their new fence and blocked the most convenient path to the park. She would have to walk all the way to the south side of Inner Circle Drive to get to the closest open path through the Pond Houses to Spring Park at the center.

From what Lupe understood, there used to be no fences around the yards of the Pond Houses, and there had been paths between the Pond Houses to the public park within. Now, though, there were only a couple paths left from Inner Circle Drive to Spring Park. The rich families of the Pond Houses had started fencing in their backyards, running their fence lines down the middle the old paths, effectively blocking the paths. As if they were trying to claim Spring Park, a public park, all for themselves. Lupe noticed she was grinding her teeth and made herself stop.

She would probably end up at Spring Park, anyway. Spring Pond might have been slowly getting overgrown with plant life and developing a film of algae around the edges, but there was a sense of the pond, something she felt when she was there. Something she liked. Plus, it was not as if she expected much to do at North Park. As a child, she had enjoyed the playground equipment there, and the old stone bridge over its dry streambed, and even the cemetery with its decaying headstones, but she was eleven now. These days, going to either Spring Park or North Park was more about enjoying the walk.

"Hey!" a voice said.

Lupe looked over and noticed Mr. Brenner's black lab, Jackson, standing on his back legs, his front legs against the chain-link fence so he could see over. She looked around for Mr. Brenner, but did not see him.

When he saw her looking at him, Jackson barked again, and she realized that no one had said *hey* to her. Jackson had just barked at her, trying to get her attention, as he always did when she walked by. Jackson bobbed his head, as if nodding in agreement with her, then barked again.

"Hey, boy," she said. She walked across Mr. Brenner's front lawn so she could give Jackson a scratch between the ears.

Jackson rested his neck on the top of the fence and stretched forward to meet Lupe's right hand. When she touched his forehead, her fingers brushing his fur and eyebrow whiskers, a tingle went up her arm as if she had bumped her funnybone. Her fingertips went numb, even the fingers on her left hand which had not touched Jackson, and her nose.

She pulled her hands back and flexed her fingers. She rubbed at her nose. Her nose felt like her cheek did after a dentist visit. The effect wore off almost immediately, though.

"That was weird," she told Jackson.

Jackson only looked at her, waiting for his promised ear scratching.

"Alright, boy, here you go." She gave him some vigorous, two-handed puppy-dog-ear-scratching. Jackson licked her face when she was finished, right on the nose. "Okay, boy, okay." She ruffled the fur on his neck, then continued on her way.

77th East Avenue reached Outer Circle Drive and its freshly repaved smoothness and new sidewalks. Not for the first time, Lupe wondered if the city would repave the North Tract Addition of the neighborhood. Or if the city would, as she suspected, finish Outer Circle Drive then find some other rich neighborhood to improve. She liked the old-style concrete streets of the North Tract Addition, cracks and all. She even liked walking on the streets. It was not like there was ever enough traffic anywhere in Spring Hollow to demand sidewalks throughout. What little front yard her house had would be almost cut in half when the work crews ripped up the street and added sidewalks. That is, if the work crews even showed up.

She turned right, walking west along Outer Circle Drive, then around the curve to the south. As she walked around a Bobcat digging a shallow trench in front of the house called Mended Bow, Lupe saw Brenna My-Dad-Makes-Sooo-Much-Money-He-Can-Build-What-He-Wants-Where-He-Wants Guin running from the porch of The Parsonage, where Mrs. Lipscomb lived, and along the torn up stretch in front of North Park, where the holly bushes had been yesterday.

Lupe used to stop in and visit Mrs. Lipscomb. She liked Mrs. Lipscomb and her stories about how the neighborhood used to be. Then Brenna had gone into a vintage-Goth-Hot-Topic-slumming phase and started visiting Mrs. Lipscomb, as well. Lupe hoped Brenna would grow out of that phase, the way the girl had grown out of playing with Lupe and the other "less fortunate" kids of the neighborhood long ago. Then Lupeta could see Mrs. Lipscomb again without worrying if she would come face to face with Miss My-Mom-Lets-Me-Buy-Whatever-Clothes-I-Want.

She saw Brenna stop, look at a section of the pruned hedge. Then, despite having on a dress with a ruffled skirt, the girl dropped to all fours and crawled into the hedge.

Lupe stopped walking to more properly stare at the heavy black boots as they disappeared. She started walking again after a few seconds, deciding that there was no telling with some people.

She reached where Brenna had crawled through and saw that the bars of the iron fence had been bent. With the severe pruning of the hedge, a new way into North Park had been opened. She recalled seeing the bent bars from the other side, within the park, but all her life the holly bushes had been more than enough of a barrier. She had never seen the holly bushes cut as far back as they were now. She hoped the new sidewalk proved worth the damage.

"–says you need to leave the park." Brenna's voice, from the other side of the hedge and the fence. Her voice sounded odd, though. Lupe did not hear Brenna from over the hedge, only from under it, through the hole in the fence.

"We just got here," said another girl's voice, a voice Lupe did not recognize.

Lupe heard a little boy–no, two little boys, she could hear the difference in their voices–playing in the park. Again, though, she could hear them only through the hole in the fence.

"It's not safe," Brenna said. After a short pause she added, "Wow."

First the attempts to wall off Spring Park, now this. Did Brenna think she owned the whole neighborhood? Just because her dad owned three car dealerships?

Lupe looked at the hole Brenna had crawled through. It was closer than the gate, and Lupe wanted to get into this argument *now*. She dropped to her hands and knees and went through the hole in the fence.

She saw Brenna's steel-studded black boots, with Brenna's thin, pale legs coming out of them, squared off against a pair of pink plaid canvas sneakers with well-tanned ankles before she saw the two girls. The other girl wore white shorts and a white tank top with horizontal yellow stripes. Her long, straight hair was light brown with streaks of blonde from the sun. She seemed the fashion opposite of Brenna, and much more appropriately dressed for a summer day in the park.

"What's not safe?" the other girl asked.

"I don't know," Brenna said. "Mrs. Lipscomb saw you and your brother crawl through the ... the hole, and she got very upset. She sent me to tell you to leave. That the park isn't safe there ... here ... on the other side. You need to leave."

"You don't own the park, Brenna," Lupe said as she came through the hole. She had the satisfaction of seeing Brenna jump almost out of her big, black boots.

Lupe stood and wiped her hands on her shorts. She looked Brenna in the eye, which was harder now than it used to be, before Brenna got taller, and said, "Just because you think you can make Spring Park private–and you can't, you know–doesn't mean you can tell people what parks they can play in."

Brenna's green eyes flashed right back at her. "This has nothing to do with Spring Park or my Dad's stupid fence," Brenna said.

As Brenna spoke, Lupe noticed the sounds of the construction on Outer Circle Drive had faded. She could still hear the jackhammer and the men's voices as they shouted to be heard, but now they sounded as if they were a couple blocks away, not on the other side of a fence. Silence lay heavy over the park, broken only by the voices of the girls and the two boys playing. The sound of the breeze as it touched the leaves of the tree and the blades of grass and even as it wound its way through the branches of the holly bushes behind her was as clear to her as the sound of the stream that wound through the park.

The smells of the construction had also faded into the background, overcome by the scents of growing grass, fresh dandelion blooms, and the smell of a stream and the wet sand and rocks on its bank that she could not even see.

The sunlight in the park, though, seemed dimmer than it had been, as if someone had put a gray filter over the sun.

And North Park itself was different. No–

This was not North Park. There was no playground equipment. The trees were different. North Park had no stream or standing stones.

"What in the world ... ?" Lupe said. Stream? Standing stones?

"This isn't North Park," Brenna said, stating the obvious. "Mrs. Lipscomb says it's not safe and we shouldn't come here. We need to go."

Lupe heard the sound of rusted metal rubbing on rusted metal just before the scent of something wet and cold–something vaguely feminine and completely *evil*–made the hairs on her arms and the back of her neck stand up. Her eyes followed her ears and her nose past the two girls, across this park that was not North Park, to the narrow south gate where only one little boy played now, spinning with his arms outstretched and his smiling face pointed up at the sky, his eyes squeezed closed.

Lupe heard-saw the boy's feet stepping on the grass and the gate opening behind him and she smelled-saw the boy's sweat and the shadow leaking from the gate behind him. She could smell oatmeal sweetened with brown sugar on the boy's breath and even hear his breathing, but she could not make out any features of the shadow except an impression of long fingers and sharp teeth. She knew, though, deep in her guts, the shadow was *wrong*.

The shadow shifted and she knew in that same deep place that the shadow was about to envelop the little boy.

"No!" Lupe shouted. "Get *back!*" She did not wait to see if the shadow heard her. She threw herself forward, past Brenna and the other girl. She wished she had worn her gym shoes instead of her sandals, because she was not sure she could get there fast enough to stop–whatever it was–whatever it was doing– She stopped thinking and focused on running.

She heard one of the girls behind her shouting. "What are you doing?"

Lupe had no time to answer. She leaned into her stride, pushing forward, a part of her mind wishing that Coach Tyson could see her now. She did not think she had ever run so fast in all her life. The south fence of the park that was not North Park, the little boy, the gate, and the shadow, all of them seem to rush at her as if she were standing still and the Earth was moving below her.

She heard more shouting. In front of her, the shadow paused and Lupe knew that it saw her. She could not see the eyes of the shadow but she could feel them see her. Old eyes, dark eyes, eyes that looked hate at Lupe and tried to stop her with a weight of malice.

Lupe suddenly felt alone. She had no idea what she was charging at, only that it was evil and it wanted to snatch a little boy out of this park that was not North Park. It was the little boy–for some reason she thought of him as a cub–that made her keep going. She had never felt more protective of anyone in her life. She would do what she had to do.

The boy was between her and the shadow. He had not seen the shadow, but he had seen Lupe running at him. She watched him stop spinning with his back to the shadow, and watched the smile disappear from his face to be replaced with growing fear. She saw he was about to step backward, away from her, toward the shadow that waited for him.

"Stay away from him!" she shouted, her voice getting louder, hoarser with each word.

She leaped forward. Before she knew what she was doing, or how she was doing it, she had hit the ground in front of the boy, rolled forward, then leaped again, this time over the boy's head. She flipped over in the air and came down in a crouch between the boy and the shadow. She felt her teeth bare and heard a low growl coming out of her throat. She tensed, ready to leap at the shadow.

The shadow did not move so much as recede, like a time-lapse film sequence, and disappear back through the gate. The gate slammed closed with a sharp ringing of iron on iron. The dark, damp, rotting smells of the shadow faded to a mere trace, a taint, just as suddenly as they had first appeared.

Lupe stumbled as the tension in her limbs fell away. Her chest heaved as she tried to catch her breath.

She turned to see the girl pick up the little boy, who was crying now. The little boy wrapped his arms around the girl's neck and squeezed tight enough that Lupe was surprised the girl could still talk.

"What did you think you were doing?" the girl asked, her eyes shouting her at Lupe even louder than her voice.

Struggling to get enough air to speak, Lupe said, "Didn't you ... see that ... that ... thing?" She gestured toward the now-closed south gate.

"You scared my brother half to death."

Lupe only looked at the girl. Why was the girl yelling at *her*? "I was just ... trying to help."

The girl shifted the little boy to her left side and sunlight flashed in Lupe's eyes, making her blink. When she opened her eyes again, she saw a pair of large, double wings, like the wings of a dragonfly, on the girl's back. Lupe blinked again, but the wings remained. "Why do you have wings?" she asked.

"What kind of stupid question is that?" The girl did try to glance over one shoulder, though. When the girl had turned enough to see the wings for herself, they disappeared with another flash of reflected sunlight.

"Weren't there ... two boys?" Lupe asked. She spotted movement behind the girl. "Oh, there he is."

The girl spun around. "Edward! Thank god. Are you okay?"

Lupe stared at the second "boy". He was not a boy at all. More like a little man in a pair of buckskin shorts. She heard the little man say something unintelligible. His voice sounded like someone shaking a child's tambourine, all jangling and tinkling. She noticed that he smelled much the same, a sort of tinny smell that made her nose tingle, like the smell of Steven's slot cars when they had been running for a while.

"Who is–" Lupe started, then stopped. Edward, the little man, was gone, his scent already fading. The other girl was walking away, still carrying the little boy. At least the boy did not seem to be crying any more.

Back at the fence, standing by the hole they had come through, Brenna said, "We need to *go*." Lupe looked at Brenna, and she could smell the girl's bath soap and shampoo–and her fear. "It's not safe."

~ 5 ~

BRENNA

LATE MORNING

"WHY DO YOU say that?" Mrs. Lipscomb asked. She no longer sounded angry or apologetic. She sounded ... worried? Scared? Brenna looked at her. Mrs. Lipscomb's face was pale.

"That little boy," Brenna said. "He just crawled through the fence. I guess there's a hole there." She pointed up the street where the girl still stood. The girl was on tiptoe, looking over the fence. Brenna noticed the girl held a short holly branch in one hand. Brenna shook her head. That girl had the fairy princess phase going strong, even if she no longer had on a sheet for a shawl and was wearing a more normal-looking, nonpink shorts and tank top ensemble.

Mrs. Lipscomb moved to the north end of the porch again.

"He was with the girl," Brenna said. "I think they're the new kids from Hawk Briar. And I guess she's going through the hole too," she added when the girl went down on hands and knees. The girl crawled forward through the unseen hole, as well.

Mrs. Lipscomb stepped back as if someone had pushed her. She dropped her pruning shears and felt behind her with both hands to grab one of the porch chairs to hold herself up. In his cage on the table, Norv stood against the bars.

47

Brenna jumped down from the stepladder. She rushed up the steps to the porch. Mrs. Lipscomb had steadied herself by the time she got there, but Brenna still put a hand on the old woman's arm. "Are you okay?"

"The dark of the Moon," Mrs. Lipscomb said, her voice a whisper that Brenna could only just hear. She turned to face Brenna. "Tonight is the new Moon. "

Brenna nodded as she placed her pruning shears on the table. She had a lunar calendar poster adorned with werewolves and vampires over her bed because she had decided to keep up with that this year. "At least it's not the full Moon," she said with a weak smile.

"Tonight is the new Moon," Mrs. Lipscomb said. "And the way is open."

Brenna just looked at her. "You're scaring me–"

"You should be scared. The way is open and tonight is the new Moon." Mrs. Lipscomb stood and faced Brenna. She put her wrinkled hands on Brenna's shoulders. "You need to tell them to get out of the park," Mrs. Lipscomb said. "The boy and the girl. It's not safe. They need to leave the park. Now."

"North Park? North Park is one of the safest parks in the city."

"Not today. Not tonight. Go, Brenna. Go."

"Are you okay?"

"I am fine, Brenna. But the girl and the boy. You must tell them to leave the park. Go." Mrs. Lipscomb let go of Brenna's shoulders. "Go! Run!"

Brenna backed away, then turned around. She saw Norv standing on his hind legs again. He looked as if he was looking out at the park, as well. He turned to look at her and squeaked, as if he too were telling her to run.

She dropped the gardening gloves on the table next to

Norv, then went down the porch steps. She ran to the big, iron gate of North Park that was always open and pulled up short. She could not see either the boy or the girl. The park was empty.

"You must go through the hole," Mrs. Lipscomb said behind her. "They are on the other side. Hurry, Brenna."

"The other side of what?" Brenna looked back at Mrs. Lipscomb. The woman did not seem crazy, just scared. Very, very scared.

Brenna backed out of the gate then ran along the outside of the fence, picking her way through the piles of holly branches and the twisted stumps left by the work crew. She wondered what the men working were thinking of the crazy girl running along the fence.

She scanned the hedge as she went. The twisted gray and brown limbs looked like earthworms frozen in place when their protecting rock was pried away. Where the girl and the boy had crawled through was obvious. The iron bars had been bent out along the bottom, as if a small car had run into the fence. Though *why* a small car would be in North Park was beyond Brenna. The branches of the holly bush had wrapped themselves around the bent bars, but not across the gap opened between the bars, leaving a space she could fit through, as long as she was willing to crawl through on her hands and knees.

Now she could hear the laughter of a little boy. The sound came through the hole.

Brenna could feel the men looking at her, and she could imagine what Mom would think of her crawling around while wearing a short skirt, new or otherwise, with or without men watching, but she did not hesitate. She dropped to her hands and knees and crawled through the hole in the fence.

~ ~ ~

The sunlight on the other side seemed to come from everywhere and reflect off everything, making it hard to see. Brenna squinted and she could just see a pair of plaid canvas sneakers not far from where she was coming through the fence. She twisted her neck and saw the girl she had seen with the little boy. She could not see the little boy because of the glare off something on the girl's back. After a second, as her eyes adjusted to the brightness, she saw that the girl had long, crystalline wings on her back, as if she was wearing a Halloween costume.

The flashing light made Brenna's eyes water. She squeezed her eyes closed for a second. When she opened her eyes again, it was still brighter than she expected, but she could see more clearly. The girl still stood there, but she no longer had wings on her back. In her right hand, though, the girl held a straight branch of holly with a few pointed, gray-green leaves sprouting from it, like a wand. Brenna wondered if she had imagined the wings because of all the glare, and the wand.

"Um," Brenna said, trying to decide how she should say what Mrs. Lipscomb had told her to say. She decided to keep it simple. "You need to leave."

She crawled the rest of the way through and stood. She wiped her hands together to get rid of the loose dirt, then used her left hand to shield her eyes. The girl had turned around. She was taller than Brenna by at least a couple inches, but she seemed about the same age. The girl had the long straight, platinum blonde hair that Brenna used to wish she had instead of her own unruly brown curls. The girl's eyes were gray with silver flecks, and her skin was pale, paler even than Brenna's, which was uncommon.

"My name is Brenna," she said. "Brenna Guin, and I'd love to meet you, but Mrs. Lipscomb says you need to leave the park."

"We just got here," the girl said. Her eyes narrowed and her chin shifted after she spoke, taking on a stubborn set.

"It's not safe," Brenna said, and wished she could be more specific. Mrs. Lipscomb had not given her much more than that, though. The sound of laughter pulled her attention past the girl for the first time, and she saw that she was not in North Park. Not the North Park she had played in and walked past a thousand times since she was a little girl. Nor did she seem to be seeing anything the way she had been seeing them her entire life. "Wow."

The tall grass, the standing stones, the huge pile of rocks, the leaves on the trees, even the girl in front of her, everything stood out to her, traced in silver and gleaming with the late morning sun. The grass looked like tiny, flexible swords waving in the breeze. The veins of the oak and maple leaves shone like filigree. The standing stones and the raw rock of the boulders where the playground equipment should be had a texture like hammered silver or platinum with flecks of gold. Colors had been reduced to pale, gray versions of what they normally were, but the texture of what she could see had taken on a level of detail she had never imagined possible.

"What's not safe?" the girl asked, pulling Brenna's attention back to her.

"I don't know," Brenna said. As she spoke, she looked at the girl again. Now she could see that the girl's hair was not really platinum colored. The girl was a blonde, but more of the mousy or dishwater variety, her eyes were blue or blue-gray, and her skin was not as pale Brenna first thought. "I told Mrs.

Lipscomb I saw you and your brother crawl through the ... the hole, and she got very upset. She sent me to tell you to leave. That the park isn't safe there ... here ... on the other side. You need to leave."

"You don't own the park, Brenna," said another girl's voice, behind her.

Brenna jumped, startled, and stepped away from the hole in the fence. She turned around to see another girl following her through the hole. She hoped Mrs. Lipscomb had sat down.

Seeing the rich texture of the new girl's wavy brown hair as it hung over her face made Brenna want to see what her own hair looked like now. She held up a hand in front of her face. The smudges of dirt that she had failed to wipe away stood out from their different texture even if she did not think she would have noticed it before.

As the new girl stood and wiped her hands on her shorts, Brenna saw her face and recognized her. Her name was ... Lupeta? Brenna remembered playing with her in Spring Park and in North Park years ago, before their parents had sent them to separate kindergartens. Lupeta to Skelly Elementary, Brenna to Miss Helen's Private School. Brenna had seen Lupeta around the neighborhood in the years since then, but only in passing, like when Lupeta and her older brother, Esteban, had walked past her house on their way to Spring Park. Thinking about Esteban made her face get warm.

"Just because you think you can make Spring Park private–and you can't, you know," Lupeta said, jabbing a finger at Brenna, "doesn't mean you can tell people what parks they can play in."

Brenna's thoughts of Esteban dissipated under Lupeta's verbal onslaught. Brenna pulled her face away from Lupeta's accusing finger. "This has nothing to do with Spring Park or my Dad's stupid new fence," she said.

Lupeta's finger dropped as the girl looked past Brenna, then at the park around her. "What in the world ... ?"

"This isn't North Park," Brenna said. She looked from Lupeta to the other girl as she spoke. "Mrs. Lipscomb says it's not safe and we shouldn't come here. We need to go," she added when neither girl seemed to be paying her any attention.

Brenna heard Lupeta suck in a breath, then Lupeta shouted, "No! Get back!"

Lupeta pushed past Brenna, forcing Brenna to step back and away to avoid being run over. She would have protested, but Lupeta had run halfway across the park toward the gate to the old cemetery on the south side before Brenna had recovered her balance.

"What are you doing?" shouted the other girl at Lupeta's back.

If Lupeta heard the question, she made no sign of it. If anything, Lupeta seemed to go faster. Brenna saw silver streamers of air swirl around Lupeta's arms and legs and fall behind her in twisting, silver-lined eddies.

The other girl stepped forward, dropped her holly branch wand, then ran after Lupeta. Brenna saw the air move around this girl too, and the wand as it fell, though slower and with less definition.

Brenna moved her hands to her face to rub her eyes, but stopped with her fingers at the level of her mouth when she finally saw what Lupeta was running at.

It stood just inside the open gate to the cemetery. She could see the edges of the shadows in the air that the thing had wrapped around itself, but the shadows were only a bit of texture to Brenna, not concealment. She could see it standing there, looking like an old woman made of stretched and distorted triangles, all warped angles and hooked claws, dripping wet and covered with damp moss, leaning over a little boy that did not seem to see it. The boy could not have seen what Brenna saw and still been spinning and giggling.

Brenna opened her mouth to shout a warning.

It was Lupeta, though, that shouted. "Stay away from him!"

Brenna saw both the boy and the–thing–see Lupeta charging at them. The boy's happy expression disappeared and he looked as if he was about to cry. The thing behind him saw Lupeta, then noticed the other girl coming behind Lupeta. Then it looked at Brenna, its black and quicksilver eyes in their wrinkled sockets locking on hers.

Brenna felt the cold and the hatred in those eyes all the way to the back of her skull.

It knew. It knew she had seen it.

The fear–her fear–like no fear she had ever felt followed the reverse route through her, coming up out of her guts to jabber in her head and tell her she needed to run–run *now*. She fought the urge to vomit. She tasted bile in her mouth. She wanted to look away, to run away. She might have done both, if there had been time, if there had not been a little boy. She swallowed against the fear, silenced the jabbering, and took a step forward.

Lupeta seemed to drop out of the air between the boy and the thing, her hair flying wild, the silver eddies of the air swirling around her. Lupeta landed in a crouch and Brenna could feel the girl's growl as well as hear it.

The thing–whatever it was–drew back from Lupeta. It flicked its eyes to each of the girls, then hissed through its teeth and went backward through the gate into the cemetery. The gate pulled shut of its own accord, the loud clang visibly shaking the air. It was gone as suddenly as Brenna had first seen it. One instant beginning to turn around–then gone, as if it had never been there. Only the fear remained and made Brenna's heart beat loud enough to shake the world around her.

"It's not safe," she said, repeating Mrs. Lipscomb's warning in a hoarse whisper. Neither of the other girls seemed to hear her.

Lupeta still faced the now-closed gate, still crouched, as if she would have tried to fight the horror that Brenna had seen.

The other girl reached the little boy and scooped him up into her arms. She held the boy awkwardly but possessively. The boy wrapped his arms around the girl's neck and squeezed.

"What did you think you were doing?" the girl asked when Lupeta turned around. The girl was not shouting, but Brenna could hear a jagged edge of anger in her voice.

Panting, Lupeta said, "Didn't you ... see that ... that ... thing?" She gestured toward the now-closed south gate with her left hand.

Movement at the edge of her vision drew Brenna's attention to one of the smaller standing stones. She saw a little man cowering under the arch of the stones. He was not a child, despite his size. He was built like a full-grown man, but much shorter. Shorter even than the little boy.

"You scared my brother half to death." The girl was still not shouting at Lupeta, but Brenna could hear that she wanted to.

"I was just ... trying to help," Lupeta said.

Brenna watched the little man watch the two girls. He had not noticed Brenna. The air around the little man glittered with gold and silver, except right behind him. Brenna could almost make out the shape of something missing, an absence that moved with the little man.

"Why do you have wings?" asked Lupeta.

Brenna looked back at the other girl. For an instant, no more than a fraction of a second, Brenna saw the dragonfly wings again on the back of the girl. Then the wings were gone, nothing more than an afterimage.

"What kind of stupid question is that?" the girl shot back.

"Weren't there ... two boys?" Lupeta asked.

The little man appeared behind the girl. Brenna blinked. She had not seen him walk or run from his hiding place.

"Oh," Lupeta said, "there he is."

The girl turned around and looked down. "Edward! Thank god." She let out a sigh of relief. "Are you okay?"

Brenna could almost hear the little man reply, but his voice never reached an audible level. She could hear only a low buzzing. When the buzzing from the man paused, the girl said, "That one's Brenna." She gestured with her head in Brenna's direction. "I don't know who *she* is," she added with a dark look at Lupeta. Another low buzzing, then, "Maybe. Look, I need to get Flub home. He's freaked out. I'm freaked out." With that, the girl turned toward the main gate of the park, and stopped, said, "Right." Then she turned again and started walking toward Brenna.

Brenna looked and saw that the main gate, which was always open in the real North Park, was closed here, locked and chained and overgrown with more holly bushes.

"Good-bye, Edward," said the little boy over the girl's shoulder. He waved where the little man had been. Brenna could not see where the little man had gone.

The girl met Brenna's eyes when they came close, but said nothing as she walked around Brenna.

"You're going to have to get down," the girl said. "I can't carry you through that."

"I don't want to go home," the boy said. "We just got

here."

"Just go, Flub."

"Don't call me Flub," the boy said, but he crawled through the hole.

"Oww," said the girl a few seconds later. "How did that happen?"

Brenna turned around to see what happened, but the girl was already gone.

The gate to the cemetery creaked and shifted with the wind. The sound sent goose bumps down Brenna's back. She saw Lupeta's head come up at the sound. Lupeta sniffed at the air, then turned back around to look at the gate.

"We need to *go*," Brenna said. This was not North Park. There should not be little men shorter than children in North Park. There should not be ... things ... like that threatening children. Her fear from when the thing had looked at her still whimpered in the back of her mind. She did not understand how Lupeta could have seen what she saw and still run at it. "It's not safe."

Lupeta's head snapped around and she looked at Brenna with eyes that should have been chocolate but that Brenna saw as dark gray. Lupeta's expression became mocking, as if she could see the fear behind Brenna's eyes. With one last look at the gate to the cemetery, Lupeta walked back to Brenna. Lupeta did not say anything when she walked past Brenna.

Lupeta paused in front of the hole in the fence, sniffed at the air, then sneezed. After wiping her mouth and nose on the tail of her shirt, Lupeta went down on hands and knees and crawled through the hole in the fence.

Not wanting to be alone with her fear, Brenna followed Lupeta. She noticed small drops of what she knew was blood, like little, dark-gray berries, on one of the holly leaves that dangled across the hole now. She pushed the leaf and its attendant branch out of the way.

When she came out of the ruined holly bush on the other side, colors had returned to the world. The sun, approaching noon, though, was still too bright. She shielded her eyes with her left hand again and kept her head down as she walked back to The Parsonage.

PART 2
THE STRANGE IN THE AIR

~ 6 ~
LUPE
LATE MORNING

FRUSTRATED THAT HER trying to help the little boy, that her trying to save him from whatever it was that she had smelled and seen had been misinterpreted by the other girl, Lupe walked past Brenna without saying anything. She resisted the urge to growl. Brenna probably thought Lupe had been trying to scare the little boy too.

How had the girl not been able to see the shadow-thing about to grab the boy? She could smell the fear coming off Brenna, overpowering the smells of soap and shampoo and fabric softener that Lupe realized she had been getting from Brenna. The other girl had been frightened too, but not this much, and she had been more angry than afraid. Angry with Lupe. And Lupe had only been trying to help.

Lupe started to ask Brenna if she had seen the shadow-thing, if that was what had scared her. Then she decided that Brenna probably blamed her for scaring the little boy and said nothing.

She smelled the fresh blood even before she reached the hole in the fence. Had the little boy been hurt by the shadow-thing–?

No. It was not the little boy's blood. It was the girl's blood. Lupe was not sure how she knew, exactly, but the metallic smell of the blood included the same scent as the girl. Not the chemical smells of soap or clean clothes, but the smell of the girl herself.

Lupe realized she could still smell the scent of the boy from when he had come into this park, and from when he had passed this way again on his way out. She could also smell the two passings of the girl. And Brenna's and her own coming into the park, as well.

She could not *see* the paths the four of them had taken, not with her eyes. She knew the traces were there, though. She could *almost* see them, with the help of her nose.

The inside of her nose tingled with all the new scents and smells and she sneezed. She thought she might sneeze again, but after a couple of seconds the sensation faded. Lacking anything else to use, she hesitated only a second before pulling up the tail of her tank top and wiping her nose and mouth. Let Brenna think of that what she would.

Lupe saw the drops of blood on holly leaf that hung over the hole. There had been no branch hanging that way when she crawled through a few minutes ago.

Had it really only been a few minutes ago?

The sun was brighter when she came out of the bush. Not as bright as it had been before she went to the other park, but still brighter than it had been in the park.

With the renewed sunshine came the odors of the construction. The tar and the asphalt and the dust from the broken concrete as well as the sweat and musk of the men working the machines, all of it rolled over her and threatened to make her gag.

She made it to her feet without losing her breakfast, but

her eyes watered and her nose began to drip. She walked to her right, hoping that would get her past the work sooner than the other direction. She sniffed to keep her nose from dripping and wiped at her eyes with her fingers as she walked.

Some of the men stopped what they were doing to watch her walk past. She heard Brenna coming out of the hole in the fence behind her. She hoped that Brenna did not think she was crying.

As she walked past Mrs. Lipscomb's house she smelled the old woman on the porch before her eyes could spot Mrs. Lipscomb in the shadows.

"Thank God," Mrs. Lipscomb whispered and let out a breath. Lupe wondered how she had heard either the prayer or the breath. Mrs. Lipscomb had not done either loud enough to have carried, especially over the construction work.

Just as the smells had done, the sounds around Lupe began to get louder and louder. The jackhammer tried to split her skull but could not drown out the men talking about all the girls crawling through that hole in the fence or passing the word that it was lunchtime and they could knock off. Beyond the construction work, Lupe could hear the wind in the trees and Brenna getting to her feet and beginning to walk the same way she had come. She could hear Mrs. Lipscomb's breathing and the sound of a half-dozen air conditioner compressors all kicking on at the same time and the birds and squirrels chattering in the trees and the breeze that brushed against the blades of grass.

Lupe did not stop at Mrs. Lipscomb's house. She kept walking, her hands on her ears to deaden the sound and to hold her head together. She thought about going home, but realized she would have to walk back through the construction–and by Brenna. She did not think she was up to either of those.

She walked past the church and along the fence that surrounded the South Cemetery. The peace of the cemetery was like a soft pillow on her right side, so when she reached the main gate to the cemetery she walked in.

The barrage of sounds lifted and the wave of scents both ebbed and became bearable again. Lupe let out a breath she had not realized she was holding.

She could still hear everything, but it was manageable now. She could tune out the men and Brenna and machines and Mrs. Lipcomb and hear only the breeze. She could still smell everything, but like the sounds, the scents had become a menu she could choose from instead of a flood trying to drown her.

Lupe looked around. She had seldom visited the cemetery, except on Dia de los Muertos with Grannie Litta and her family and a few other neighborhood families that had loved ones buried there. She had heard people talk about the peace they felt in cemeteries before, and Lupe had assumed they were just trying to sound brave. Now, though, she felt that peace. Not as if the world or time had stopped, but as if both had agreed to intrude as little as possible.

Breathing easier, her head no longer trying to explode—or collapse—and her nose no longer burning and making her eyes water, she walked to the nearest bench and sat.

She looked across the neat rows of windworn headstones and pedestals and tried to make sense of everything that had happened in the last ten minutes. Or was it even that long? A park that was not North Park. A wet and evil shadow-thing. A little man. A girl with wings that were there one second and gone the next. Being able to smell the different types of grass—

She stopped.

Earlier this morning, grass was just grass. Some grass was cut. Some needed cutting. That was about the only distinction she had ever noticed. Now, though, she could identify, just from their scent, six types of grass within a few yards of where she sat. The only one she could name was, she thought, Bermuda grass, and maybe the darker green grass with the pointed blades was crab grass, but other than that, she had no idea. The grass growing around the feet of the bench was different from the grass growing over most of the graves and different from the grass getting long around the base of the nearest headstones.

The wind shifted and the grass bent in the new direction, flashing silver under the still-muted sunshine. The wind brought her a different scent, one that made the hairs on the back of her neck stand up.

The shadow-thing had passed this way.

The scent was faint, almost nonexistent, as if the cemetery itself had been laid on top of the scent. But it was there. Unmistakeable. She heard the growl in her throat before she realized she had done it.

She remembered that the shadow-thing had retreated into the cemetery through the gate from North Park– No, not from North Park. From the other park. Was there another cemetery? The thought made Lupe's head ache.

Whether there was another cemetery–and where it might be in relation to this one–Lupe pushed those thoughts out of her head. She concentrated on the scent of the shadow-thing.

She stood and moved upwind to see if she could find where the shadow-thing had passed. She wrinkled her nose against the wet wrongness of the stench when she stepped into the middle of the route the shadow-thing had taken. The scent was stronger, but still masked, only a hint of what it would have been if the shadow-thing had come this way in this cemetery. Instead of–

She would think about that later.

A couple steps farther into the cemetery confirmed that the shadow-thing had come this way. The trail came around the church and along the edge of the cemetery adjoining the churchyard, then out of the cemetery through the gate. How she had missed that smell before, when she came through the gate, Lupe could not guess. Her nose must have really been burning.

She followed the scent out of the cemetery.

The shadow-thing had not walked along the streets of Spring Hollow, but it was headed toward the center of the neighborhood, to Spring Park. Lupe did not have to walk across people's yards to know where it led. She had the trail now, faint as it was. She could almost see the trail in the air, fading in the sunshine, eroded by the breeze.

She could still smell everything else, though. The scents of all the different flowers—

Before today, Lupe had mostly distinguished flowers by color. Purple ones with white edges, yellow ones, red ones with white centers. The only flowers she had been sure of were lilies and roses. Now she realized there were dozens of different types of flower that she had considered all the same. Each smelled different, even the varieties of roses.

Then there were the scents of all the different trees—

Her house had a huge, fifty-year-old red oak dominating the backyard, and Mr. Henry across the street had a maple in his front yard, the leaves of which turned a shimmering gold in the fall. Those and pines were the only trees she knew by sight. Now, though, she could distinguish a dozen or more varieties based on the smell of their sap, and the sound their leaves made when the wind rubbed them together.

And the scents of all the different animals—

She could smell the trails of birds and squirrels and rabbits and dogs and cats and more. The faint hint of skunk told her that a small family of the animals had passed through the neighborhood within the last month.

Spring Hollow, her home for her entire life, had become a new world.

Lupe thought she might have stepped through the hole in the fence into a different world, but she seemed to have come back through the fence to a world even more different than that one.

As she passed houses, dogs barked at her through mail slots or from behind cedar fences. Her ears heard the barking and she could distinguish one dog from the other. She could almost picture the dog in her mind. Even more unusual was that all the dogs seemed to be barking, "Hey! Hey, you!"

Lupe stopped walking and shook her head to clear it, before her ears and her nose overloaded her brain again. Her forehead ached from the strain of keeping everything inside. After a few seconds, she was able to start walking again.

She followed the scent of the shadow-thing up Sew Spoke Drive, then had to make a decision. The trail continued inward toward Spring Park, but none of the houses on the west side of Inner Circle Drive still had trails leading through from the street to the park. She would have to go around to the south trail still open between Sparrow Hawk and Briar Rose.

Or, she could cut through someone's yard.

Lupe bared her teeth in a grin. She knew just the yard to cut through. She went left, toward Spring Beach.

Brenna's father, Mr. Gawd-Is-That-Annoying-Car-Commercial-On-Again Guin, had built their new fence to withstand a siege of the common folk. The eight-foot-tall red-brick fence stretched from the sides of Spring Beach to the property lines, with supporting towers of gray stone every twenty feet or so. The corner posts had been made taller and given crenellations so very small archers could stand behind them and shoot arrows out at the armies of the poor and downtrodden who got too close. The one gate, on the south side of the house, was heavy iron, wide enough to let a pickup truck through.

Lupe thought about going through the gate–and leaving it open, of course–but that seemed too easy. Instead, she went to one of the support posts. She used her fingers and the toes of her sandals to climb and was up and over almost before she had picked out her fingerholds and toeholds. She jumped from the tower and landed in a crouch, hands and feet deep in the thick cushion of green grass that smelled expensive and, once summer arrived for real, thirsty.

Only when she stood, dusting her hands off on her shorts did she realize she had just leaped from the top of an eight-foot-high fence. When she started climbing, she had assumed she would do a hanging drop. Once she was up there, though, even as high as it was, leaping down had seemed the obvious choice. She turned and looked up the fence to the top. Now it looked higher than before. Her head became light and she took a step back as the top of the fence seemed to spin and she lost her balance.

The fence and the rest of the world stopped spinning with the help of her fingers pressing her temples. Then she looked over the Guin's backyard.

The backyard resembled a bricked-in golf course more than a place where children would play or a dog would be allowed to run. Another iron gate opened in the rear of the yard and Lupe could see Spring Park through its bars.

As she walked through the backyard, she smelled traditional Mexican cooking, like Grannie Litta made. Of course, the Guins *would* have a Hispanic cook. She remembered the preschool Brenna always came to the park with a Hispanic nanny.

Lupe heard someone tapping on a window behind her. She did not turn, but she could have pointed to the window without looking. She had never heard sounds so acutely–or so accurately–before. She ignored the rapping and continued walking to the back fence.

The back fence proved as easy to climb as the front had been. She did not leap down this time. The grass outside the fence did not look as soft to land on as that inside the fence. So she did a hanging drop, which was still easy. Lupe decided she would have to walk across fenced-in yards more often.

Spring Pond had seen better days. Lupe had seen pictures of Spring Park from the 1960's and even earlier. In those days, the park had been beautiful. Spring Park was still beautiful, but marred. The owners of the Pond Houses, and the city of Tulsa, had been battling the growing incursion of some kind of leafy, green underwater plant and its accompanying algae longer than Lupe had been alive. Nothing tried had worked for long. The plants and the algae had turned the eastern side of Spring Pond, where the Spring that fed the pond bubbled forth, into an ugly green swamp.

The geese, like the Guins, preferred the still-clean, uncluttered western side of Spring Pond with its imported sand "beach" that gave the Guin's house its name. The geese honked as Lupe came over the fence.

Seeing the geese–smelling the geese; had they always smelled that bad?–reminded Lupe of the baggie of stale bread she had brought with her. She pulled the baggie out of her pocket and walked toward the geese.

The geese, though, were walking away from her, wading into the water and swimming away.

She stopped at the water and looked at the tail feathers of the retreating geese. For a second she thought about splashing into the pond after the birds and shouting at them and making them flutter into the air in a sparkling shower of water drops. The feel of the cool water on her right foot, drenching her sandal, startled her and made her take a step back.

Her head felt light again as she stepped away from the water. She shook her right foot to get the water off, then shook her head. She had no idea where the thought had come from, and no idea why she had almost acted on it. This morning was getting weirder and weirder.

The geese were halfway across the pond now, clustered around the circle fountain in the center of the pond, close to the line of unkillable waterweeds. These geese were neighborhood regulars. They recognized people with bread crumbs and would waddle in flocks around anyone with food, honking and snapping at crumbs on the ground or even still in the air. Then honking and snapping and waddling away in a snit when the food ran out. Lupe had never seen them run away from someone with food.

She scattered some bread crumbs along the beach. A few geese watched her do it, but none of them made to swim back to shore.

Lupe shrugged and put the baggie back in her pocket.

Under the many smells of geese, geese droppings, stale water, algae, and more, she caught again the scent of the shadow-thing–which was not even the first weird thing of the day–and remembered that she had come to Spring Pond for another reason than feeding geese.

She followed the scent around the southern edge of the pond until she was opposite where she started. The geese had watched her as she walked. Now they started swimming back to the western beach and the bread crumbs scattered there.

The scent of the shadow-thing was stronger here, but the trail had stopped. And, though stronger, it was still more a shadow of a scent than a real scent.

As Lupe looked around the edge of the pond and tried to peer into the dark, algae-coated water of the pond, she noticed that the scent was fading, becoming even less real. Within a few minutes, the scent was gone as if it had never been there. She could still smell everything else—especially the algae—but the scent of the shadow-thing was gone. Not even a trace remained.

After a few more minutes, she gave up and walked the rest of the way around the pond back to Spring Beach. Those geese that did not get back into the water waddled away from her as she walked, keeping the pond between them and her.

Not sure what else to do, Lupe scattered the remaining bread crumbs on the ground, then left the park through the path between Sparrow Hawk and Briar Rose.

~ 1 ~

FAYE

NOON

FAYE WALKED OUT on her balcony. It was noon, and the sun was as directly overhead as it ever got in Tulsa. Her shadow, only a small pool of darkness under her feet on the marbled white tiles of the balcony floor, pointed slightly north.

She looked west, over the torn up section of Outer Circle Drive and into North Park. The real North Park, with the playground and the dry streambed. There was no sign of North Park Other, with its standing stones and bubbling stream. No visible sign, anyway. Somehow, though, Faye could still *feel* North Park Other. She could point to where the standing stones would be, and she could sense the real forest that surrounded North Park Other even if she could see only the handful of scattered trees planted by the city of Tulsa and the residents of Spring Hollow over the years. She had thought the trees in Spring Hollow were old, what the real-estate agent had called "established", but the impression of age she had received from the trees in and around North Park Other made the Spring Hollow trees seem like saplings.

North Park Other, Edward Pennyfeather, and whatever had happened on the other side of the hole in the fence, all of

72

it seemed like a dream now. How could any of it have been real?

The fingers of her left hand touched the three Band-Aids positioned over the scratch on her shoulder. That, at least, had been real. So had being grounded to the backyard for the rest of the day when they got back. First, because of the bloody scratch on her shoulder, then because the wild story Flub told Mom. The way Flub described what happened made it sound as if he and Faye had been involved in a turf war with a gang of bloodthirsty biker girls.

Flub had been a brat all the way home, of course. First he did not want to go home so soon. Then he had wanted her to carry him again. Then he had climbed on the Bobcat digger left as the men working on the road stopped for lunch. After she had told him to get down or she would tell Mom, he had looked at her and his eyes had become wide.

"You're bleeding," he said. "Did that girl with the teeth and claws scratch you?"

Faye had looked at the scratch on her right shoulder where the holly leaf had dragged across her skin. What had been just a thin scratch had become a line of swelling beads of blood. The hole in the fence, and the branches of the holly bushes, had pressed close around her as she crawled out, and one of the leaves had poked her and scratched her. As she watched, one of the beads had dripped, leaving a long, red stripe. She had wiped the blood away with the fingers of her left hand, which she then had to wipe on the grass to get clean. At least she had not bled on her white tank top.

Mom, however, had not seen the white shirt spared, only the bloody arm scratched. So Mom had freaked out—the first time—washing the scratch, dabbing it with hydrogen peroxide, then applying three Hello Kitty Band-Aids. Then freaked out again when Flub told his version of what happened and Faye argued with him about it.

Faye had eaten a silent, sullen lunch at the kitchen table because Mom had nixed her original idea of eating lunch on her balcony. Now she was back in her room and back on her balcony. And unsure what she would do with the rest of the day.

She saw Mrs. Lipscomb and a girl in a floppy garden hat walking along the fence in front of North Park. Faye did not recognize Brenna under the brim of the big hat until she noticed the red and black dress and the black boots. Brenna carried a basket in her left hand while Mrs. Lipscomb held Brenna's right arm for support. The pair reached the hole in the fence and stopped. Brenna handed something from the basket to Mrs. Lipscomb who bent over so she could reach the hole. Faye wondered what they were doing. The real-estate agent had said Mrs. Lipscomb was about eighty and had lived in the neighborhood for a long, long time. Maybe Mrs. Lipscomb was just upset about how badly the men had mutilated the holly bushes.

The day was already getting warm. Faye turned to go back inside. She stopped when she noticed something odd about her shadow. When facing north so the sun overhead was behind her head, the shape of her shadow extended to her sides, both left and right, more than she expected, as if she had her arms stretched. Except her arms were not stretched.

She stretched out her arms. The shadows of her arms moved over the other shadow, and were darker, as if the other shadows–the not-her-arms–were cast by something translucent, or crystalline.

She leaned forward, her arms still extended, to stretch her shadow out lengthwise. As she did, the extra bit of shadow resolved itself into her arms and two–

Wings?

Faye straightened and looked over her shoulder, trying to see her back. She could not see her back, but she could also not see ... anything else either. She looked up in the sky. There were still no clouds. Nothing she would think that would throw a shadow over her. She put off looking down again for a few seconds, then leaned forward and saw—

"Admiring your wings?"

Faye jumped and made a squeaking noise that Flub always found hilarious, even when she was chasing him down the hall, yelling at him for scaring her.

"Flub–" she started, then stopped. Flub was nowhere in sight, on the balcony or in the front yard.

"Over here," said the voice.

Faye's eyes found Edward Pennyfeather perched on the corner of her balcony long seconds before she allowed herself to believe that she was actually seeing the little man. Edward's eyes met hers, and he waved.

"You're real," she said.

Edward's eyes looked left, then right, making him look more like a large bird than he already did, squatting there with his knees pulled up to his chest and his feet on the balcony railing. "Well," he said, pulling a face as if considering the validity of her statement. He seemed to reach a conclusion, and gave her a quick nod. "Yes. Yes I am."

Faye decided to ignore his sarcasm. She noticed that one of his small eyes looked swollen. "What are you doing here?"

"I thought I would come visit," he said, looking away. "I do not often have a chance to get out and about over here." He paused. "May I come in?"

"What? Oh, sure. Come in, please. I don't have any place to sit, though."

"No matter. Now that I have been invited in, I will make myself comfortable here on the railing."

"You're already sitting on the railing."

"Yes, but now I will comfortable."

"You haven't moved."

Edward turned his head and looked at her from the sides of his eyes. "I like to think of comfort as a state of mind." His left eyebrow arched at her.

Faye shook her head. This was too much like talking to Flub, except that Edward had perfect enunciation and much better grammar.

She looked down and saw that her shadow had returned to its normal, nonwinged Faye shape. She spread her arms and leaned forward, then back again. No wings.

"They are still there," Edward said.

Faye just looked at him.

"Your wings," Edward added.

"My wings?"

"Yes. They are still there. Just, for lack of a better word, hiding."

"I don't have wings," Faye said, then remembered. "I mean, yes, I have a pair of wings–that I wore for Halloween when I was seven. But that was three–almost four–years ago, and they're packed away in a box in the attic. Plus, they're not real."

"Some wings are real. Yours are. Mine–" Edward stopped.

"I don't see any wings on you."

"Well, that is hardly saying much, is it?" Edward asked, his tone testy now. "You cannot even see your own."

"I don't *have* any wings to see."

"Fine." Edward looked around the balcony, then at the front of the house and the roof line. "This is a very pretty house.

Hawk Briar, is it not?"

"I don't have wings," Faye said again.

Edward shrugged, still not looking at her, seeming to examine the gutters over her head. "That is what you keep saying."

Faye was about to insist again, but Edward turned to face her.

"I almost forgot," he said, "I was going to give you this." He held out his left hand. A straight branch of holly with three sprigs of green, pointed leaves appeared in his fingers. "I saw you had dropped your wand, and thought you might like it back."

Faye looked at the wand, then at Edward's face, then at the wand again. She wondered where he had kept the wand–

No, not a wand. It was just a holly branch. She did not want to think of it as a wand. She did not have wings. And that ... stick ... was not her wand.

"Shall I hang on to it then?" Edward asked. "I do not mind."

Not sure what else she should say, Faye said, "If you would, please."

Edward gave another nod, and the fingers that had held the holly branch then held nothing.

"Where ... ?"

"Just some place handy."

"This is all very confusing," Faye said.

"In what way?" Edward asked.

"In every way that I can imagine. Who are you? I mean, *what* are you? You look like ... like a man, but you're ..." She gestured with her hands trying to indicate how tall he was.

"You already know my name, but I do not mind giving it to you again." He stood on the railing. "I am Edward Pennyfeather, and I am pleased to make your acquaintance."

He bowed as deeply as before when he first gave her his name, then he settled back into his squat. "As to the other, I am certain that you already know the answer."

"No," Faye said. "You can't be. You're not a ..."

Edward looked at her, his left eyebrow arching again.

"You're not a fairy," Faye said. She felt foolish just saying it. She felt even more foolish saying it to a man less than two feet tall. What else could he be?

No. She refused to consider it.

"Are you saying you do not believe in fairies?" Edward asked.

"There's no such thing as fairies," Faye said.

Edward's face became pale and he clutched at his chest, gasping.

"Are you okay?" Faye asked.

Edward did not answer. He coughed and seemed to lose his balance. He fell backward off the railing, arms flailing.

"Edward!" she shouted and rushed to the railing and looked over.

Edward floated in the air just below the level of the balcony, reclining, with his hands behind his head. He smiled up at her. "Got you," he said, and laughed.

"You're as bad as Flub," Faye said. She turned her back on Edward and walked off the balcony back into her room.

Edward appeared on the balcony railing, then just inside the French doors as she pulled them closed. Faye thought she saw him move, but she could not be sure. The little man was so quick he seemed to vanish from where he started and appear where he stopped.

He looked up at her, still smiling. "Your cheeks take on the color of spring roses when you are angry," he said. "It is a most agreeable look for you, Miss Faye Woods."

Faye felt her cheeks grow warm, but did not respond. She went to her bed and sat on it.

Edward followed her and perched on the white footboard of her bed. "You are talking to a fairy, and you have fairy blood in your own veins, Miss Faye Woods. So fairies must exist."

Faye shook her head.

"You can shake your golden-brown locks from now until ... until the Spring itself dries," Edward said, "and it will all have been for nothing. Fairies will still exist, and you will still have their blood in your veins. I should know," he added. "I saw some of it on the way here."

Faye touched the Band-Aids on her shoulder again. "The bush scratched me."

"You should be more careful," Edward said.

"Can you heal the scratch, Mr. Fairy?" she asked.

"Not now," Edward said. "The blood is too dry. You have to work quick to–" He stopped, and seemed to think. "Blood is best when it is fresh," he went on. "Though there are still things that can be done, even with ... and I can see I am boring you. Or making you ill."

Faye swallowed. "How can I have fairy blood?"

Edward shrugged. "These things happen sometimes."

"How?"

"I have only the vaguest notion, I am sure," Edward said, looking away. "A fairy falls in love with a human and, you know, these things happen."

"But you're so ... small ..." Her voice trailed away as Edward grew until he was nearly the size of Dad, but still perched on the footboard of her bed. The frame of the bed shifted from his new weight, but Edward did not seem to notice. Faye saw that one of his eyes was swollen and discolored. He would have a black eye soon. There were also bruises around his neck. Then Faye found herself uncomfortably aware of Edward's bare chest, and his shoulders. And the muscles in his arms. She looked away, feeling her face getting hot.

"To me," Edward said, "the real mystery is what a fairy sees in a human. Humans are fun to play with, of course, but so are bees and cats and even trogs and trolls. You never hear about those having fairy blood in their veins, though."

Faye nodded. Not because she agreed but because some response seemed necessary. She did not want to look at Edward again. Not now.

The bed frame settled. Faye risked a peek out of the side of her eye and let out her breath in a sigh of relief. Edward was back to his former size. Much less threatening. Much less ... man-like.

"What happened to your eye?" Faye asked.

Edward looked away, hiding that eye from her. "Nothing," he said. "Just ... your friend was right. It is not always safe on the Other Side."

Faye thought of the shadow in the gate and the other girl running straight at Flub, and she shivered. "She's not my friend," Faye said. "She just ... showed up."

"You have pennies!" Edward said. He disappeared from her footboard and reappeared on her tall, five-drawer dresser beside the half-full glass vase of pennies there. He dipped his hand into the coins and pushed them around. The pennies were the size of small Frisbees to him. "Old pennies too."

"You like pennies?"

"My name, you will recall, is Edward *Pennyfeather*."

"Right," Faye said. "Mom and I ..." She paused. "Before Flub was born, Mom and I use to go through batches of pennies, picking out the old ones and putting them in that vase. Just one of many things that used to happen *before* I had a little brother."

"May I have this one?" Edward asked, holding up a penny so she could see. As if she could see which it was from across the bedroom.

She shrugged. "Sure. You collect pennies?"

Edward rolled his eyes at her, then bowed again. "Thank you, Miss Faye Woods, for your generous gift."

"Sure."

Edward appeared perched on her footboard again. He held the penny in front of his face, smiling at it as he turned it over in his fingers. "If I could show you my wings, you would see what is possibly the finest collection of pennies–"

"Edward!"

Faye groaned as Flub charged into the room. The child could never just *walk* anywhere, especially in the house, and he seldom seemed to talk in anything except exclamations.

Edward turned and smiled, then looked surprised when Flub caught him in a hug and lifted him off his perch on the footboard.

"Got you!" Flub said.

"Finn Reilly Woods," Edward said, laughing. "It is a pleasure to see you again, as well."

"You're it!" Flub shouted, and dropped Edward, who was still laughing. Flub ran back out of Faye's room, his shoes stomping loudly on the hardwood floor of the hall, then down the stairs.

"Flub!" Faye shouted after him. "Stay out of my room!"

"What's going on?" Dad asked, calling down the hall.

"Nothing," Faye called back. "Just Flub being Flub."

"Keep it down, please."

"Sorry," Faye said. Edward had resumed perching on her footboard when she turned back to him. The gift penny was nowhere to be seen. "Does Flub also have fairy blood in his veins?" she asked.

Edward shrugged. "I do not know, Miss Faye Woods. I have not seen his blood."

"That doesn't make any sense. He's my brother."

"That doesn't make any sense," Edward said, echoing her words in a voice that sounded almost like hers–but with a definite mocking tone. "He's my brother." Edward rolled his eyes. "So now you believe in fairies?"

"Well, no, not really. But I'm pretty sure about genetics. Unless the Discovery Channel is lying to me."

Edward shrugged again. "I have not seen any wings adorning Finn Reilly Woods, but wings can be ... such fickle things." His shoulders twitched as he talked. "I would have to see his blood to know for certain."

"Wait a bit," Faye said. "He'll probably injure himself soon. Or me. That seems to be the nature of little boys."

"Snips and snails and puppy dog tails," Edward said in a singsong voice.

"Something like that. Oh, no, here he comes again. I wish–"

Edward did his disappear-and-reappear trick again, this time appearing right in front of her, his right hand over her lips, shushing her. "People with fairy blood in their veins," he said, "should be careful when saying 'I wish'." Then he was perched on her footboard again.

The stomping and clomping of Flub-sized feet that had started as a low rumble on the staircase crescendoed into an explosion of Flub into her room–again. Startled by Edward, flustered by Flub, Faye took in a breath to create an explosion of her own.

"You were supposed to chase me," Flub said.

"Flub!" Faye shouted. "Get out of my room!"

"But you're It," Flub said to Edward. "You're supposed to chase me."

"He can't chase you in my room–"

"Enough!" Dad's disembodied voice rolled like aggravated thunder down the hall from his office, amplified by the naked walls and the hardwood floor. "I asked you to keep it down."

"But, Dad, Edward–" Flub started, turning to face up the hall.

"Shh!" Faye said, putting her finger to her mouth. She moved to the edge of her bed, preparing to forcibly eject Flub from her room if that should prove necessary.

Flub faced the other direction. "Mom! Faye is shushing me."

Faye could hear Mom coming up the stairs. "Outside," Mom said. "Both of you. Outside for a bit."

"Can we go to the park?" Flub asked, moving to the door.

"No," Mom said, as she came into view outside Faye's bedroom door. "You already got in trouble at the park. Go play in the backyard. Both of you."

Faye jumped up from the bed and walked to the door to keep Mom from seeing Edward. Flub assumed she was coming for him, and he retreated behind Mom's legs. Faye ignored him. "Why do I have to go outside?" she asked.

"To keep an eye on your brother."

"The backyard has a fence," Faye said. "It's not like he can escape."

"I can too escape," Flub said, and darted down the hall, then down the stairs, his steps as loud as before.

"Go," Mom said, pointing after Flub.

"Fine. If he gets out of the backyard, though, do I have to chase him? Or can we just call the dog catcher?"

"Go," Mom said again. "Watch your brother."

Faye looked over her shoulder, but Edward was no longer perched on the footboard of her bed. She heard Mom taking a breath to repeat herself. To head her off, Faye said, "I'm going. I'm going." She pulled her door to her bedroom closed as she followed Mom down the hall. "I wish I didn't have a brother," she muttered.

"What was that?" Mom asked.

"Nothing," Faye said, then shivered. A shadow passed over her, making the hallway seem like a tunnel, and a chill gave her goosebumps on her arm. Mom did not seem to notice either the shadow or the chill.

Flub was already outside when she came out the back door. He was under the redbud tree, jumping up, trying to grab the hand that Edward dangled before the little man could pull it back out of reach.

Edward met her eye, and his smile faded. He sighed and shook his head.

"What?" Faye asked. "I didn't mean it. I was just mad."

"Didn't mean what?" Flub asked.

"Miss Faye wished she did not have a brother, Master Finn."

"How could you tell him that?" Faye asked, surprised that Edward would just up and say that to Flub.

Flub spun to face her, his mouth already beginning to pout and his chin to tremble. She saw the sense of betrayal in his eyes.

"Mom!" he called out. "Mom! Faye wished I didn't exist."

"Flub," Faye said, "that's not–"

Flub ignored her. He ran past her, back through the door into the house.

Feeling like the worst big sister ever, Faye watched him go. Edward appeared beside her. "I didn't mean it," she said to

Edward. "I was just mad." Edward only nodded. "How can I ... How can I take back a wish?"

Edward looked away. "Sometimes," he said, "you can take them back easy. Other times, though, you must take them back the hard way."

The back door opened and Mom came out, looking angry. Edward disappeared before Faye could ask him about the *hard way*.

~ 8 ~

BRENNA

NOON

AS SHE WALKED home for lunch, Brenna found herself squinting and averting her eyes from the glare of sunlight off the roofs and windows of houses, off the windshields of cars, and off the street. Even the trees and the bushes seemed to be angling their leaves to shine reflected sunlight into her face and eyes. The wide-brimmed, straw garden hat that Mrs. Lipscomb insisted she borrow did little to help.

"You're no help either," she told Norv, squinting down at him. The rat was curled up in his cage with his eyes under his tail. The metal bars of his cage glinted in the sunlight. Norv did not respond. He did not like the sunlight either.

She stopped in the shaded shelter of the old white oak in front of Thimble Nest on Sew Spoke Drive because the glare gave her a rest there. She could almost see normally, though anywhere the sun touched outside the shade of the tree seemed brighter, whiter than it should be. She could see the edges of things, but much of the color and detail were washed out by the brightness.

Almost the same as she had seen the world on the Other Side.

The Other Side. That's what Mrs. Lipscomb had called it. Despite the bright sunlight and the increasing summer warmth in the air, Brenna shivered, remembering.

~ ~ ~

Mrs. Lipscomb had been waiting for her on the front porch of The Parsonage after Brenna had come back through the hole in the fence.

The old woman met her at the top of the steps. "Thank God," she said, then pulled Brenna into a hug.

Brenna was surprised. Mrs. Lipscomb had never hugged her. Before she recovered herself enough to return the hug, Mrs. Lipscomb pushed Brenna away, though still holding Brenna's shoulders. Mrs. Lipscomb looked over her glasses into Brenna's eyes as if trying to see through them into Brenna's head. Embarassed by the hug and the scrutiny, Brenna looked away.

"No," Mrs. Lipscomb said. "Look at me, Brenna. Look me in the eye."

Reluctantly, Brenna met the old woman's eyes again. Mrs. Lipscomb had dark green eyes with flecks of gold and brown. Something about the way Mrs. Lipscomb hunched over Brenna, her wrinkled hands gripping Brenna's shoulders, made Brenna remember the–the *thing*–she had seen in the park. The thing with its black eyes and long, clawed fingers, as it had loomed over the boy–

She pulled away from Mrs. Lipscomb and sat at the table on the porch. She did not want to remember that–whatever it was.

Mrs. Lipscomb followed her, and rested a hand on her shoulder again. "You sit right there, Brenna. I'll fix us some Chamomile tea. I think we both could stand some calming about now." Then she shuffled into the house, leaving Brenna alone on the porch.

Brenna followed her into the house less than a minute later, not wanting to be alone.

"The Other Side is beautiful," Mrs. Lipscomb said when tea was ready and the two of them were seated at the small cherry-finished table in her tiny kitchen. "Terribly, terribly beautiful. I still dream about it."

Brenna held her cup with both hands. She did not want to think about what she had seen.

Mrs. Lipscomb took a sip. "Not all the dreams are good, though."

Brenna nodded. She did not want to think about sleeping. She did not want to think about what her dreams would be like after seeing that–*thing*.

"Drink up, dear. You'll feel better."

Brenna finally took a sip of her tea. The warmth and flavor of the tea, the sweetness of the honey, had a calming effect. Brenna felt herself relaxing and only then did she realize how tense she had been.

"I hope I didn't scare you," Mrs. Lipscomb said. "Getting all upset like that. I just ..." She paused. "It's been so long, and it all came back in a rush."

Sitting in Mrs. Lipscomb's kitchen with its organized clutter of vintage aluminum cookware and glistening displays of Depression glassware, sipping tea while looking out the window at the old church, made everything seem normal again. Brenna was almost able to think that crawling through the holly bush and the hole in the fence, and what she had seen there–and how she had seen–had been a dream. The–thing–seemed less and less menacing, the whole experience less and less real, with each sip.

"I'm curious what you saw," Mrs. Lipscomb said.

Brenna tensed as the dream became real again.

"But you don't have to tell me right now," Mrs. Lipscomb added. Brenna relaxed.

When they finished the tea, Mrs. Lipscomb had Brenna fetch a big basket of ribbon and twine from the guest room. When Brenna came back with the basket, Mrs. Lipscomb held a bundle of twigs in her right hand, and a floppy straw garden hat in the other. She dropped the twigs into the basket, and gave the hat to Brenna.

"You're going to need this, dear. The sun is just too bright for that delicate skin of yours." When Brenna started to protest, Mrs. Lipscomb only laughed. "I'm eighty-one years old, little girl. There's not much left of me that needs protecting. I'm well aware the hat doesn't go with your dress or your boots, dear. Just humor an old lady."

Once they walked down the steps of the porch into the sunlight, Brenna was grateful for the hat. Without it, the sun would have been too bright. As it was, she still kept her face down and followed Mrs. Lipscomb, wondering what they were going to do.

"We're going to patch this hole," Mrs. Lipscomb said, as if she had heard the question in Brenna's mind. "Before there's any more mischief. Or before ..." She paused. "You mentioned the Spring Hag before. So I'm sure you've heard the story about the Spring Hollow boy who went missing long ago?"

Brenna nodded. Every child in Spring Hollow knew that story. Four-year-old Billy Tippens was famous, even if the details of his disappearance and presumed death were so vague that it had invited more than 50 years of speculative embellishment. Tulsa's own Lindbergh baby, mystery still unsolved. "Is that why they never found him?" she asked. "He was taken ... over there?" She shivered, touched again by the chill of seeing the thing. She wanted to ask Mrs. Lipscomb about the thing, but– Not yet. She did not want to know too much. The boy in the park this morning was safe. She did not need–certainly did not want–to know.

"I didn't live here then," Mrs. Lipscomb said as they walked. "So I'm not sure. But, yes, that's what I believe. We had moved away after the war. Bobbie and I were already married when we first heard about the Tippens boy." She paused again, and sighed. "Anyway, now you know why not all my dreams of the Other Side are good ones. And why we need to patch this hole."

The two of them walked to where the hole in the fence was visible through the truncated holly bushes. Brenna watched, handing items from the basket when asked, as Mrs. Lipscomb tied twine and ribbon to the bent bars and the branches of the bush. Then Mrs. Lipscomb wove the twine and ribbon with the twigs she had brought, muttering under her breath as she did.

Brenna tried to listen, but she did not understand what Mrs. Lipscomb was saying. Brenna could speak Spanish almost as well as she did English, and had started learning French at school the previous year. What words she was able to hear, if they were words, sounded like none of those languages.

"Is that really going to stop anyone who wants to get through?" Brenna asked when Mrs. Lipscomb stood straight again. The woven twine and ribbon and twigs resembled Native American dreamcatcher ornaments, but did not look like it would be strong enough to stop a determined kitten. Certainly it would not stop the thing Brenna had seen.

"You would be surprised," Mrs. Lipscomb said, then stepped around Brenna, walking back to The Parsonage. "The iron in the fence is good for most things. But not everything, obviously. As long as we don't see another of *those*, though, this bit of ... hmm ... *patching* ... should do the trick."

As she looked at the unusual "patch", Brenna thought she saw the hint of a pattern in the twists and the knots and the positions of the twigs. Then she blinked and whatever pattern she thought she had seen faded. Still, she realized she felt calmer, less frightened, now that the patch was there.

She followed Mrs. Lipscomb back to The Parsonage, then picked up Norv's cage to walk home for lunch.

~ ~ ~

Wishing she had another cup of Mrs. Lipscomb's Chamomile tea to drive away the chill that had touched her, Brenna also wished she could move from the shadow of this tree to the shadow of the big mulberry across the street in front of the house called Lady Mulberry.

She held Norv's cage up to her face. "It's only June," Brenna told the rat. "Can you imagine how bright it's going to be in August?"

Norv did not answer. He did not wish to imagine anything, it seemed.

"Maybe if we run?" Brenna asked. "You wouldn't mind if we ran, would you? You can stand a little shaking up, right? A little exercise?"

Now Norv opened his eyes and looked at her.

"So it's OK then?" she asked.

Norv shook his head, then curled up in a tighter ball than before, his eyes squeezed shut.

Brenna lowered Norv's cage and looked at the pool of shade around the trunk of the mulberry tree. When she had been younger, about five or six, that mulberry tree had had branches low enough that she and other neighborhood children–including

Lupeta, she remembered, and her brother, Esteban–could use the tree as a sort of combination clubhouse and monkeybars. The couple living in Lady Mulberry at the time, though, had been less than thrilled with kids playing in their tree. Brenna remembered Eloísa calling the couple "Mr. and Mrs. Grumpypants". One day, Mr. Grumpypants took a chainsaw to the lower branches of the tree. In that one afternoon, the tree had become unclimbable, and no longer such a fun place. Brenna could still see the stubs where the branches had been cut off. At least one good thing had come from the ire of Mr. Grumpypants. Brenna could get under the tree today without having to duck and crawl past the lower branches.

She got ready to make a dash through the sunlight. She hugged Norv's cage to her chest, hoping that would keep him from being too shaken. She focused on the shade under the mulberry tree. She took the first step.

She tripped over something and nearly dropped Norv's cage as the mulberry tree rushed at her. The tree seemed to *slide* at her, as if she had stood still and the world had moved under her, bringing the mulberry tree close enough to touch in less time than it took her to gasp.

She finished her gasp, then touched the tree, her outstretched right hand grabbing one of the flat, sawed off branch stubs to keep from falling.

"Did you see that?" she asked Norv. Norv was no longer curled in a ball. He was flat against one side of his cage, his claws gripping the wire, his eyes wide open. "I'll take that as a 'yes'."

Brenna turned to look behind her, at the oak where she had been standing just a few seconds before. She did not remember running. She had taken only the one step.

"How–?"

Norv had no answer for her. Not even a squeak.

Brenna left the shade of the mulberry tree with more caution, focusing on putting one foot in front of the other. Walking. In a normal, non-world-sliding, no-tripping-over-trees manner.

The world did not slide. She tripped over no trees. She saw nothing that she did not wish to see.

She reached the corner of Sew Spoke and Inner Circle and crossed to the other side. The sun seemed to shine especially bright off the smooth, new pavement of Inner Circle Drive, making it all but impossible to see, but she and Norv managed to cross without getting run over. Less than a minute later, she was walking in her own front door.

The smells from the slow cooker were even more amazing than when she'd left. But just under the wonderful smells that would eventually be dinner, she recognized the spicy, floral scent of perfume that meant her mother had come home for lunch.

"Is that you, Brenna?" Mom called from the kitchen. She did not sound happy.

"I think it has to be," Brenna said in a low voice, "If it was Dad, he would have come through the garage."

"What was that?"

"Hi, Mom," Brenna called back. "I gotta put Norv up."

"Did you take that rat out again today?"

Brenna did not answer. She tried to take as long as she could going up the stairs. Walking to her room. Marvelling at the neatness and organization Eloísa had achieved. Choosing a place to set Norv's cage. Deciding that his usual position by the window would do. Hanging Mrs. Lipscomb's floppy hat on the knob of her closet door. Leaving her room.

She could hear Eloísa cleaning the hall bathroom upstairs, and if it had been any other room than the upstairs bathroom–

also known as "Brenna's bathroom"–Brenna would have gone in to say hello.

Having exhausted the options for dragging out seeing her mother, she finally went back down the stairs. She thought about clomping down the stairs–what good are heavy boots if you can't clomp with them?–but decided she did not need that lecture/argument.

Mom was, unfortunately, still in the kitchen when Brenna got there. She was at the island counter, putting together a salad of mixed greens, grated carrots, and sliced mushrooms. All very healthy, Brenna knew, but she would really rather have a burrito made by Eloísa.

"Wash your hands," Mom said. She scooped up a handful of the mushrooms she had just sliced and dropped then in the bowl with the greens. "I'm almost finished."

Brenna moved to the sink.

"I cannot believe that girl," Mom said. She snapped the cover on the salad bowl.

"What girl?"

"I don't know her name," Mom said, shaking the bowl to toss the salad. "One of those kids from the North Tract. She climbed over the fence, walked across our backyard, then climbed over the fence–again!–to get to the park."

"When was that?" Looking out the window over the stainless-steel sink as she washed her hands, Brenna could see Spring Park. The geese were massed in the middle of the pond, near the old fountain. The bright sunlight washed away most of the colors, but she could still make out the feathers on the geese's back. And she could see Lupeta standing on the far side of the pond, looking around and–sniffing?

"Just now. A few minutes before you got home."

"Lupeta?"

"I already said I don't know her name." Mom put the salad bowl down on the island counter so it thumped. "Just makes me mad."

Brenna wiped her hands with the towel hanging by the sink. "I told you the fence was a bad idea."

"No, this shows why the fence was necessary in the first place."

Brenna rolled her eyes. She moved her lips, mouthing the words Mom always said.

"Spring Park used to be so pretty," Mom went on, ignoring Brenna. "That's why we have to restrict access to it, to make it pretty again. We can't have just anyone going in there, leaving their trash behind–and their dog poop. Get two salad bowls from the cabinet, please, Brenna."

"Just our dog poop and trash then? Nobody else's?"

"That's not what I mean, and you know it. We don't even have a dog. Spring Park needs help. We're the ones who can help it."

Brenna opened the cabinet. As she stretched to reach the salad bowls, she asked, "So, once you make Spring Park pretty again, does that mean you'll take the fence down?"

"Of course not, Brenna. Because then it will be our responsibility–the responsibility of all the Pond House families–to keep the park clean, and make sure it stays pretty." Mom put the salad in the center of the breakfast nook table, then arranged the salad tongs and a bottle of "light" Italian dressing beside the bowl.

"So, either way," Brenna said, putting the bowls on the table, "you don't want Lupeta playing at Spring Park?"

"Who is Lupeta? That girl? If you mean that girl who walked through our backyard, then, no, I don't want her at Spring Park. She's not the kind of person I want there. Don't forget the forks, dear. We can't eat with our fingers." Mom took the salad bowls and put one on either side of the table.

"What kind of person? Mexican? Or just poor?" Brenna grabbed two forks from the everyday silverware drawer and dropped them on the table.

"Brenna," Mom said, wincing at the noise and disorder, "stop trying to turn this into some kind of race thing or class war." She arranged the forks beside the bowls.

"You're the one keeping out the poor people." Brenna sat.

Mom used the salad tongs to fill Brenna's bowl with more salad than Brenna had any intention of eating, then also sat. "If she's not going to respect property rights–"

"It's a public park, Mom." Brenna would have preferred ranch dressing, but knew Mom would then lecture her about calories and fat and blah blah blah cellulite. So she settled for dousing her salad with Italian dressing. She put the bottle of dressing down beside her bowl.

"That has nothing to do with it, Brenna. Spring Park need protecting. Please, Brenna, I would like some dressing too."

Brenna moved the dressing bottle so it was in front of Mom. "Mrs. Lipscomb was telling me the other day," she said, "about how the family that lived in Spring Beach would host an annual Easter egg hunt. All the families who lived around the pond would decorate eggs and hide them. And they would invite all the children in the neighborhood, and the surrounding neighborhoods." And earlier today, she did not say, Mrs. Lipscomb told me about how little Billy Tippins disappeared. Nor did she say anything about the Other Side. Or about the thing. Easter egg hunts were normal. Unlike sliding from one shadow to another, and tripping over a tree.

Mom wrinkled her nose and her shoulders shook with a shiver. "Eww," she said. "Have you ever smelled an Easter egg that's been left out too long because no one found it?" She poured a small amount of dressing on her salad. Her expression became stern as she set the bottle down beside the salad in the center of the table, once again balanced by the salad tongs. "I don't like you spending so much time with Mrs. Lipscomb."

"It's more fun than spending all day here alone."

"If you would have stuck with the volleyball team—"

"Mom, I hated volleyball."

"I thought you wanted to go to volleyball camp?"

"No. That was you. All they do at volleyball camp is–get this–*play volleyball*. And talk about boys. I don't mind the boy talk, but I don't want to play volleyball." Brenna rolled her eyes and shook her head. "I wanted to spend the summer reading, writing, and helping Mrs. Lipscomb."

"Whatever, Brenna. I just don't want you spend so much time over there."

"I'm just helping her out. She's fun and tells great stories."

"That's another thing. If you're helping her out, I want you to talk to her about paying you for your time."

"What for?"

"You should learn what's important in life. And what's important is getting paid for your work."

"I'm not going to ask her to pay me, Mom. I like her."

Mom sighed. "Brenna," she said, "I just don't want you to grow up to become a crazy cat lady."

"Mrs. Lipscomb is not a crazy cat lady."

"Eat your salad, Brenna."

Brenna speared a forkful of greens and sliced mushrooms doused in Italian dressing. "I'm trying," she said.

~ 9 ~
LUPE
AFTER SUNDOWN

THE HARSH, CHEMICAL smells of the "orange-scented" dish soap made Lupe's eyes tear up as she washed the dishes. Yesterday, the week before, all her dishwashing life until now, she had liked the smell of this dish soap. Tonight, though, she could smell all the component chemicals–including the one that pretended to smell like oranges–and rank them by how much she hated them. That is, if she had any idea what the names of the chemicals were. She had never thought of dish soap as anything but dish soap. Now she knew better. She hoped her nose would survive.

To keep the smells of the dish soap and the increasingly grimy dishwater from overwhelming her, she opened the window above the sink.

"Hey," Steven said. Her older brother, he stood beside her, drying the dishes and putting them away as she washed and rinsed them. "You can't do that. The air-conditioning is on."

Lupe ignored him. The scents of grasses and flowers and trees and small animals came in with the warm air of the evening and Lupe could breathe again.

"You can't open the window," Steven said. "Not while the AC is on."

"I'm washing the dishes, aren't I?" Lupe asked. "That means I can open the window. That's what you said back in the winter. At least it's not freezing–"

"That was different." Steven tried to look superior. At fourteen, he stood nearly a foot taller than Lupe, so he had more than enough height to look down his nose at her.

"Esteban," Momma said from the living room. She was not shouting, but her voice was raised. Lupe could hear the edge of irritation. "Stop telling your sister what to do."

Lupe stuck her tongue at Steven and put her hands back in the warm water. She had tried to beg off washing dishes tonight, but Steven refused to swap. He had accused her of being so complimentary at dinner just to avoid doing the dishes.

Which was a lie. Dinner had been incredible. Possibly the best dinner she had ever eaten. Momma had made her customary stacked enchiladas–what Daddy called her "Texmex casserole"–with seasoned ground beef, black beans, corn, and cheese. Lots of cheese. Momma claimed she had done nothing different, but Lupe could not remember it ever tasting so good before. She had had a third, large helping, which was sitting a bit heavy in her stomach now, but had been worth every bite.

The truth was that the first whiff of dish soap as it squeezed out of the bottle and into the white double sink had been enough to make her gag. She had refused to throw up such a delicious meal, though, which Esteban took as proof that she was not sick. Certainly not sick enough that he had to do the washing on her night.

What made the chore bearable tonight was that in addition to how intense everything smelled, she was also hearing a whole new world. The sound of the water traveling through the pipes and coming out the tap and pattering on the bottom of the sink or rolling off the glass plates. It all fascinated her. Even the plastic cups and the silverware jostling together in the soapy water had music to them she had never heard.

Steven's voice also had a surprising number of layers to it tonight, as well. So did his breathing. She could hear his irritation at being thwarted by Momma, and the impatience that Lupe was not finished washing everything yet, and his distraction about something–some*one*, probably–on his mind that had nothing to do with Lupe, Momma or dishes. His whining, though, sounded the same as it always did.

"Will you hurry up, Lupeta?" Steven said, emphasizing her full name. "I'm supposed to be going over to Jimmy's."

"I'm going as fast as I can, *Esteban*. If you wanted it done faster, you should have swapped with me."

"I'm not going to swap with you, you little buttkissing faker."

"Momma–"

"Esteban, that's enough."

Steven growled in his throat.

Lupe felt the growl in her own throat before she knew she was doing it. The sound rumbled in her ears and surprised both her and Steven. He stepped back from her.

"You don't scare me," Steven said.

Lupe only smiled. She curled her lips back to show her teeth. Her smiled faded as she heard something move outside the window.

"What was that?" she asked.

"I said 'you don't scare me'."

"Not that–" A new scent came with the breeze from the backyard. The scent of something *bad*. Something she had first smelled that morning, then smelled again on the edge of Spring Pond.

She pulled her hands out of the dishwater and let them drip as she went to the sliding door by the kitchen table. The sound of the door sliding open almost–*almost*–masked the sound of the backyard gate closing. The hairs on the back of her neck stood up, her teeth bared, and a part of her brain wondered what she thought she was doing as she stepped outside into the darkening twilight.

"Where are you going?" Steven asked behind her. "You're not done yet."

Her eyes were finding it hard to see, harder than she expected. The sky was still bright enough, she thought, but anything at ground level wanted to melt together. It was difficult to distinguish one object from another. Her ears and her nose, though, seemed to be working overtime to compensate. She could not see the tire swing that hung from the tree branch overhead, but she could smell the rubber, the rope, even the bit of moisture that had collected in the tire. And she could hear the wind moving over the rope and across the inside of the tire. All of that was secondary, though, to the stench of the shadow-thing.

The scent of the shadow-thing was strong this time. But not fresh, she realized. The scent was secondhand. The shadow-thing had not been in her backyard–which made her light-headed with relief–but something, or someone, who had been with the shadow-thing *had* been in her backyard. Looking in her kitchen window. At her.

"You're not done yet," Steven said again.

And possibly looking at Steven, she allowed. But she doubted it. Who would look twice at Steven?

She sniffed the air. After a few seconds, she could make out the scent of whoever had been there. The scent was weaker, but metallic, almost powdery, like dried beach sand and slotcars. As she isolated the scent, she realized she had smelled it before, in the North Park that was not North Park. She had been too distracted–and winded–by her running leap at the shadow-thing that she had not noticed it. It was not the scent of the little boy, or his sister. Or Brenna. Lupe tried to remember who else had been in the not North Park.

"Mom," Steven called. "Lupe isn't finished yet."

The other little boy. The one who was not a little boy. She found it hard to think of him, as if even the memory of him was trying to elude her. She could remember nothing specific about him. Just his smell.

"Lupeta," Momma said from the sliding door behind her. "You need to finish the dishes. Then you can go outside."

Lupe took in another lungfull of air through her nose, creating a more permanent scent memory. "I'm coming," she said as she let the air back out.

It would be dark when she finished the dishes. She did not think that would slow her down, though. Not now. She had the scent.

~ 10 ~

BRENNA

AFTER SUNDOWN

BRENNA FOUND HERSELF watching the dinner movie alone within thirty minutes of the opening credits. Eloísa had left for the night after plating their dinners and putting away the leftovers. Mom, Dad and Brenna had sat on the oversized leather sofa facing the sixty-inch family TV, Brenna in the middle, each with a plate of rice and refritos and a beef and onion tortuga sandwich. Dad had his nightly beer and the remote, Mom had a glass of filtered ice water, and Brenna sipped a sugar-sweetened "Mexican Coke".

Dad made it twelve minutes into the movie before his phone chirped for his attention. He left the remote on the coffee table in front of Brenna, then took his plate with its half-eaten sandwich and his beer when he stood. He had his Blackberry phone balanced on his shoulder as he walked from the living room, talking about a missing shipment of four-door sedans. Brenna did not expect him to come back. He seldom did.

Ten minutes later Mom finished her rice. Though she had only nibbled at her refritos and her sandwich, she declared herself full and took her plate back to the kitchen. She did not come back. Brenna could hear the fan of Mom's laptop whirring on the table in the breakfast nook and she could hear Mom's fingers tap-tap-tapping on the flat keyboard. So, obviously, Mom was not coming back either.

Brenna used the last bite of her tortuga to scoop up what was left of her rice and refritos. She sighed as she chewed, still balancing her empty plate on her lap. At least dinner had been as good as she expected. The movie might have been too, but she was not in the mood to watch it alone.

She reached for the remote control with her right hand, just as Norv's whiskered face appeared beside her left knee.

Her muscles all tried to jump at once as she pulled back, and a tight squeak escaped her control.

"Norv," she said after she managed to breathe again and her heart had slowed to almost normal. "What are you doing down here?" She leaned forward to put her plate on the coffee table as Norv climbed into her lap. As she leaned back again, he stood on his hind legs and looked up at her. "You better not let Mom see you down here. How did you get out of your cage?"

"Shh!" squeaked Norv. "Not so loud." After a few seconds, he added, "And close your mouth. That thing is huge. All those teeth." He shuddered. "Big teeth."

Brenna left her plate on the coffee table and the movie running as she scooped up Norv and ran up the stairs to her room. She tried not to think about hearing Norv talk. She focused on getting Norv back to her room. Before Mom saw he was out of his cage. Before–

It would have been easier to concentrate, to pretend she had heard nothing, if Norv had not kept talking.

"You're ... squeezing me," Norv said as they went up the stairs, his words coming out as high-pitched squeaks. "I don't ... want to fall ... but I al– ... –so want ... to breathe ..."

She heard the squeaks, but in her mind the squeaks became

words and rearranged themselves to make coherent sentences. Each squeak-word-sentence echoed in her head and mocked her. She was hearing a rat speak. Not just squeak, but actually speak. Words. To her.

She wished Eloísa were there to tell her that she was not going insane. That she needed to stop spending so much time with El Rata, and that she needed to straighten her closet or take a walk in the park–

Except she had seen something–some *thing*–in the park already today that had scared her and made her stay in her room all afternoon wondering if she were losing it. She did *not* want to go back to the park. Or any park. Not tonight. Maybe not ever.

And she could still hear Norv speaking.

Once in her room, she tossed Norv–"Aaaaah!" Norv squeaked as he flew through the air–on her bed and closed the door. She leaned against the door–or braced it closed–and paused to get her breath. She noticed the door of Norv's cage hanging open. Behind his cage, her bedroom window was open like she had left it when she went down to dinner–but open wider now. And it looked like one corner of the screen had been pried up.

"You're scaring me," Norv said. He had moved behind one of the Gund bears that populated her bed and was peeking out from behind it. "Really really scaring me."

"I'm ... I'm scaring *you*?" Brenna managed to ask.

"Yes," Norv said, nodding. His whiskers twitched. "Yes yes yes. You're huge and you're breathing hard and you just threw me tail over teakettle across your room."

Brenna pushed herself away from the door and stood straight again. She shook her head to clear it. To stop hearing the high-pitched, rapid-fire voice of her rat.

"And did I mention you're huge?" Norv added. He shrank back farther behind the Gund bear when she looked at him. "And have big teeth? Really really big teeth?"

Brenna took a breath to say something, but decided that she did not know what she should say. "I'm ... sorry?" Then, covering her mouth with one hand, "And my teeth aren't that big."

"Just so long as you don't do it again." Norv came out from behind the Gund bear. "The throwing me part, I mean. Not the being huge and having big teeth. There's not much you can do about that, even if you do apologize for them. But none of that matters right now." He stood on his hind legs. "You need to follow me."

Norv was talking too fast. She could understand him. She just could not get her mind to focus properly to keep up. Then the last thing he had said began to register. "Follow you?"

"Yes yes yes. Follow me." Norv went back down to four legs and moved to the edge of the bed. He turned and did a hanging drop to the floor, then walked around her to the door. Brenna moved her feet out of his way and shifted so she could see what he was doing. He stopped at the doorframe and stood again.

"You'll have to open it," he said. "I mean, I *could* open the door, it would just take longer." His eyes flicked around the room while his right claw stroked his whiskers. "I would have to go up the curtains first," he said, "to get some elevation. Then over to that shelf with the round-headed cat that has–thankfully– no mouth. And no visible claws, but then cats are tricky and you can't trust them. Ever. Anyway, then I would–" He stopped. "The details aren't important," he said. "But we do need to go. Your friend said you needed to be there."

Brenna stared, trying to fit the movements of the tiny rat

lips with the words she heard in her head. There was no correlation. It was like watching a poorly dubbed manga animation on fast-forward. "Go? Wait. What friend?"

Norv rolled his eyes. "Like I know all your friends." He took a breath. His whiskers twitched. "The tall one," he went on. "But not as tall as you. Male? I guess? Kind of smelled that way, but I didn't get a chance to check. Whatever. He climbed up to the window and asked if he could come in. I told him you weren't in. He offered to let me out of my cage if I would invite him in. That seemed a fair trade, so I did and he did. Then he told me to bring you to the Hole in the Fence. I told him that I wasn't in the habit of bringing you anywhere, and that if I was going to bring you somewhere, it wouldn't be a place where people bring their *dogs*. But he insisted and made me promise. So I need to bring you to the Hole in the Fence. But you have to open the door first."

"Are you always–?" Brenna stopped. She squatted, and leaned over so she could look at him more closely. She wondered if her supposed "friend" was the little, glowing man she had seen on the Other Side talking to the girl and her brother. Norv had not been with her there, though, so she could not ask. She had something more important to ask, anyway. "How am I able to understand what you're saying?"

"Am I going too fast?" Norv asked. "That's a problem with us rats. High metabolisms. We go-go-go and we can get carried away–"

"No," Brenna said. "Stop. Slow down. I mean, you're speaking. And I understand you. How ... ? How is that possible?"

"Oh." Norv paused a second. "Oh." Then shrugged. "I don't know. How come you couldn't understand me before? It's not like I didn't try to talk to you. I used to tell you every time I took a whiz so you could clean it up, but you just seemed to think it was cute, me making all those 'squeaking' noises. So I had to learn to do that sort of thing in one corner of the cage. Didn't want to have to sleep on that. I mean, yuck. Sure, I'm a rat, but–"

"Stop, please."

Norv stopped talking and drew into himself. "Sorry. Sorry sorry."

"So you've tried to speak to me before." Before Norv could reply, she held up a hand. "Yes or no."

"Yes." His nose wrinkled and his whiskers twitched, but he did not say anything else.

"You want me to–"

"It's not like I could understand you either, by the way. All that chatter-chatter-chatter. All I got out of it, I think, is that you call me 'Norv'."

"Right," Brenna said. "Your name is Norv. And you can talk to me. And you want me to follow you."

"That is what I have been saying, yes. Nice, neat and tidy. With all your chatter before, I never expected you could summarize something so succinctly–"

"Wait. Can you tell me more about ... about my 'friend' that let you out of your cage."

Norv seemed to consider the question for a second. "You're bigger," he said. "By a lot. A lot a lot. But he was still tall. He reminded me of a lightning bug, for some reason. Too big to be one, of course, and he climbed up instead of flew, but the similarities were still–"

"Norv," Brenna said. "Please. You're going too fast."

"Sorry."

Brenna took a deep breath, then let it out slow. She did not know what else to do, so she decided to just go with the flow. Even if it seemed insane. "Do I have to follow you?"

Brenna asked. "Or can I carry you?"

"If you're going to put me in the cage, I'd rather you followed."

"I can just carry you." Brenna put out her hand, palm open.

"You're not going to squeeze me again, are you? Or throw me? I didn't like being thrown. Not at all. Not at anything. Even the bed, which is soft—"

"No, I won't throw you. I'm sorry about that."

Norv crawled into her hand. She stood and held him against her stomach as she moved to the bed. She set him down on the bed and he crawled off her hand.

"I thought we were leaving?"

"I need to get my boots on," Brenna said.

Norv peered over the edge of the bed at her feet as she took off her slippers. "Could I have one of those?" he asked. "In my cage, I mean. I think it would make a better bed than cedar shavings. Softer. Warmer. Much more comfortable."

"Ask me again later," Brenna said.

When she had her boots on, she picked up Norv again and opened her door. She walked down the stairs as quietly as she could. She had no doubt Dad was still busy with his work. Mom, though, was less predictable. She managed to get down the stairs and to the front door without being noticed. She thumbed the latch and held it while she pulled the door open, then let it up slowly.

"You're being too loud," Norv said. "You're going to wake up everybody in the neighborhood. Everybody everywhere. Your friend wasn't this loud—"

"Shh," she told him, whispering. "No talking."

"Brenna!" Mom called from the family room. Brenna froze just as she was about to close the front door. "You left your plate, and you didn't turn off the TV."

"No squeezing," Norv said. "No squeezing, no squeezing!"

"Sorry," Brenna said, then said it again louder after putting her head around the door.

"Next time," Mom said, "don't be sorry. Just do it. I get so irritated when I have to clean up after you."

Brenna rolled her eyes. As if Mom ever cleaned up after anyone. She had no doubt her plate was still where she left it on the coffee table. "I'm going to be in my room," she said.

"Fine," Mom said.

Brenna pulled her head back through the door, then pulled the door closed. Her heart was racing nearly as fast Norv's. She could feel his heart beating against her fingers.

Norv sniffed the air, then struggled against her grip. When she loosened her fingers, he crawled out of her hand and up her arm to her shoulder.

"Can we stop by the garbage cans on the way?" Norv asked. "I've always wanted to stop by the garbage cans. They smell wonderful. Every day."

"No," Brenna said. She looked around as they walked down the front sidewalk. The sun was down now, but she could see as far as she could ever see. There was no color, though. Not even the washed out colors she had seen under the noon sun. Everything was bright silver and shades of gray, like watching an old black-and-white movie, but she could still see. Everything was in sharp focus. Her hand in front of her face. The leaves on the trees. She could not see what color they were, but she could have counted the blossoms on Mrs. Schmidt's begonias, across the street and two houses down. Brenna had never seen such detail before, nor so many textures.

Norv squeaked in her ear. "Are we going or not? I don't think it's coming to us, this Hole in the Fence, whatever that is. You know, I don't know your name. Is it Brenna? Is that what the Woman Even Bigger Than The Huge One But Not The One That Hates Me called you? Brenna?"

Brenna had not realized she had stopped walking. She started again, still looking about her, trying to see everything because it seemed like everything was right there, waiting for her to see it. "Yes," she said. "My name is Brenna."

"Oh, good," Norv said. "I was hoping it was something short like Brenna, and not what I've been calling you all this time. The Huge One. Which was short for The Huge One Who Feeds Me And Cleans My Cage." He sniffed the air again. She felt him shudder. "Be careful," he said. "There are some big dogs around. Big dogs. Big, big dogs."

~ 11 ~
FAYE
AFTER SUNDOWN

AT HER DESK in her room, Faye laid a fresh sheet of tracing paper over the base drawing of her manga character, Yosai Nomori. Yosai faced out of the page, her hips swivelled and her right leg extended in a forward-kicking attack pose. Her face expressed a sort of feral joy that Faye had worked hard to get right over the past weeks. Faye picked a point that should be between her manga self's shoulder blades and drew double, dragonfly-like wings out to both sides. She gave the wings an up-and-back angle, and drew in tiny veins. Then she took the tracing paper where she had already copied Yosai alone, and overlaid it on top of the paper with the wings. She adjusted the position, trying to find one where the wings looked *good*. Instead of goofy. Or like an angry Tinkerbell. Maybe she could give the wings a bit more of an angry slant, or harder, rougher edges and details. Something–anything–to get rid of the Tinkerbell vibe.

She resisted the urge to ball up this set of wings and toss them into the wastebasket with the other failed attempts. For one thing, she thought she was getting closer–finally–to a useful result. And because she was beginning to run low on the pack of tracing paper Mom had bought just before the move. If Mom saw the pile in the wastebasket, she would probably have a fit. Mom had thrown enough fits in her direction for the next week or so, Faye thought.

Faye had not been grounded to her room after dinner. She had decided to retreat there on her own. A preemptive withdrawal from the field of annoyed and exasperated parental looks and irritating young sibling whining before such grounding–or worse–could be meted out. She had unpacked some of her clothes and hung them in her closet, and moved other clothes from the boxes to the new chest of drawers. She had stopped unpacking, and started drawing wings on Yosai–or trying to–after she decided she had organized about as much of her room as Dad had his office.

She heard the scratching at her door and let out an impatient sigh. Flub had been clingy all afternoon and through dinner.

"I already said I'm sorry," she said without turning around. In a lower voice, she added, "How many times do I have to say I didn't mean it? Little brothers. Sheesh."

The scratching came again, and she realized it was not coming from her bedroom door, but from her balcony door. She leaned back in her chair to look at the balcony doors, wondering if a squirrel had climbed up, or a bird.

"Or an Edward," she said aloud. The little man–she still avoided thinking of him as a fairy–had his face pressed to the glass, bugging his eyes and puffing out his cheeks as he blew against the glass. It was difficult to be certain, but she thought he might be crossing his eyes too.

"You really are as bad as Flub," she said when she opened the balcony door. Edward lost his balance and fell into the room, laughing. "You know," Faye added, "only other guys think that's funny. The rest of the world just thinks it's gross. And now I have a big, glowing yellow smudge on my window. Thank you."

Edward rolled over to his back and smiled up at her. "It is good to see you again too, Miss Faye Ellen Woods."

Faye started to ask how he had learned her middle name, then noticed that he had pronounced "Ellen" with a slight wuh-sound, "Eh-wen". Just like a certain, pain in the butt little brother.

"Eff, ee, double-you," Edward said, again sounding like Flub. "Few!"

"No one calls me that," Faye said. "Either one," she added before Edward could ask. "Just call me Faye."

Edward bounced to his feet, almost too quickly to be seen, then he leaped up to the footboard of her bed and perched there. He was still moving fast, but Faye could see him move now. He did not just disappear and reappear.

"Faye, Few, Faye, Few, Faye Ellen Woods, Few, Few, Few," Edward recited.

Faye did not sit on her bed this time. She went back to her desk chair, spun it to face Edward on her footboard, and sat. "Why are you in such a good mood?"

Edward turned his head until he was almost facing directly backward. "Why are you so gloomy, Faye, Few, Faye, Few, Faye Ellen Woods?" Edward asked, pulling a long face as his body turned to get in line with his face. The effect was disturbing.

"Stop calling me that. Just call me Faye."

"That I shall, Miss Faye, but I do have one request of my own. Or two. Yes, two," he continued in a singsong voice, "two requests to ask of you."

"Will you stop with the not-quite rhyming? It's giving me a headache."

Edward's head bobbed up and down like a bobble-head doll.

"You really are in a good mood, aren't you?"

"A new Moon is a good Moon for a good mood," Edward said with a grin. Before Faye could respond, he asked, "Why do you call your onetime brother, the Honorable Finn Reilly Woods, whose initials, eff, are, double-you, and spell nothing, Flub?"

Faye rolled her eyes. "He's still my brother, you know."

Edward cocked his head to one side, but did not say anything. He just looked at her, waiting.

Faye shook her head. Men and boys. "Eff, ell, bee," she said after a minute. "Faye's, little, brother. I didn't start calling him Flub until he started calling me Few. He was just learning to read and write, and he wrote out my initials in huge, block letters. And his initials. And Mom's and Dad's. At first, he pronounced it fee-wuh. Then Dad had to correct him, tell him that eff, ee, double-you spelled 'few'."

"But 'flub' also means 'mistake', does it not? An action you take that you wish to take back?"

"No," Faye said. "Well, yes. He thought me calling him Flub was funny until he learned what flub meant. Then he didn't like it so much."

"Snubbed Flub rubbed wrong," Edward said. "My other request is less personal, though it does require your person."

"What? You're not making a lot of sense."

"I am feeling more myself," Edward said, "and more myself is less your sense. I cannot go home, Miss Faye. The way has been stayed. The fence has been mended. The hole has been held. And so I need your help."

Faye worked to unravel the rush of words. "The fence? The hole in the fence? Someone fixed it?" She remembered seeing Mrs. Lipscomb and the girl in the floppy hat doing something at the hole. She did not think anything in the basket the girl carried would be sufficient to fix a bent iron fence. Maybe the men working on the street had done something more permanent.

Edward nodded with enough energy to set his brown hair in motion.

"You know, I can't bend iron–"

"The burning iron of the fence still retains its several bents," Edward said. "Stretched string is the wretched thing barring my way."

"String? Someone fixed the fence with string? Can't you just pull it off?"

"No," Edward said.

"I could loan you some scissors–?"

"I just want to go home, Miss Faye Ellen Woods, but I need your help."

Faye was trying to think how she could ask Mom to go to the park after dark without sounding like a crazy person–and without Flub–when the door to her room opened. Flub stood just outside the door, in the hall, looking sad. He had been looking sad all evening. Faye realized how sad he must feel when he did not rush into her room as the door swung open. Even after he saw Edward. He just stood there, hanging his head.

"You could have knocked," Faye said.

"Can I come in, Faye?"

"Yes. Come in. And close the door before Mom or Dad sees–" She gestured at Edward, who was looking smug and pleased with himself.

Flub shuffled into the room and closed the door. "Are you still mad at me?" he asked, and sniffed. His eyes were shiny when he looked at Faye. Then he looked away.

"Only because you're being whiney," Faye said. "If you would just get over it–"

"But you wished–"

"Stop. I was just– I didn't mean it. Look, if you're going to go through this again, you can go back downstairs and watch TV. Or go to your room or something."

Flub nodded. His lower lip trembled.

"Stop crying."

"I'm not crying."

Edward leaped from the footboard, twisted in the air, and landed in front of Flub. "Grin, Finn, and spin!" Edward said and did a pirouette. "It is the new Moon soon and gloom and doom will not do. Not at all. Tonight is a glorious night. Though," he added, his voice losing some of its manic happiness, "maybe not for you." He spun to face Faye again. "But it will be nothing for nobody, Miss Few Faye Few, if you do not unmend the fence."

"You can't wait until morning?" Faye asked.

"Few things, Miss Few, can wait until the morning dew. They must be done before the sun or there is no fun."

"Enough with the rhyming. Stop, please."

Edward's face was all grinning teeth and batting eyelashes.

"Fine. I'll do it." She stood. "I'm not sure how I'll get past Mom and Dad, though."

Edward pointed to the door to the balcony that hung open.

Faye shook her head. "I'm not going to jump off my balcony. No," she added, when Edward gave her a look of exasperation. "I've never tried to sneak out of the house before, and I'm not going to start tonight."

"There is no need to sneak if they are asleep," Edward said, as if "sneak" and "sleep" rhymed.

"You don't know my parents," Faye said. "They don't go to bed until after midnight."

Flub sniffed. "They used to be my parents too."

"They're still your parents," Faye said.

"Wish them asleep," Edward said.

"I can't just– Fine." She looked up at the ceiling. "I wish my parents were asleep. Are you happy–?" A chill touched her and sent bumps down her arms and as the lights in the room dimmed, then came back. She blinked and hugged her arms to her body to suppress a shiver. She looked at Edward. "What ... ?"

"And it is done," Edward said, smiling. "They will sleep until the sun."

"How did you–?"

"I did not."

"This is crazy," Faye said. She walked past both Edward and Flub to her door and pulled it open. "Mom?" she called out. "Dad?" She could hear the TV playing in the living room, but nothing else. She walked down the hall to the head of the stairs. "Mom," she said, louder. "Dad." Still nothing but the sounds of a TV crime drama.

She went down the stairs, through the foyer and under the arch into the main living room. Mom and Dad were sitting together on the loveseat, as they usually were. Dad had his chin on his chest, the book he had been reading still held open, but beginning to droop in his hands. Mom's head leaned against Dad's shoulder. Both of them were breathing slow, heavy breaths.

The chill came back and she shivered again. "This is crazy."

"I brought your sandals," Edward said behind her, surprising her and making her jump.

She turned to look at Edward. He held her sandals in his

arms. Her sandals were as big as Boogie Boards in his tiny arms. He raised his arms and the sandals dropped to the white tiles of the foyer. "I will stay here with the Esteemable Finn Reilly Woods while you are gone."

Flub came down the stairs but he stopped at the landing. "Don't go, Faye," he said. A tear escaped and ran down his cheek.

"Will you stop crying?" Faye said. She bent down and pulled on her sandals. "I'll be back in a minute." She paused at the door. "Be quiet," she told Flub. "Don't wake Mom and Dad."

Flub nodded.

Faye flipped the switch for the porch light, but nothing happened. "Just great," she said, and went outside. She pulled the door shut behind her, then let the glass storm door close as her eyes adjusted to the dark.

The neighborhood seemed darker tonight than it had the last few nights. The nearest streetlights were out, including the big light that illuminated the park. She decided that the construction workers must have disconnected the lights.

She walked across the front yard, then picked her way across the torn up street. The hole in fence proved easy to find, even in the dark. The web of twine and ribbon that had been stretched across the hole gleamed in the faint light of the stars.

Her first thought was to just grab the twine and ribbon and pull it free, but when she reached for it with her fingers, she found she did not want to touch it. It looked too much like a spider web. And the darkness behind the web looked ... too dark. Too inky black and menacing.

"I wish I had brought scissors," she said, then jumped back and squeaked as something cold touched her hand then fell clattering to the ground. She stumbled against an exposed root of the holly bush, but managed not to fall. She looked for what she had hit–or what had hit her. She could just make out a pair of Mom's scissors on the ground.

"This is crazy," she whispered. She squeezed her eyes closed, then opened them again. The scissors still lay on the ground.

She squatted and picked up the scissors, carefully, not trusting them to not disappear as suddenly as they had appeared. The plastic grips of the scissors were cold in her hand, but felt solid. Real. She slid her fingers into the grips and did a few practice snips. Finally, she took a breath and reached forward.

When the scissors cut the first string of twine, the divided pieces sprang back with an audible "snap".

"What are you doing?" A girl's voice, calling to her from the darkness to her left.

Faye ignored the girl and peered at the web. The inky blackness behind the web seemed to twist, then pushed against the web.

A panicked squeaking erupted out of the darkness as the girl who spoken before repeated her question. "What are you doing?"

The web bulged. The tension caused threads to snap.

From her right, Faye heard running footsteps and another girl's voice. "Look out!"

The web fell apart, the remaining strings breaking all at once, and something dark and dank poured out of the hole.

Faye dropped the scissors again as she pushed backward, scrambling out of the way of whatever it was that coming out of the hole. She cried out as something sharp and wooden punctured the palm of her right hand. She thought she saw a piece of the darkness swinging at her head just before everything went bright with the pain of impact, then darker than ever.

PART 3
THE DARK OF THE MOON

~ 12 ~
FAYE

: NIGHT

COLD, WET DARKNESS pressed down on Faye's face. The smells of rotting vegetation and stale, standing water forced their way into her mouth and down her throat, trying to suffocate her or drown her or worse. She could not see. There was only the darkness. But she could feel a hungry presence sniffing at her, tasting her as it rolled over her, its rough tongue so cold it burned where it touched her right hand and the right side of her face. She wanted to scream, but she could not breathe.

Then the darkness was gone, and its sniffing and tasting, but still she could not scream. She could only cough, trying to get rid of the foul, damp airs that had been left in her lungs.

She felt hands on her shoulders as she coughed. Then the same hands holding her hair away from her face as she rolled over and gagged, her dinner threatening to come up. She tasted bile in her mouth, but managed to stop the coughing without vomiting.

She heard the panicked squeaking again, then a girl's voice. "I don't know where it went." More squeaking. "Yes, I can see that. Thank you." In a softer tone, the voice asked, "Are you OK?"

Faye started to say something, then thought better of opening her mouth. She did not want to breathe that stench again. If she did, she did not think she could stop the gag reflex. Not yet. So she just nodded. Her eyes were watering. She blinked away tears and tried to sit up.

"Can you see straight?" the girl asked, letting go of Faye's hair. "I thought I saw it hit you."

More squeaking. It sounded right next to Faye's ear.

"She can't understand you. Hang on."

Faye turned to her left as the girl moved around beside her and squatted. Faye recognized Brenna, the girl from the park, the one she had seen wearing the floppy hat. Brenna still had on the same dress and boots. Instead of the hat, though, now the girl had a rat perched on her shoulder. Brenna leaned forward to look at the side of Faye's face, where the darkness had struck her. The rat leaned forward too, also looking at Faye's face.

"Oh," said Brenna. "That's ... does that burn?"

The rat squeaked a question.

Faye looked down at her right hand. Her palm still felt hot and sticky, but she could see no blood. A jagged, white scar traced across her palm, though, as if the cut had been seared closed with a supercooled poker. Her right temple, just above her eye burned, as well. When she touched it with the fingers of her left hand, her fingertips felt warm. The skin felt rough in the center.

"I hope that didn't leave a scar," she said.

The rat squeaked.

Brenna said nothing. She just drew back a bit and bit her lip.

Faye sighed. "Fine. I *wish* that didn't leave a scar–" Heat, as intense and searing as the cold had been, touched her temple.

She felt nothing with her fingers, which she now pressed against her skull to keep it from exploding. Her cry of pain frightened the rat so it ran down the other girl's back out of sight. The heat and pain passed almost as quickly as they had started, leaving Faye holding her head with both hands and panting.

"Are you OK?" Brenna asked after a minute.

Faye tried a quick, single nod. When that did not make her head fall off her shoulders, she nodded again. "Yes. I think so." She paused, then added, "That really hurt."

"Let me see," Brenna said, and touched Faye's hand, the one covering the burned spot. The rat's eyes seemed to glow as it peeked out from under the girl's arm.

Faye moved her hand out of the way.

Brenna's expression changed from concern to surprise. "How did you do that?"

"People with fairy blood in their veins," Faye said, still breathing hard, "should be careful when saying 'I wish'."

"What does that mean?"

Faye shook her head. "I have no idea."

An abrupt howl like a wolf or a coyote echoed through the darkness, cut off into a yelp of pain.

"What was that?" Faye asked.

"It came from your house," Brenna said, looking over Faye's shoulder.

The rat squeaked.

"My house?" Then Faye remembered Flub. And the thing in the park that morning. "Oh-my-god-Flub," she said, and went to stand. "Is that ... is that where it went?"

Brenna helped Faye steady herself. Faye's head still did not want to stay on straight, and the world rocked back and forth. With Brenna's help, Faye turned around and stared across the street. The street was darker now than it had been. The only lights came from her upstairs bedroom, and through the open front door.

"I didn't see where it went," the girl went on. "I saw Lupeta run after it–"

"My front door is open," Faye said. "I didn't– Oh my god, what did I do? Flub!" she shouted. She pushed away from Brenna and ran, stumbling across the street. "Flub!"

She was not sure how she crossed the broken street without tripping. All she could think of was, *What did I do? What did I do?*

The glass storm door's hydraulics had pulled it closed, but the solid front door behind it hung open, inward, letting out the light from the foyer. When she pulled the storm door open, the front door moved on its own and closed in her face.

"Flub!" she shouted, and banged on the door. "Mom! Dad!"

Her hands scrambled to find the doorknob, to grab it and turn it. The door resisted when she pushed on it, then opened. She felt a breeze blow against her as she stepped inside. The breeze tugged at the door.

"Flub! Mom! Dad!" she shouted as she ran into the living room. The wind caused the door to slam behind her.

Mom and Dad still slept on the loveseat. The TV still played. Behind Mom and Dad the double French doors to the backyard stood open. She could not see or hear Flub. There was no sign of Edward either.

Mom stirred and opened her eyes. She looked at Faye, blinking. "Tell your brother," she said, "to stop jumping on the bed." Then Mom put her head back down and resumed the slow, steady breathing of sleep.

Faye stared at Mom, but the woman did not stir again. She ran through the living room, past the loveseat to the double doors and looked out at the backyard. The doors shifted as the front door was opened again.

"Hello?" Brenna said from the front door.

The backyard was darker than the street because of the tall trees. Faye flipped the switch to the back porch light. The light did not come on.

"I wish the light would work," Faye said. The double light socket on the porch arched and popped but gave out no light.

"Did you know your front porch light was broken?" Brenna asked as Faye saw the tiny shards of broken lightbulb on the back porch.

"Flub!" Faye shouted, stepping out on to the porch. "Finn!"

"Hello?" Brenna said again. "Mr. and Mrs. ... um ... Hello?"

"They won't wake up," Faye said. She did not add Edward's singsong words that repeated in her head. *They will sleep until the sun.* "Go look upstairs. I'll check out here. I wish–" She stopped and stared at the darkness. *People with fairy blood in their veins–*

The darkness of her backyard was as thick as black velvet, and it seemed to roil and twist like the inky black behind the web she had cut away from the hole in the fence. She could see nothing. She could hear nothing. Their backyard–the backyards of their neighbors–had become a void. She tried to make herself move, to open the screen door and step off the porch into the backyard. Flub could be out there, scared, waiting for her.

She heard Brenna walk up behind her and stand in the door.

"I can see," Brenna said. "In the dark." The rat squeaked. "I wasn't telling you."

"I'll go look upstairs then," Faye said. She spun and pushed past Brenna. The rat ducked behind Brenna as Faye got close.

Faye ran through the living room and the foyer and up the stairs. "Flub? Finn? Edward?"

The door to Flub's room hung open, as it always did, showing his perennially unmade bed and the chaos of partially unpacked boxes and toys. The door to her bedroom was closed. She hesitated only a second before opening the door. Also empty. The French doors to the balcony were closed. The smudge of Edward's face still glowed on one of the lower panes of glass.

Faye looked in Dad's office with all of its glowing green, red and amber lights from his computer and other equipment, then she looked in all the closets and, finally, the upstairs bathroom. It was like when they were younger, she was only eight and he was three, and they used to play hide-and-seek. Their old house had been so small, but Flub had been so thin and flexible, he could hide anywhere. He had once managed to hide from her and Mom and Dad for more than an hour. All of them had been looking throughout the house, pulling boxes out from under beds and getting more and agitated and worried, until his little head had popped out of the denim diaper bag that had hung, unused for months, from a closet doorknob. None of them had looked there, of course. There was no way he could have even fit, the bag was too small. Except he did fit. He thought it was the funniest thing ever. They had laughed about that for hours. Flub still tried to fit into anything, no matter how tight or small.

She kept hoping Flub's head would pop out and he would be laughing at her for not finding her and for being so worried.

He was not upstairs. She was at the top of the stairs, about to head down to search the first floor just as thoroughly when Brenna appeared at the bottom of the stairs.

"Hey!" Brenna shouted. "I'm sorry," she added in a softer voice. "I didn't expect you to be there. I found Lupeta."

Faye did not know who Lupeta was. The face of the

other girl from that morning appeared in her mind. The dark-haired girl who had charged at Flub and scared him and Faye both. Faye ignored Brenna and whoever Lupeta was. She was not looking for Lupeta. She was looking for Flub. For Finn. For *her brother–*

–should be careful when saying "I wish".

"He's still my brother," she said in a tight whisper.

"What?" Brenna asked.

"Never mind. You didn't find Flub? I mean, Finn."

"Not yet, but Lupeta–" Brenna gestured helplessly with her hands.

"Who's Lupeta?"

"She's–" Brenna looked toward the back door. "She's unconscious. In the backyard. I can't wake her up."

~ 13 ~
LUPE
NIGHT

A SHARP PAIN in her left earlobe, like getting that ear pierced again, woke Lupe.

"Oww," she said. She could not see–or maybe her eyes were not open yet, she was not sure–but she could hear and smell the night around her. A rustling in the grass as something small, like a squirrel or a rat, moved away from her. And the sounds and scents of two people, girls, her age.

Then, louder, she said, "Ah!" as she started to sit up but the pounding in her head, right at the base of her skull, stopped her by threatening to push her eyes out of their sockets. She lay back again, very slowly, the pain in her earlobe forgotten, her hands coming to her head to help hold it together.

"Oh, thank god," said a girl's voice. Brenna? Why would Brenna be here? "Does it always hurt so much when you wish on people?"

"That wasn't me," said another girl's voice. This girl's voice sounded familiar, but Lupe could not place it. "At least," the girl added, "I don't think it was me. She didn't wake up until your rat bit her."

"Rat?" Lupe said. "Bit me?" Her earlobe remembered the

pain, then forgot it again with the next heartbeat that tried to swell her head. "Ah," she said again.

"Shh," said someone, and soft fingertips that smelled of Brenna and rodent brushed across Lupe's forehead. "You had a nasty fall. Or something hit you on the head–"

"Something hit me," Lupe said. She tried to open her eyes but managed only a slit. She could just make out the two girls leaning over her. She was lying in damp grass that had been mowed less than two days ago. She could smell the exposed chlorophyll of the cut grass and the faint hint of lawnmower engine exhaust.

"Did you see my brother?" the other girl asked. Now Lupe remembered her. The girl from the park. The one with the little brother. The one who had yelled at her.

"I didn't ... see it," Lupe said. She paused, trying to remember what had happened. "I saw the boy–your brother, I guess–and the little ... man ..." She almost shook her head to clear it, but the throbbing insisted she not do that. "God, my head hurts. Help me sit up."

Both girls helped, one with a hand under each shoulder. "I saw them," she went on when she was sitting, head between her knees, still held with her hands. "In the tree. I guess it knew I was ... coming. Waited for me. Never saw it ... before it hit me. Or after."

"We heard a howl," Brenna said. There was a series of squeaks. "Right, then a yelp. Like a dog. Or a coyote."

Lupe twisted her head–slowly–and tried to see if that was really a rat perched on Brenna's shoulder. The shadows made it hard to be sure. The musky smell of rodent, though, and the faint odor of cedar shavings, was definitely coming from the shadow on Brenna's shoulder.

"That might have been me," she said. She looked back at the grass between her ankles. She could remember running through the house, past the sleeping man and woman in the loveseat, out the back door, then off the porch into the grass. She had smelled the little boy and the–she wished she had a better word or phrase to use–*little man* in the oak, both of them clinging to the lower branches as if they had just climbed there. "It must have put them in the tree, then waited for me." Had she howled? "I thought I was shouting at the boy to hang on, or maybe shouting for someone to come help, I don't remember now. I don't remember *howling*, though. I'm not a dog, Brenna."

"I didn't say you were a dog–"

"Why do you have a rat on your shoulder–?"

"What happened then?" the other girl asked, interrupting them.

"Then ... nothing," Lupe said. "I guess it hit me. Whatever it was. The shadow-thing. The scent of it was still there, as strong as I had ever smelled it. I knew it had to be there, but I couldn't see it."

"So it's gone? And it took my brother?"

"Sorry," Lupe said. "I tried–" She stopped. She remembered walking down Outer Circle Drive, approaching North Park. She remembered seeing someone–or hearing them, anyway–cutting string with scissors, right before–

"Did you let it out?" Lupe asked, squinting at the girl. "You were there, at the fence."

"Yes, she did," said Brenna at the same as the girl said, "I didn't mean to. I didn't know it was there."

"What did you think you were doing?" Brenna asked before Lupe could.

"I thought I was," the girl started, then stopped. The expression on her face sagged and Lupe could smell the girl's fear and frustration, smell the salt of the tears on her cheek. "I thought I was helping a friend."

Lupe squeezed her eyes closed, then opened them wide. The night was still dark, but her eyes seemed to be working again. The throbbing in her head no longer felt as if someone was trying to inflate her like a balloon. She kept her hands ready, though. Just in case. "A friend?" she asked, then another couple memories connected. "The little man from the park?"

"Yeah," the girl said. "His name is Edward. He said he couldn't go home ..." Her voice faded as she spoke until it was just a whisper. "... he said I needed to cut the string ..."

"It–the thing," Brenna said after a minute. "It was waiting for you."

"I guess so," the girl said. "As soon as I cut the string, it came through." The girl sighed. "I feel so stupid." Her eyes met Lupe's. "I'm sorry," she said. "About yelling at you. This morning. I thought– I didn't understand. I'm sorry." She sighed again and sat back on her heels. "My brother's gone and it's all my fault. What am I going to tell Mom and Dad?"

"I have my cell phone," Brenna said. "We could call the police."

Lupe almost shook her head. Of course little rich girl would have a cell phone.

"What?" Brenna asked.

"Nothing," Lupe said.

"What would we tell the police?" Faye asked. "An evil fairy took my brother?"

"I don't know," Brenna said. "But we have to do something." She paused. "We should go talk to Mrs. Lipscomb," she said after a few seconds. The rat on her shoulder squeaked and seemed to be nodding in agreement.

The other girl looked at Brenna while Lupe kept her eye on the rat. "What?" asked Lupe, resisting the urge to growl a warning at the rat. The rat seemed to sense her hostility, though, and pulled back until it was peeking over Brenna's shoulder.

"Mrs. Lipscomb," Brenna said. "She seemed to know about ... the Other Side." She shivered. "She's the one who sent me to warn you this morning. In the park."

"How's that going to help my brother?"

"I don't know," Brenna said. "But it's a place to start. Especially if that–that *thing*–took your brother to the Other Side."

"The Other Side?" Faye asked. "You mean North Park Other? Why would it take him there?"

Lupe sniffed the night air. She smelled the three of them, plus the rat, and more. "No," she said. "If you two will help me stand up, I think we can start from here."

"What do you mean?" asked the girl. She held out a hand for Lupe.

"What's your name?" Lupe asked as she took the hand. She took Brenna's hand too, once the girl offered it. "I'm Lupe. Lupe Garcia." She pulled against the girls and the three of them rose to their feet.

"Faye Woods," the girl said. She did not let go of Lupe's hand. She looked into Lupe's eyes. "What do you mean we can start from here?"

"What I mean, Faye, is that I can smell them," Lupe said. She let go of Faye's hand. She took a deep breath through her nose, let it out through her mouth. "The boy, the little man, and whatever that thing is." She pointed east, into the darkness at the back of the yard. She could not *see* it, but the trail was as obvious to her as a flashing, neon sign. "They went that way."

~ ~ ~

"I thought you said they went the other way," Faye said as she and Brenna followed Lupe up the steps of the porch and back through the house. Lupe could walk without help, but she did not think she would be running soon. Or climbing.

"They did," Lupe said, "but I'm not sure I'm up to climbing any more fences just yet."

On her left, Brenna chuckled.

"What are you laughing at?" Lupe asked.

"My mom saw you climb our fence today," Brenna said. "She was so pissed. It was funny."

"I wasn't trying to be funny–"

"Why are we going this way?" Faye asked, cutting her off.

"Why aren't they waking up?" Lupe asked, looking at Faye's parents. "That–the shadow-thing–came through here carrying your brother, and then I came through here. They never moved. So far as I can tell, they still haven't moved."

"She wished them asleep," Brenna said. "Faye did. Just like she wished–whatever it was she wished on you–to get rid of the swelling–"

"What?" Lupe asked. Her right hand went to the back of her head, which still tingled.

"How can you smell my brother?" Faye asked. "Aside from the obvious, I mean? How can she," she went on, pointing at Brenna, "see in the dark?"

"I don't know," Lupe said.

"Exactly," Faye said. "None of us know. Now, why are we going this way? I'm more than willing to push you over fences if I have to."

"Because I think I already know where they're going." Lupe looked at Brenna as the three of them walked to the foyer. "You can see in the dark?"

"What?" Faye asked. "Where?"

"Sort of," Brenna said. "I still think we should go talk to Mrs. Lipscomb. We're going to walk right past her house–"

"She also talks to her rat," Faye said. "Now, where do you think they're going? Where are they taking Flub?"

Lupe looked at Faye. "Flub? Oh, your brother. And people say I have a weird name," she muttered.

"His name is Finn. I call him Flub. Where are they taking him, Lupeta?"

"My name is Lupe. *Loo*-pay. No one calls me Lupeta except my grannie or my mom, when she's mad. And I think it–that shadow-thing–is taking your brother to Spring Pond." She paused. "I smelled it there this afternoon. That's where it seemed to go. After the park."

Faye pulled the front door closed behind them.

As they crossed the lawn to the street, Lupe told them about following the strangely faded scent from the cemetery to the far side of Spring Pond.

Brenna looked across the street at The Parsonage as they walked past it around the southern curve of Outer Circle Drive, then back at it when they had passed it. Lupe might have been convinced to stop. She was still feeling a bit heavy-headed. Faye, though, had no interest in stopping. Lupe decided she did not blame the girl. If Steven were in trouble, she would be the same way. Do what you can as fast you can.

Faye kept the three of them walking at a speed that tested Lupe's sense of balance. If she had not been able to hold the arms of the other girls when she needed to, she did not think she would make it. As they walked, though, Lupe felt her strength coming back.

They took Sew Spoke Drive to Inner Circle Drive, where it seemed the streetlights were still working. Faye wanted to head right, straight to the last public entrance to Spring Park, but Lupe insisted on going left. "I want to find the trail again," she said. "I want to make sure."

"I thought you were sure," Faye said. "I wish you would be sure."

"I am sure," Lupe said, feeling more than a bit annoyed–of course she was sure–and feeling an odd chill that touched her neck and sent goosebumps down her back. "But I want to cross their trail again, just to be more sure, before we walk all the way around." She shuddered, trying to shake the chill. "Did you just wish on me?"

"Sounded like it," Brenna said.

"Stop that."

"Can we get on with this?" Faye asked.

As Lupe had thought, the trail of the shadow-thing with the boy, Finn, and the little man, Edward, crossed Outer Circle Drive directly east of Hawk Briar. The trail came down the driveway of Dawn Fingers and proceeded across the street to Spring Beach. Brenna's house. So did the trail of broken streetlights and front porch lights.

"It was easy earlier today," Lupe said, looking at the silhouette of Spring Beach and its tall fence, "but I don't think I'm up to climbing your fence again."

"There's no lock on the gate," Brenna said. "And the alarm hasn't been hooked up yet."

"Let's go," Faye said.

"Are you really going to put an alarm on your fence gate?" Lupe asked as the three of them crossed the street and started across the lawn of Spring Beach. "That's so ... like a rich person, I guess. What next? Security cameras? Another maid?"

"*I'm* not going to," Brenna said. "My dad probably will, though."

"You have a maid?" Faye asked.

"Same thing," Lupe said.

"I'm not my dad. And, yes, what of it?"

Faye shrugged.

Brenna opened the gate for them, then closed it behind them. The huge yard seemed even larger with only the stars for light.

Lupe looked up at the sky. "Where's the Moon?"

"New Moon tonight," Faye and Brenna both said.

"A new Moon is a good Moon for a good mood," Faye whispered.

"What?" Lupe and Brenna both asked.

"Nothing," Faye said. "Just something stuck in my head."

Brenna opened the back gate for them, and Lupe led them around to the north side of Spring Pond. The trail was still fresh, only a little disturbed by the slight breeze, and getting stronger as they walked. Combined with the stale, rotting smell of the pond and the geese droppings, the scent of the shadow-thing made Lupe nauseous. It also raised the hairs on her neck. She was torn between wanting to throw up and wanting to attack something. She had the scent, though, she was not going to stop–

The rat's squeaking and Faye's hand on her arm were all that stopped her from walking into the pond. Lupe stopped with her left foot just above the water. The three of them–plus the rat–had come around to the east bank of the pond. The trail went straight into the reeds and the dirty water. Where the shadow-thing had gone into the water the algae were still displaced, creating the shape of a wide-open mouth with long, twisted teeth.

"It went into the pond," Faye said.

Lupe nodded.

"I can almost feel Flub," Faye went on. She held out her

hands, as if she was groping the air. "Like he's right here. Right *here*," she insisted. She tried to hug something that was not there. Then she collapsed, her legs giving out and making her sit, hard, on the damp ground. She sobbed.

Brenna's rat emitted a high-pitched squeal of warning right before Lupe heard the water start bubbling.

"Look out!" Brenna shouted and pushed Lupe out of the way of the dark, wet shape that came out of the water.

Lupe tripped, but rolled along the edge of the pond. Her knees and shoulder got wet and smeared with mud and goose droppings, but nothing else. She came to a stop in a low crouch, facing back at Brenna.

The wet shape of something that looked like a cross between a dog and a panther had Brenna pinned to the ground. Brenna had her hands up, keeping the soggy, blunt muzzle away from her face.

Lupe released the growl in her chest as she sprang forward. Her shoulder rammed into the beast's ribs and knocked it off Brenna. Her momentum carried her over Brenna with the beast. She tried to get both arms around its torso, but it was slippery, like trying to grab a garbage bag full of cold, dank water. The beast twisted out of her arms, then turned toward Faye. Lupe caught the beast before it could spring and the two of them, girl and beast, rolled across the mud and the grass. Lupe's mouth closed on the vinyl-like skin of the beast's throat before she knew what she was doing. She did not stop herself, she did not try to avoid the nauseating, slimy taste. She only felt the shock and the pleasure as she felt her teeth penetrate, lock and *pull*.

The beast collapsed into a cold, smelly puddle of water and rotting vegetation. Lupe fell to the ground on top of the remains of the beast. She spit out the long, slimy wet blades of water weeds in her mouth. Behind her she heard Brenna moan, and the rat give a single, soggy squeak. She could not stop the gagging this time and threw up the best meal of Mom's stacked enchiladas she had ever eaten.

~ 14 ~
BRENNA
NIGHT

BRENNA HAD NEVER been afraid of the dark. Not even in her earliest memories. Somehow–maybe Eloísa had first told her, whispering words of comfort into her baby ears; maybe it was Dad, when he used to hold her in arms and she would sleep–she had never been afraid of what she could not see. Unlike Mom, who still got freaked out in power outages and could not watch scary movies, Brenna embraced darkness. In the light she felt exposed. Darkness, night, was a shroud of protection she could wrap around herself and feel safe. In the dark, she could close her eyes and know she was safe.

Now, though, she could see in the dark. And in the dark she had seen monsters. Real monsters that attacked little boys or jumped out of the water and tried to drag her under–

The smell of dirty diapers burned her eyes and nose, then her lungs when she gasped, fighting against the ammonia smell and the memory of the cold, wet thing with the paws and the mouth full of writhing tendrils. She coughed and convulsed into a sitting position.

"Wow, those do work," said a girl's voice. "I always wondered."

Somewhere near, Norv coughed and squeaked. "Yuck."

A woman's hand held Brenna's shoulder while another hand patted her on the back. "Cough it out, dear, you'll feel better." Mrs. Lipscomb's voice.

"I mean," the girl's voice went on, "you see it all the time on old movies."

"See–" Brenna coughed and blinked tears out of her eyes. "–what?"

"Smelling salts," said another girl's voice. Lupeta. Or Lupe. Her voice sounded muffled.

Brenna watched Mrs. Lipscomb put the stopper back in a small bottle and set the bottle on her coffee table, then stand. Mrs. Lipscomb had been leaning over Brenna. On the other side of the coffee table, Lupe and Faye sat in the antique armchairs that matched the couch Brenna was on. Lupe had her hand over her mouth and seemed to be breathing shallow. Her eyes were watering as much as Brenna's. Faye looked unaffected by the smelling salts. Norv perched on the back of the sofa, near Brenna's left shoulder. He had his paws over his nose, similar to Lupe. His whiskers twitched.

"How did we get here?" Brenna asked.

"The other Huge Ones," Norv said through his paws. "The Two-Legged Dog and the Big Fairy. They helped you. I had to run to keep up." He started panting as if he had just finished running all the way there.

"You don't remember walking?" Faye asked.

"Two-Legged Dog?" Brenna asked. "Big Fairy?"

Norv nodded.

"Or us dragging you?" Lupe added, still talking through her hand. "What are you talking about? Who's a big fairy?"

"You walked most of the way," Faye said.

Lupe snorted.

With a last, long look at Norv, Brenna swung her legs around so she was sitting on the couch instead of reclining on it. She coughed one more time, trying to get rid of the last traces of diaper pail in her lungs. "Those are nasty," she said, pointing at the innocent-looking stoppered bottle.

"You have no idea," Lupe said.

Behind her, Norv squeaked his agreement with the Big, Two-Legged Dog.

Mrs. Lipscomb picked up the bottle of smelling salts and took them into the kitchen.

Now that she made an effort to do so, Brenna did remember the other girls helping her to her feet, and stumbling along the sidewalk, wondering where they were going. Trying to tell them about the monster that had attacked her.

"Why are we here, though?" Brenna asked as she felt Norv crawl from the back of the sofa to perch on her shoulder. She felt better just by him being there. She reached up with her right hand and rubbed his belly with her index finger.

"You said we should come here," Faye said. "We didn't know where else to go."

"I told them to take us home," Norv said. "But they didn't listen me. I had to run to catch up."

"And," Lupe said, "you said your mother would kill you if she saw your dress."

Brenna looked down at herself. The front of her dress was torn and muddy. There were also lots of little paw prints from Norv. One section of her bodice was untorn and untouched, except a perfect, muddy paw print bigger than Norv. Her knees were as scratched and muddy as her dress, so were her boots. She touched her hair, then her face.

"You're a wreck," Lupe said, sounding smug.

Brenna looked at Lupe. The girl met her gaze with a smirk. Brenna rolled her eyes, then looked at Faye. "Can you wish me clean?" she asked.

"What?" Faye asked, then shrugged. "I wish–"

"No!" said Mrs. Lipscomb from the archway to the kitchen. She held a tray with a teapot and four sets of cups and saucers. The cups rattled against their saucers, Brenna started and Norv ducked behind Brenna's shoulder as Mrs. Lipscomb said it again. "No! You can't just wish like that, all willy nilly." She placed the tray on the coffee table and sat beside Brenna. The three girls just looked at her. "I'm sorry," Mrs. Lipscomb said. "I didn't mean to snap. I just ..." She paused. "I just wish Tink were here."

"Tink?" Faye said, an odd edge to her voice. "Like 'Tinkerbell'?"

"We called her Tink," Mrs. Lipscomb said. "She thought it was funny." Faye shook her head. Mrs. Lipscomb ignored her. "Her real name was Debbie. She ..." Mrs. Lipscomb sighed. "She could explain it all so much better than I could. But she's ... Never mind all that." Mrs. Lipscomb put a hand on Brenna's knee. "Could you pour the tea, dear? I'm ... It's been a long day with a lot of old memories. And then seeing you ..."

Brenna nodded, then saw her hands were as muddy as the rest of her. "I need to wash my hands."

"Don't worry about it, dear," Mrs. Lipscomb said. "Just only touch the handle and we should be fine."

As Brenna poured the tea, Mrs. Lipscomb said, "People with fairy blood in their veins–"

"Should be careful when saying 'I wish'," Faye said. Her face had become darker, closed. "Yes. I've heard that before today."

"Don't interrupt, dear. But, yes, you should be careful.

Very careful. You have to know what you're wishing for. You have to be specific, at least in your own mind. Or ... you don't know what could happen."

Brenna put down the teapot. Lupe leaned forward out of her chair and took one of the cups of tea.

"Do you know where my brother is?" Faye asked. She made no move toward the tea.

Lupe tasted the tea, then wrinkled her nose. She leaned forward and picked up the plastic honey bear and squeezed honey into her cup. Brenna picked up a cup and sipped. This was not the same tea that Mrs. Lipscomb had fixed for her before lunch. She had been hoping for the relaxing effect. Still, the heat and the flavor seemed to help.

"You know where he is," Mrs. Lipscomb said. "You could sense him, couldn't you?"

"It was like he was right there," Faye said. "I kept expecting to turn around, and there he would be. As if I could hear his breathing just over my shoulder." She stopped and rubbed at one eye. "He does that. He comes up behind me when I'm reading, trying to scare me. I hate that." Her lower lip trembled, but only for an instant. Then she looked at Mrs. Lipscomb, her jaw set. "Where is he? Is he in North Park Other?"

"He is on the Other Side," Mrs. Lipscomb said. "If you ... felt him ... by the pond, though, then he is not in North Park Other. He's at the Source of the Spring. Which means ..." She took a deep breath.

"What?" Faye asked.

"It means," Mrs. Lipscomb said, "that the Spring Hag has him. And you must rescue him before the sun rises. Or ..."

"Billy Tippens?" Brenna asked. She suddenly felt cold.

Mrs. Lipscomb nodded. "Yes," she whispered.

"The kid that went missing?" Lupe asked. "You're saying the same thing happened to him? And the shadow-thing is the Spring Hag?"

"I wasn't living here then," Mrs. Lipscomb said. "So I can't be sure. But, yes–"

"Who is Billy Tippens?" Faye asked. "Who–or what–is the Spring Hag? No, I take that back. I really don't care. Just tell me where I can find my brother."

"If the Hag went into the pond," Mrs. Lipscomb continued, "then there must be a Hole there, as well. But not one that would be safe for you to use. And it might be only one way. In fact, since the Hag did not use that Hole to cross over before now, it is almost certainly one way. So I think it's best if you went through the Hole in the fence again, and made your way to the Source of the Spring from there. Then you will know the way back to the Hole in the fence."

Faye nodded. "Fine. Then I better–" She took a deep breath. "Then I better be going."

Brenna stared at the girl, shaking her head. "No," she said. "No no no." She could not control the quaver in her voice. "You haven't seen that thing. You can't–"

Faye met her gaze. "You think I'm not scared sick? Can you imagine how scared Flub is?" She stood. "I have to go. This is all my fault."

"Sit down," Mrs. Lipscomb said, her voice sharper than Brenna had ever heard.

Faye sat, but she did not look happy about it. Before Faye could speak again, Mrs. Lipscomb held up her hand.

"I wish I had time to tell you everything you need to know about the Other Side," Mrs. Lipscomb said, "but I don't. You don't have time to listen to an old woman ramble on, but I can help. First, you can't go alone. All three of you will need to go."

Brenna shook her head. "No, I can't."

"I will go alone," Faye said. "This is my fault—"

"It is *not* your fault," Mrs. Lipscomb said.

"I wished my brother away—"

"It doesn't work like that, dear."

"—and I have to take him back the hard way," Faye said, refusing to be interrupted. "That's what Edward said. Some wishes you have to take back the hard way."

"I wish I had time to ask you who Edward is, but I don't. Your wish did not cause this, even if it did play its part. The Spring Hag is a legend that goes back hundreds of years, before the settlers came, even before the first conquistadors came through this part of the country." She looked at the girls and read the confusion on their faces. "Yes, the conquistadors— Never mind, you'll learn about them in Oklahoma History someday.

"Spring Hollow was a potent place to the Native Americans who lived near here before anyone else," Mrs. Lipscomb went on. "The story of the Spring Hag dates to them. I wish I could sing you the full song, but there's no time. The short version is that a young mother brought her new son to the Spring Pond on a night of the new Moon and he drowned when he could not see the water's edge. Overcome with grief, the young mother threw herself into the pond after him. She did not die, though. She became the Spring Hag. On nights of the new Moon she would come up out of the pond to kidnap the young sons of other women to replace her own. The children never survive the 'mother love' of the Spring Hag, they always drown, so she is constantly looking for new sons." She took a deep breath. "Somehow, possibly through the Hole in the fence, she must have come through in 1954 and ... taken ... Billy Tippens. Just like today. You have until the sun rises to rescue your brother. After that ..."

"So what are we waiting for?" Faye asked.

"What if we called the police?" Brenna asked. "We could lead them through the hole ... the Hole ... in the fence. Then they could ..." She let the idea go as Mrs. Lipscomb shook her head.

"Even if they believed you, dear, even if they could fit through the hole, there's an ... age limit ... of sorts."

"So it's up to us," Lupe said.

Mrs. Lipscomb nodded.

Brenna shook her head. "I don't think I can do it."

"I think I'm ready to go now," Faye said. "With or without her," she added, pointing at Brenna. Brenna felt her face become warm with shame. "Or her." Faye pointed at Lupe. "If sunrise is the deadline, I don't want to waste any more time talking."

"Hey," Lupe said. "I'm coming. Just let me call my parents first."

Brenna could not make herself say the same thing.

"And tell them what?" Faye asked.

"Hush, Faye." Mrs. Lipscomb directed Lupe to the phone in the kitchen, then said, "Wait for her, Faye. And wait for Brenna. And me." With that, the old woman stood and walked out of living room, ignoring the look of frustration on Faye's face, and Brenna shaking her head again.

"I thought you said there was an age limit," Faye said.

"I'm not coming with you, dear," Mrs. Lipscomb called from the other room. "Even if ..." She did not finish the thought. She came back into the living room carrying an old-fashioned wicker picnic basket. She set the basket down on the coffee table beside the tea service as Lupe returned from the kitchen.

"I told my Mom I'm staying over at your house, Brenna,"

Lupe said. "She was confused, but she was all for it. I guess she figures you'll loan me money or something."

Brenna looked at Lupe, brow furrowed. "What's that supposed to mean?"

Lupe met her gaze. Her expression was slightly sneering. "Forget it."

"Girls," Mrs. Lipscomb said. She turned to look at Brenna. Brenna had a hard time meeting her eyes. "Don't you need to make a call too, Brenna?"

Brenna shook her head.

Mrs. Lipscomb touched her shoulder. "You have to go, Brenna," she said, her voice soft. "You are the only one who will be able to see when it becomes darkest."

Lupe gave a snort.

Norv squeaked a weak squeak.

Brenna took a deep breath, then let it out slow. "OK," she said.

Mrs. Lipscomb nodded. "I wish I had the time to more properly tell you all that has begun today. I wish I had seen this coming. I feel like I should have known ... But there is no helping what has been done. Wish in one hand–though, not you, dear," she added quickly, looking at Faye, "only some of us can be free with our wishes."

She lifted the lid on the picnic basket and took out a small, worn leather pouch with a drawstring. She held the pouch in her hand, looking at it with a wistful expression. After a few quiet seconds, she held the pouch out toward Faye. "Take this, dear. It was Tink's. I know she would want you to have it."

Faye looked at the pouch, then at Mrs. Lipscomb. For an instant, Brenna thought Faye would refuse the gift. Then Faye stood, stepped forward, and took the pouch. "What is it?" she asked. "Fairy dust?"

Mrs. Lipscomb pursed her lips and shook her head. "No, dear. It's just a pouch. But Tink always found it handy, in case she forgot something."

Faye looked at Mrs. Lipscomb as if the old woman were crazy. She did not give the pouch back, though. "How do I use it?"

"Tink would say something like, 'I wish I hadn't forgotten my whistle', then she would reach into the pouch and pull out whatever she had wished for. Most of the time. She said it helped her keep the wishes small. And it helped her to not drop things. She also carried bubble gum in it. If you hold it to your nose, I think it still smells of bubble gum."

Lupe wrinkled her nose. "Yes. It does. Old, stale, long-chewed bubble gum."

Faye looked at the pouch more closely now. She pulled up open the drawn top and peeked into it. Then she shrugged.

Mrs. Lipscomb reached into the basket again. This time, she came out with a small, curved, sheathed knife. "This is for you, Lupe," she said, holding the knife hilt first toward Lupe. "You never know when you might need an extra tooth."

Lupe took the knife and pulled it out of its sheath. The four-inch blade was the color of bone, and did look like a long, sharp fang.

"Be careful," Mrs. Lipscomb said. "It's sharp. I think it was carved from the tusk of a saber-toothed tiger, but it might have been a wooly mammoth."

"She gets a knife?" Faye asked, looking from the ivory blade to her worn leather pouch.

"I ... found ... that knife ... on the Other Side," Mrs. Lipscomb went on, ignoring Faye. "I kept it as a ... as a souvenir. But I think, now, you might find it useful. I hope– No, never mind. You will do what you have to, I have no doubt."

Mrs. Lipscomb reached into the basket once more and took out something dark and folded. It looked like an old, charcoal-colored blanket with frayed edges. She held one edge of the bundle, and shook it out, and the blanket unrolled to reveal a well-worn wraparound cloak with a hood, sized for a girl. The details of the cloak were hard to see, dark gray on dark gray, but there seemed to be fasteners and loops down the front. The edges of the cloak that had looked frayed at first, Brenna now saw were not frayed, only that she could not focus on them. The cloak seemed to be trying to blend with whatever was visible behind it.

"That's making me cross-eyed," Lupe said. She still had the knife out of its sheath.

"I'm sorry it's so dusty," Mrs. Lipscomb said. "Can you believe this used to fit me?" She folded the cloak across her forearm, then handed it to Brenna. "I think you will find this will help you."

Brenna took the cloak. The material felt softer than it looked, like a coarse silk. She had seen women wearing similar cloaks at the Rennaissance fair, and had been tempted to buy one. Mom had been adamant, though, refusing to buy anything so obviously handmade and not designed by a European or constructed in an Oriental sweat shop.

"Well, put it on," Mrs. Lipscomb said.

Brenna moved Norv from her shoulder to the couch cushion, then stood and pulled the cloak on. The material of the cloak shaped itself around her. Where the cloak touched her bare skin, it felt cool. The cloak smelled of dust and ... twilight. A gray, shifting sort of scent like the night air after the sun has set but before the stars have come out.

Lupe sneezed. "Dust," she said. "And ... I can still see you. But now it's really making me cross-eyed."

Faye was looking at Brenna with her head at an angle. "It's not easy to look at you. My eyes keep wanting to slide off you." She turned back to Mrs. Lipscomb. "How come she gets a magic cloak?"

On the wall in the kitchen, Mrs. Lipscomb's cuckoo clock began cuckoo-ing eight o'clock. Or maybe, Brenna thought, the little bird was giving his opinion of all of them, individually. Twice.

Mrs. Lipscomb stood. "It's time for you to go, girls. Be brave."

Brenna almost took off the cloak and handed it back.

"No, you wear it," Mrs. Lipscomb said. Her met her eyes and smiled. "You were brave once tonight, Brenna. You will be brave again." Then Mrs. Lipscomb kissed her on the cheek.

~ 15 ~

FAYE

NIGHT

"SO CAN WE go now?" Faye asked. She stuffed the leather pouch Mrs. Lipscomb had given her into a pocket. She watched Lupe sheath the curved, tooth-knife, then turned to walk to the front door. She hoped the two girls would follow her, but knew that she was going through the hole–or was it *the Hole?*–in the fence whether they came with her or not. She hoped she was being brave, or at least looked brave. She knew she was scared. She had no idea if what had come through the Hole in the fence really was a Spring Hag or some other kind of nightmare, but it had Flub.

And the reason it had Flub was her fault. She had wished him away. She had to get him back. Hard way or not, it was the only way. She was not going to give up her little brother.

She had to go. The other girls, Brenna and Lupe, they did not have to. Flub was not their brother. They had never seen either her or Flub before today.

She hoped they would follow her.

She opened the front door, pushed past the screen door and walked out. The screen door did not slam closed behind her. She turned and saw Lupe coming through the door.

"Wait up," Lupe said. She held the sheathed knife in her left hand, hilt forward. She held the screen door so it did not slam, then she walked to Faye. Her brown eyes were black in the darkness, with only two small gleams. "I know you're scared," she said. "So am I. But we'll get him back." She paused. "Why do you call your brother Flub?"

Faye looked away. "It's just a nickname."

"My older brother, Steven, used to call me Loopy. I hated that."

"Did he wish you away?"

Lupe gave a low laugh. "Probably. Maybe he still does. If he did, though, maybe he gets his wish tonight."

Faye gave Lupe a sharp look. "Don't say that. Don't even think it."

"Just trying to be funny," Lupe muttered.

"There's nothing funny about that ... that *thing*," Brenna said behind them as she stepped out of the house.

"You both need to calm down," Lupe said. "Lighten up."

Mrs. Lipscomb followed Brenna out on the porch. "It's OK to be scared," she said. "There are scary things on the Other Side, and you've only seen one of them. But if you stick together, well ... just stick together."

Faye tried to decide if that was supposed to be encouraging. "Let's go," she said. She walked down the steps and turned left, heading for the Hole in the fence. Lupe followed her down the steps. She heard Brenna come a few seconds later.

"Good luck, girls," Mrs. Lipscomb called after them. "Be strong."

Faye did not feel strong. She felt as if she was pushing against a stiff wind with every step, a wind of fear that was trying to blow her away. She wanted to run home and try again to wake up Mom and Dad. Maybe she could wish them awake.

But then she would have to face telling them she had wished Flub away, and that she had made it possible for some black nightmare creature called the Spring Hag to come and take him and drown him.

Her scissors still lay on the ground by the Hole where she had dropped them. The metal blades were a dull gray "X" on the ground. She bent over and picked up the scissors. Not sure what else to do with them, she put them into the pouch, which she then hung by its pull straps on her wrist.

"Maybe Brenna should go first," Lupe said. "She can see in the dark."

Faye turned to look at Lupe, and saw the white oval of Brenna's face floating in the dark behind the other girl. Faye shook her head in disbelief. Lupe got a knife made from a saber-toothed tiger. Brenna got a cloak that made her all but invisible in the dark. She, Faye, got a leather pouch that had a pair of scissors in it. And she had to put the scissors there herself. Maybe it was all part of her punishment for wishing Flub away. "I'll go first," she said.

Lupe reached forward and grabbed Faye's arm just above the wrist. "No," Lupe said. "I know you feel guilty. I can– I can smell it on you. We're here to help you, Faye. Not just follow you. Let me go first, or Brenna. Either of us is a better choice than you going in blind."

Faye pulled against Lupe, but the girl's grip was stronger than Faye expected. "Fine," she said.

Lupe did not let go Faye's arm as Brenna caught up to them. Lupe did a double-take as Brenna appeared beside them. "I can barely hear you when you walk," Lupe said. "And I can barely make out your face. The rest of you is– Just not there. If I couldn't smell you, I would hardly know you're there. So," she went on, "you or me, Brenna?"

Brenna did not answer right away. A bit of the darkness around Brenna's face moved and two tiny gleams appeared just before Brenna's rat squeaked.

"Norv says he'll do it," Brenna said. She bent down and put the rat on the ground.

Lupe let go of Faye's arm as Norv moved to the Hole and stood, sniffing. Then he went back on all fours and disappeared through the Hole.

"Norv?' Lupe asked.

'His name is Norvegicus Rattus,' Brenna said. "I call him Norv."

"If you say so."

Faye rubbed her wrist. The night in Spring Hollow was quiet. Beyond the trees, Faye could hear the cars moving at high speed on the crisscrossing highways. The wind moving through the leaves of the trees dampened the sounds but could not eliminate them. She had laid in bed last night listening to the trees and highways. Where she had lived before had been near one of those highways, miles to the west. Even though they had been farther from the highway, the big trucks and the cars had been louder there than here in Spring Hollow. Last night, her first night sleeping in Hawk Briar, had seemed *too* quiet, almost. Tonight was even quieter. And darker. She could hear the breathing of the other two girls as well as her own, but she could only just see them.

She did not know how long it was before Norv came back through the Hole. Her eyes had become more accustomed to the dark, but he was still little more than a bit of moving darkness. He stood on his hind legs again and squeaked up at Brenna.

"He says ... he says there's no one in the park," Brenna said. Norv squeaked again. "No one that he could see or smell, anyway."

"Then let's go," Faye said. She was down on her hands and knees fast enough that she startled the rat. She followed him through the Hole into North Park Other.

~ ~ ~

The faint sounds of traffic disappeared as Faye came out of the Hole, replaced by a silence that was almost a presence of its own. She could still hear the wind in the trees, and the sounds of insects, but that was all. Not even enough noise to obscure the sounds of Norv the rat as he moved away from her through the grass.

She stood. Above her the stars were brighter than any stars she had seen before. They seemed close enough to touch. As if someone had set off fireworks and the sparkling embers hung in the air just over her head. In the middle of the east sky, the new Moon hung like a black disk. It seemed to absorb the light of the stars nearest to it, dimming them. The sight gave Faye a chill in spite of the warm, spring air.

Faye heard one of the other girls coming through the Hole as she stepped over Norv and walked down the line of the fence toward the big, closed gate. The holly leaves were a glossy black under the starlight. The few visible branches beneath and behind the pointed leaves looked like twisted, gray bones. The black iron of the fence itself was lost in the darkness, visible only where it obscured the leaves and branches of the holly bushes. The pointed tops of the fence were lost in the night sky when she looked up, as if the bars of the fence extended into infinity.

"Oh my god," Brenna whispered. In the silence of the park, her whisper almost echoed. So did Norv's answering squeak.

"Shh," Lupe said, also whispering. "Just listen to it. It's ... It's wonderful." She breathed deep, then let the breath out slow.

Faye felt a pang of jealousy at what Lupe must be smelling. Even to her normal nose, the night air of North Park Other smelled of pure spring. Trees and grass growing. Flowers blooming. With Lupe's heightened sense of smell, the girl must be overwhelmed.

After a few seconds, Faye heard Lupe and Brenna following her.

Faye reached the big, double gates that looked exactly like the gates in the real North Park. The real-estate agent had told her parents that the gates of North Park had never been closed that she had ever seen. Here in North Park Other, though, the gates had been pulled closed so long ago the holly bushes had grown across the gap, just as they had grown along the fence. Further, the gates were held shut by a heavy chain and an old padlock as big as Faye's hand.

Faye could not see past the bushes to what was beyond the gate. The bushes were too tall. She spotted the black line that was the lower, horizontal bar of the gate, and tested it with her foot. It seemed solid. So she grabbed two bars of the fence to pull herself up and see over the top of the bushes.

The metal of the bars was cold to the touch at first, then became a searing, burning pain that made her cry out and fall back, away from the gate. She fell into the tall grass, her hands still burning. She could even feel heat through the sole of her right tennis shoe, where she had stepped on the gate.

She rubbed her hands on the cool grass, and that helped, but it did not stop the pain. She held her hands in front of her face, but she could not see them clearly. They were just hand-shaped grayness in front of her, a few shades lighter than the night sky. She blew on her palms. She hoped she was not feeling blisters form.

"What's wrong?" Lupe asked, appearing beside her.

"The fence," Faye said, between breaths, still blowing on her palms. "It burned me."

"Iron," Brenna said.

"Let me see," Lupe said. She took both of Faye's hands in hers and held them to her face. She sniffed at them. "I smell burning, but not from heat. It's like ... I don't know. Freezer burn?"

"Cold iron," Brenna said.

"What are you talking about?" Lupe asked, turning to look up at Brenna's face.

"People with fairy blood in their veins," Faye said. "I guess we should also avoid touching iron."

"This smells like a burn," Lupe said. "You need some aloe vera. Or maybe you can wish the burn away?"

Faye thought of the aloe vera lotion Mom had used on their sunburns after working in the yard all day at the old house, before the move. Had she seen the bottle of lotion since the move? She remembered what the bottle looked like. She hoped that was enough. She closed her eyes and thought of the plastic bottle, and the pouch on her wrist. "I wish I had brought the aloe vera," she said. The leather pouch expanded like a balloon and became heavy.

"Whoa," Lupe said, letting go of Faye's hands and pulling back.

Faye took the pouch of her wrist and opened it. She used her fingertips to pull the bottle out of the pouch. She could not read the bottle's label in the darkness. It felt like the right bottle, though. She held the bottle up in the direction of Brenna's voice. "What's this?" she asked.

"Aloe vera lotion," Brenna said. "One-hundred-percent pure aloe vera."

"Let me help," Lupe said, then took the bottle from Faye. "Hold out your hands."

Faye did as she was told. A few seconds later, she heard the plastic top of the bottle pop open, then soothing coolness pooled first in her right hand, then her left.

"Rub them together," Lupe said.

Faye did. When she was finished, Lupe asked, "What do I do with this?"

Faye took the bottle and put it back into the pouch. "I wonder," she said. She thought about the bottle and her desk in her bedroom. "I wish ..." She had only said those two words before the pouch was empty again.

"I'll swap you the knife," Lupe said, "if you can give me a few wishes."

"I'm not sure it works like that," Brenna's disembodied voice said.

"I'm not sure how it works at all," Faye said, then got to her feet.

"I don't think we're going to be able to go this way," Brenna said, her face appearing beside Faye as the other girl pushed the hood of the cloak off her head. "Faye can't climb the gate, and even if we had the key to the lock—"

"I could wish for it, maybe?" Faye said.

Lupe was shaking her head as she stepped close to the two of them.

"No," Brenna said. "Even if we did have the key, assuming that the padlock could still be opened and isn't rusted permanently shut, we have no way to get through the bushes. It would be like walking through a meat grinder."

"So what does that leave us?" Faye asked.

The wind shifted and behind them the gate to the cemetery moved with a squeal of rusted metal hinges.

"I was afraid you were going to say that," Lupe said.

~ 16 ~

BRENNA

NIGHT

BRENNA TURNED TO look at the smaller gate in the south fence of the park. Like the east fence and the gate, she could not see past the border of the park. Her flat, silver night vision stopped at the gate. Beyond the fence, beyond both gates was just ... gray darkness. Like night air that had become solid substance.

The sky above the park was the same gray color, and the stars were swirling dark stains. She could not see the stars move, but when she looked away, then back, she was certain that their shapes had changed, as if they had danced around while she was not looking.

"Are you sure?" Lupe asked. "Maybe we can lift Faye over?"

"I think she's right," Faye said. "Can you smell if the ... the Spring Hag came that way."

"Yes," Lupe said, drawing out the final "s" into a long hiss. "I can smell it. It came that way, through the cemetery. Just like it did this morning."

The Spring Hollow Cemetery had never frightened Brenna. She did not know if this cemetery was different from the one she had spent so much time in, or if it were as alien as

North Park Other was to North Park. She could feel it was a different place, even from this distance, and what she felt through the gate was not unpleasant.

She could see the gate to the cemetery was not fully closed. It hung open a fraction of an inch, its simple catch turned up, rusted in the open position. She wondered how long the gate had been left like that. Years, at least. Maybe decades. The idea that the gate had been open longer than she had been alive thrilled her, somehow. Silver light shimmered through the narrow opening of the gate. The light did not shine through into North Park Other, but she could see the light moving around behind the opening.

North Park Other scared her. Iron fence bars that burned Faye's hands when she touched them scared her. That Lupe could smell Brenna's fear scared her—and shamed her. But this silver light from an old cemetery did not scare her. It called to her.

"There's no other way," Brenna said. She walked toward the gate. She heard Faye and Lupe move to follow her.

"You're sure the Two-Legged Dog can't throw the Big Fairy?" Norv squeaked up at her. He had found a pocket on the front of the cloak, just over her left breast, and he rode there. "I think she could."

"Hush," Brenna said. "And their names are Lupe and Faye."

Norv sniffed the air. "I don't like the smell of that place," he said. "Or the rest of this place. Or that Really Huge Black Thing."

"What's he saying?" Faye asked.

"He's being a fraidy rat," Brenna said.

Norv squeaked a nonverbal protest.

"That sounds like all of us," Lupe said.

"Be careful," Faye said as Brenna reached the gate.

Brenna gave the gate a quick touch, but it felt like nothing but cold metal to her. She pushed the gate open and stepped through before she could talk herself out of doing either one.

~ ~ ~

The color of the night brightened from gray to silver. Around her transparent shapes traced in white stopped what they were doing to turn and look at her and Lupe and Faye entering the cemetery. Men and women and a few children stood in groups or sat on gravestones. The clothes they wore had the same transparent tracing as their faces and hands. Many of the men wore suits, single-breasted and double-breasted, some with waistcoats and watch chains, bowlers or tophats or hats she had no names for. The women and children were dressed up, as well, as if they were on their way to church. One group of men, women and children, separated from the others, were dressed very differently. They wore no hats over their long, plaited hair, though a few wore headdresses of various sorts. They wore simple clothes that seemed very plain next to the Sunday-Go-To-Meeting finery of the rest. None of the people were talking, but the air seemed stilled, as if everyone had stopped talking at once.

Brenna stopped and Faye walked into her. Behind them, she heard Lupe give a low growl.

Norv buried his head in the pocket.

"There's something here," Lupe said.

"I feel it too," Faye said.

The men, women, and children all began to talk at once. Their voices matched their visible form, hollow-sounding with a ring of time and distance. Most of them spoke with southern accents, though some sounded foreign. Brenna recognized British accents, and German.

"What's this, then? Who are they?" "I don't like the look of that dark-skinned girl." "What scandalous outfits they are wearing." "They have a lot of nerve, barging in on us." "So young, don't you think?" "Do you recognize them? I think the one in the cloak looks familiar, don't you?" "My Reginald used to visit every Sunday, but I have not seen hide nor hair of him since I'm sure I don't know how long." "I think she sees us." "Do you think they have family here?" "Girls again? Remember the last batch?" "Watch your stones, everybody. These young ones are all hooligans." "Don't call them stones. They're monuments." "Come along, children, do not get too close."

"Brenna," Faye said, her hand on Brenna's arm. "What do you see?"

"People," Brenna said. "Lots and lots of people."

"Ghosts?" Lupe asked.

Brenna did not answer.

"Are they blocking the path?"

Brenna shook her head. "No. They're just ... talking. No," she added as men adjusted their hats, and the women adjusted their skirts, and all of them began walking toward the girls, "now they're coming over."

"All of them?" Lupe asked.

"Close enough. Come on, let's walk along the path." The path through this cemetery traced the same route as the Spring Hollow Cemetery she had visited so many time. The path here on the Other Side, though, was not paved with gravel. Instead rough, flat stones had been arranged to mark the path. She could see the path went to a small, stone bridge, just as she expected. But she could not see beyond the bridge, or beyond the stream the bridge crossed. There was only dark-gray night again.

"Are you sure?" Faye asked.

"No. But the only other way is to climb the gate back there. Just stay on the path. I think."

Not all the ghosts were coming toward them. The children stayed back, some of them peeking out from behind marble headstones. None of the Native American spirits moved either, except to watch the girls walk.

The ghosts lined the path, men in the front, mostly, but a few of the women, as well. None of them stepped on the path. The shorter ghosts had no problem seeing through the taller ghosts, so there was surprisingly little jostling. The faces of the ghosts, men and women both, seemed more curious than anything else.

"They're close now, aren't they?" Lupe asked. "The smell of ... age, and decay, suddenly got strong."

Faye sniffed. "I can't smell anything."

The ghosts, who had been silent as they gathered, began talking again, all at once. "Well, I never–" "The very nerve–" "Who is she calling old?" "I think, for our ages, which are none too spring-like, you must admit, that we are all in excellent condition." "In my day–" "In your day? You were all a bunch of young whippersnappers–" "Sniffing at us like day-old garbage–"

"Shh," Brenna said. "They can hear you."

The ghosts fell silent again. A man who stood near the front of the group cleared his throat and stepped forward. He wore a tophat and tails and had wide, trimmed sideburns and a mustache waxed to curling points that dominated his face. Brenna stopped and faced him.

"Of course, we can hear you, young lady," the man said. "We're not deaf, you know." He punctuated himself with a curt nod. "The surprise here is that *you*, young lady, can hear *us*."

"Why have we stopped?" Faye asked.

166 / DAVID MICHAEL

"Don't be alarmed by Preston, dear," said a woman who appeared next to the man, her arm intertwined with his, as if they were walking arm in arm in the "good ol' summertime". The woman wore a long dress trimmed with ruffles and lace across her bodice and down her sleeves. She had a wide-brimmed hat covering her curly hair, and gloves on her hands. Brenna wished she could see the color of the materials and fabric instead of just silver tracing. "It's just that this hasn't happened in some time," the woman went on, "us getting visitors at all, much less visitors who can see us–"

"Or who don't try to play tricks on us–"

"Hush, Preston," the woman said, patting the man on his arm. She looked at Brenna. "We are Mister and Mistress Preston Conners."

"A pleasure," Brenna said, then introduced herself with her best attempt at a curtsy.

"What's going on?" Faye asked.

"The pleasure is all ours, isn't it Preston? You can call me Bitsy. Guin, you say? That's Irish isn't it?"

"I think she's talking to dead people," Lupe said.

Brenna ignored Lupe and Faye and gaped at the woman. "You're Bitsy? Elisabeth Bitsy Preston?"

"Who's Bitsy?" Faye asked.

"You have me at a disadvantage, Miss Guin. Have we met?"

"No," Brenna said. "It's just, I've sat by your grave–"

"Oh, dear me, that god-awful monstrosity? I'm so embarrassed."

"No," Brenna said. "It's lovely. It's my favorite."

"It used to be mine," Lupe muttered.

"You're too kind, dear," Bitsy said. "Poor besotted Preston," she added, reaching up to pat the man on the cheek with a gloved hand. "He was so distraught to lose me, but he never had any taste. Or restraint."

Faye put her hand on Brenna's arm. "We don't have time for this."

Brenna shook off Faye's hand. "And I live in Spring Beach. That is, I live with my family in Spring Beach."

"Do you really?" Bitsy said, her face brightening. She sighed and looked wistful. "How I wish I could see the old place again."

"Brenna," Faye said.

"I would love to sit and talk with you, Miss Guin–"

"Call me Brenna, please."

Bitsy nodded. "Brenna, I believe your friend requires your attention more than a couple of old ghosts. Do come back and visit us, though." Behind her, many of the other ghosts, especially the women, nodded.

"I will," Brenna said. "I will. And I will bring pictures of the house."

"That would be lovely, dear."

"Come on," Faye said, grabbing Brenna's arm this time and giving a tug.

"I'm coming, I'm coming." Faye did not let go until Brenna was walking. Both Prestons nodded and waved good-bye to Brenna.

"About time," Lupe said.

Many of the ghosts walked with the girls. Brenna could see them talking to each other, but she could no longer hear them.

Brenna rubbed her arm where Faye had grabbed her and looked at Lupe. "Can you believe that?" she asked, still feeling excited. "I just met Bitsy Preston!"

"Who is Bitsy Preston?" Faye asked.

Lupe reached out and grabbed both Faye and Brenna. "Wait," she said. Her voice was low. Brenna could almost hear her growl.

Brenna followed Lupe's gaze to the stone bridge that crossed the stream. "What? Did you see something?"

"I can barely see at all," Lupe said. "But I can smell ... something ... is waiting for us. Under the bridge."

"That will be Sad and Angry," said one of the ghosts, a young man dressed in an ill-fitting suit with a wide collar.

"Sad and Angry?" Brenna asked. She looked at the bridge. She saw a gnarled, clawed hand reach out from the underside of the bridge and take a grip on the stonework. "Oh, my."

"What?" asked Faye.

Lupe let go of their arms and went into a crouch. "Get behind me," she said.

Brenna stepped behind Lupe as another hand appeared, followed by an arm that looked like it had been made of old vines, twisted together. In her pocket, Norv stirred. He poked his head out to see what was going on.

"They're quite harmless," the man said. "As long as you pay them."

"What are they?" Brenna asked. After the hands and arm came another arm, then the dome of a bald, bumpy head, as it crawled up the side of the bridge.

"Bridge trolls," the man said.

"Eww." The troll was a twisted caricature of a person, smaller than the girls. It looked like it– No, Brenna realized, *he*. "Eww," she said again, and looked away. *He* was wearing only a bit of rough leather wrapped around *his* waist. It did not cover much.

"I wish I had a flashlight," Faye said, and reached into the pouch Mrs. Lipscomb had given her.

"No, you don't," Brenna said, shaking her head, trying to keep her eyes averted.

Faye's right hand came out of the pouch holding the long, black handle of a flashlight big enough to scare a night watchman—and too big to have ever fit inside the small pouch.

"Really. Don't."

Faye ignored her and thumbed the switch.

"Eww," Faye said.

Screeching wails erupted from the two trolls squatting on the bridge. They had their hands in front of their faces, shielding their oversized eyes. "Turn it off!" one of them shouted, waving a hand back and forth. "Turn it off!"

"What are those things?" Faye asked.

Brenna added her own "Turn it off!" to the din raised by the trolls. The flashlight was as bright as a spotlight, and seemed to be punching a hole in the darkness. The light bounced off the gray skin of the trolls and the stones of the bridge and forced her to squint and cover her eyes. She let out a sigh of relief when Faye switched off the flashlight and the trolls stopped screeching.

She risked a peek at the trolls and saw that they had resumed squatting. Their long, knobby arms rested on their knobby knees with their hands hanging between their legs where, fortunately, their loin cloths covered—not everything, but enough. The faces of the trolls were wide, with eyes that seemed much too big, unless they were compared to the huge noses that hung over their mouths. Their mouths were only thin slits. The set of the eyes of one troll made it look tired and melancholy, as if it could expect no better than to be hit in the face with the overbright beam of an oversized flashlight. The other troll looked very upset about the same thing. Their skin had the same texture as the stone of the bridge.

"Sad and Angry," Brenna said.

"Who is sad and angry?" Faye asked. She still held the big flashlight.

With choreographed precision, both trolls held out one hand, palm up. The sad troll, on the left, sniffled and held out his right hand. The other troll, the angry one, snarled and held out his left.

"To go this way," they said in unison, "you must pay."

Faye groaned. "Not more rhyming," she said. "I have a flashlight, and I will use it."

Lupe growled, then asked, "What do we have to pay?"

The trolls again moved with precise choreography as each raised their other hand and pointed at Brenna.

Brenna took another step back, fright hitting her like a blow, stopping her heart, then making it beat faster than ever. Norv ducked back into the pocket of the cloak.

"We're not going to give you Brenna," Faye said. She held the flashlight like a weapon. "That's just sick."

"Not the girl, you silly shrew," said the angry troll.

"Her squeaky, little rat will do," said the other.

Brenna felt lightheaded with relief, then felt her anger rising. "No," she said. "You can't have Norv." Norv, still in the pocket, out of sight, gave a muffled squeak of agreement. "We'll just go around."

The ghosts standing around, watching, shook their heads.

"Everybody pays," said the young man who had spoken before. He lowered his voice to a whisper as he added, "Even the Spring Hag pays."

"We don't have time for this," Faye said, glaring at Brenna.

Brenna met her glare with one of her own. "We're not giving them Norv," she said.

Faye turned to face the trolls again. "You need to let us

pass," she said. "We need to go. The Spring Hag has my brother–"

"The Spring Hag is trouble," said the sad troll.

"And so you must pay double," said the angry troll.

"Double?" Faye shouted.

"The price for there and back," said the sad troll with a sniff.

"Because you won't be coming back," said the angry troll.

Brenna watched Faye try to stare down both trolls, her eyes shifting from one to the other. After a long minute, Faye said, "I wish you would let us pass."

"We will let you pass, Little Wishy Missy," said the sad troll.

"As soon as you pay, Little Missy Wishy," said the other.

"Fine," Faye said. She tucked the flashlight under her right arm and held the pouch in front of her with her left hand. "I wish I could pay you." She reached into the pouch.

Brenna felt Norv's warmth and weight disappear from the pocket as Faye's hand came out of the pouch holding a very upset Norv. Faye looked as surprised and scared as Norv sounded. Both girl and rat squeaked. Norv wriggled out of her grip and fell to the path with the big flashlight. Norv rolled when he hit, then leaped over the handle of the flashlight and ran toward Brenna. Brenna squatted as Norv leaped and landed against her chest. She caught him as his claws scrambled for purchase on the smooth material of the cloak.

"It's OK," she told Norv. "It's OK." She glared at Faye. "How could you–?"

"I didn't mean to do that," Faye said. "I didn't think–"

"Shut up, both of you," Lupe said.

Brenna and Faye continued to stare at each other as Lupe said, "Let us pass." Then she growled and her muscles tensed.

The trolls did not flinch or change their expression. They still held out their hands, waiting for payment.

"We're not giving you Norv," Brenna said, tucking Norv back into his pocket. "We'll just go around. The stream isn't that wide."

Brenna stepped off the path and ran at the point of the stream just beside the bridge where it was narrowest.

"No!" shouted many of the ghosts, but she ignored them. She just needed a running start. The stream was only about eight feet across. She had jumped longer distances in PE. The ghost of the young man had moved in front of her with his arms spread to stop her. She noticed him only as a slight chill as she ran through him. She reached the bank of the stream and leaped.

She came down on the other side like a gymnast executing a perfect dismount. She spun to look back across the stream, her arms stretched to both sides in triumph. "See?" she said. "Simple."

Her perfect landing fell apart as she stumbled in the turn. Her balance was thrown off as her eyes struggled to focus on Faye and Lupe and the ghosts. They were all closer than they should be. Then she looked down and saw she stood on the same point she had leaped from, right beside the bridge.

"What–?" she managed to say before her balance deserted her and she fell backward.

She flailed with her arms, the cloak billowing about her as she fell. She reached for the stone rail of the bridge, but it retreated away from her as she fell. She took longer to fall than she thought she should. She watched her boots come up as her head went lower.

She could not hear the stream below her. She could only hear her own breathing and the sound of the cloak in the breeze and Faye and Lupe shouting in distress.

She still did not hit the ground or the stream. Or anything. The night sky became a narrow, sparkling band of blue-black above her. Everything else was gray darkness.

She kept falling. The band of sky became narrower.

She fought back panic as she flailed about with her arms, trying to find something–anything–to grab.

Her fall slowed as she moved her arms, then stopped. She could feel nothing below her holding her up.

She changed how she moved her arms, moving them in sync, as if the billowing cloak were wings and she was flapping them. She righted herself, putting her head back above her feet again, spinning slowly in the middle of nothing. She began to rise. Or she hoped she was.

A few, long seconds–or minutes–maybe hours?–later she was over the bank of the stream again, her arms still flapping. Lupe and Faye were still where she had last seen them, so maybe less time had passed than she thought. She flapped to push herself to the bank, then stretched her right foot.

When her boot touched the grass, whatever had been holding her up let go again. She felt the fall beginning again.

Lupe appeared in front of her, reaching with both hands, grabbing the front of the cloak and *pulling*. Brenna and Lupe fell together on the grass by the path.

Around them the ghosts applauded with little claps, as if Brenna had scored a birdie in one of her father's charity golf tournaments.

"You don't want to fall into the stream, dear," Bitsy said as Brenna and Lupe regained their feet.

"Good heavens, no," Preston said. "That would be ... bad."

Brenna nodded.

"You should just pay the toll, dear."

Brenna nodded. Then shook her head. "No, I can't just give them my pet."

"Is there anything else we can pay you?" Faye asked the trolls.

"Two pennies each, plus two," said the sad troll.

"We prefer the rat, but that will do," said the angry troll.

"How much to get rid of the rhyming?" Faye asked.

"Eight cents?" Lupe asked. "That's it? Why didn't you say that in the first place?"

"There are four of you," said the sad troll.

"The rat, the bat, the dog, the shrew," said the angry troll.

"Plus the child you want to rescue."

"So ten pennies, there and back, paid in advance, will do."

"Now you're counting the rat?" Lupe asked.

"Whatever," Faye said. "I wish I had brought my pennies."

Brenna watched as Faye pulled a glass vase full of pennies out of the pouch. "How did that fit in there?"

"I don't think it did," Faye said. Looking back at the trolls, she asked, "Do you have a preference? A favorite year?"

"Ten pennies."

"For all you ninnies."

Lupe growled.

Faye squatted and set the glass vase on one of the flat stones of the path. She pushed the leather pouch into a front pocket of her shorts, then reached into the vase. She counted ten pennies into her left palm.

"Here," Faye said, holding out the hand with the coins.

The trolls did not move.

"Fine." She stood and walked to the trolls. She hesitated only a second before holding out her hand, palm up.

The angry troll grabbed her wrist.

"Hey!"

Brenna saw Faye try to pull back, but the troll's grip was too strong. First the angry troll took five pennies, then the sad troll took the rest. The angry troll let go of Faye's wrist and both trolls climbed the railing of the bridge, then down the side and under, out of sight.

Faye rubbed her wrist as she went back to the vase of pennies and picked it up. She sighed. "Now what? I wish I didn't have to carry this."

Lupe grunted in surprise as the glass vase appeared in her hands. She almost dropped it. "I'm not going to carry it," Lupe said, holding it out to Faye.

Faye took the vase back, then muttered something that Brenna could not hear. The glass vase vanished.

"Let's go," Faye said, and led the way across the bridge.

Once Brenna stepped on the bridge, she could no longer see the ghosts who had been standing there. The normal night had resumed. Except when she looked down, over the railing, she could no longer see the bubbling stream. Instead, there was only a gap. A nothingness between the two banks that extended down farther than she could see. She shuddered, remembering her fall.

She could see nothing on the other bank of the stream until she stepped off the bridge. Then the night was again lit by the silver tracings of ghosts.

She smiled as the ghosts turned to look at her and Faye and Lupe.

"I know that knife!"

The screech was like a thumbtack against her eardrums. Her smile faltered as she saw the faces of the ghosts and her eyes met theirs.

"What do you see?" Faye asked.

"I know that cloak!"

The wail grated against her mind, or her soul. She put her hands to her ears. She squeezed her eyes closed to block the hideous faces that rushed at her.

"Hello, little girl," said a voice in her ear. *"Would you like some candy?"*

~ 17 ~

LUPE

NIGHT

LUPE GROWLED. She could smell the death and decay all around her, she could feel it rushing toward her as if blown by a wind, but she could not see anything. It was too dark. She could see only the brightest stars overhead, and they gave very little light down here in the cemetery. The flat stones of the path were only dim gray shapes.

"What do you see?" she asked Brenna.

"You don't want to know," Brenna said. Brenna was almost doubled over, her hands pressed to her ears, her eyes squeezed shut. She smelled of fear. More fear than any girl should be able to handle. "Just run for the gate. Please."

"Faye! Can you see?"

Faye shook her head. "Only just. It's so dark– Hang on." She whispered, "I wish I had that flashlight again."

"You forgot the flashlight?" Lupe asked. "How could you forget–?"

There was a click, then a beam of light burned away the darkness in front of them. "No," Faye said. "I didn't."

Lupe growled again, but she grabbed Brenna's arm and pulled. Brenna followed, stumbling but not falling.

"Stay on the path," Brenna said, her words almost a sob. "Stay on the path."

Faye grabbed Brenna's other arm and that helped. They ran with the flashlight beam bouncing in front of them. The light reflected off the worn marble and granite headstones and threw long, black shadows that looked like teeth or fingers trying to grab at them.

"Shut up!" Brenna shouted. "Please! Shut up! Shut up shut up shut up shut up!" Her words became a wail that made Lupe want to bite something.

Lupe led them along the path, trying not to think about what Brenna must be hearing. If the ghosts on the other side of the stream had been friendly, almost helpful, the ghosts on this side did not seem to be either. Lupe had always liked the path that wove through the cemetery, never a straight line for long, taking the stroller past all the graves of important Spring Hollow residents and providing picturesque views of the Old Church. Tonight, though, on the Other Side, Lupe wished the path went straight from the bridge to the gate. The headstones and statues were grotesque in the unsteady beam of the flashlight, and when the light touched the windows of the Old Church no light reflected, making the church look like a home of death.

"Stay on the path!" Brenna screamed, then she was crying, with huge sobs shaking her. The sobs made Lupe want to protect her. Lupe itched for something to strike, to bite. She did not know how to fight an enemy she could not see. So she continued running and kept to the path.

The cemetery's east gate finally appeared before them. Lupe pulled at the gate while Faye held Brenna. Brenna had her arms around Faye and her face pressed against Faye's neck. Lupe could just hear Norv squeak, squeezed between the two girls.

The bars of the gate were cold in her hands. The gate gave a little when she pulled, then stopped, as if something were holding it. The latch was up, so that was not the problem. There was no holly bush here, but there was a leafy vine of some sort twisted around the lower part of the gate. It was the vines that were stopping her. She started to pull at the vines with her hands, wishing she could get at them with her teeth when she remembered the knife Mrs. Lipscomb had given her. *You never know when you might need an extra tooth.*

"Hurry up," Faye said. "I think she's losing it."

"I'm hurrying," Lupe said. She took the knife out of her pocket. She held the sheath with her left hand and the hilt with her right. The curved, ivory blade glowed a soft yellow in the darkness when she pulled it free. Lupe felt her lips pull back off her teeth in reply to the call of the blade in her mind. She wondered if her teeth glowed, and would have asked Faye. A wet, coughing sob from Brenna reminded her of her purpose.

The knife cut the first vines like teeth through a tender steak. She did not have to cut all the vines. After the first few, the rest pulled away from the gate, curling away into the darkness on the other side. Still holding the knife in her right hand, she pulled open the gate.

Brenna ran past her and collapsed just outside the gate. Faye followed her out, then bent over her. Faye still held the flashlight and shown it on Brenna. Lupe came last. She pulled the gate shut, then dropped the latch–just to be sure.

"Are you OK?" Faye asked Brenna.

Brenna had her hands over her face now, shielding her face.

Lupe heard a squeak, and saw that Norv the rat had freed himself from Brenna's cloak pocket. He stood on his hind legs beside Faye, looking from Brenna to Faye, squeaking as if he were trying to tell Faye what was wrong.

Faye clicked the flashlight off. "Brenna," she said. "Are you OK?" She put the flashlight on the ground, then squatted beside Brenna, putting one hand on Brenna's shoulder.

Brenna sobbed, then whimpered. "I ... I think so." To Lupe's sensitive ears the girl sounded as if she was beginning to calm down.

The night was different here, outside the cemetery. The smells of death and decay had receded, leaving a more typical smell of vegetation and a slight breeze. She had not realized until now how still the air inside the cemetery had been. She and Faye and Brenna–and the rat–had been the only things moving in the cemetery once they crossed the bridge.

As her eyes readjusted to the darkness, she looked around. She was not sure what she expected to see. The cemetery, North Park Other, even the Old Church had all looked at least superficially like their counterparts in the–real?–world. Would the named houses of Spring Hollow have doppelgangers over here on the Other Side? Or ...

"What in the world?" she said aloud.

The color of the night had shifted from charcoal gray to a more normal indigo, but there was still very little light. What she could see, all around them, was a mass of leaves. Vines with leaves the size of her hand covered everything, turning trees and bushes and anything else into anonymous mounds. A few mounds had bare branches or broken poles sticking out of them, but nothing that could identify whatever lay beneath the leaves. As Lupe watched, the breeze moved and set off a ripple through the leaves. Only the patch of bare dirt they stood on just outside the cemetery gate was free of the vine with its creepers and leaves. A narrow trail snaked away from them headed east before it twisted sharply north. The trail was also bare dirt except a few creepers that stretched across it.

Lupe had seen trees overwhelmed by Virginia creeper and fields covered with kudzu, but she had never stood in the middle of such a thing before. She had never been this close. So close she worried the vines would grow up and over her and the other girls if they stood still too long.

"I don't think we should stay here," Lupe said, watching a vine unroll itself onto the dirt. "I think we should keep moving."

"Can you stand up, Brenna?" Faye asked.

Lupe kept her eye on that vine. It definitely moved. She heard something like snakes–lots of snakes, all around them–sliding slowly across dirt.

"We need to go," Lupe said. She turned to look at the other girls again.

Brenna pushed herself into a sitting position, then nodded. "I'll ... I'll be OK."

"What did you see–?"

"No," Brenna said, shaking her head. "Don't ask me that. Never ask me that. I want ..." She took a deep breath. "I want to forget it. Like a nightmare. It's already ... beginning to fade. Please. Don't ask me."

Faye nodded. "Let me help you."

Faye helped Brenna to her feet. Faye went to put her arm around Brenna, but Brenna indicated she could stand on her own. At her feet, Norv squeaked. "Can you pick up Norv for me?" Brenna asked.

Faye hesitated, then bent over. Norv held up his front paws and she picked up the rat, her fingers under its forelegs. She held it at arm's length as she handed it to Brenna.

"We need to go," Lupe said again. She adjusted her grip on the hilt of the knife. "I don't like the look of these vines– Faye! Your flashlight!"

A vine had wrapped itself around the flashlight where it lay on the ground. The vine retracted, pulling the flashlight with it.

Faye scrambled after the flashlight, but could not catch it before it was pulled out of sight in a mound of quivering leaves. "I can just see it in there," she said. "I can see a gleam off the glass." She started to reach into the mound.

In two, long steps Lupe was beside her, grabbing her arm, pulling her back. "No. That would be a bad idea."

Faye looked at her, surprised. Lupe caught a whiff of anger, but it passed. "Sorry," Faye said. "I wasn't thinking." She looked around. "But where do we go from here?" she asked. "The vines are everywhere."

"There," Lupe said at the same time Brenna said, "That way." They were both pointing at the trail bare of vines that headed east.

"Is that the way Spring Hag went?" Faye asked.

Brenna shrugged. Lupe sniffed the air. "She has gone that way before. Plus, it's the only way we have. We can't go back through the cemetery."

Brenna shuddered and shook her head.

"Can you see anything?" Faye asked.

Lupe looked back at Faye, then realized she was asking Brenna. Brenna shook her head again. "Just leaves," she said. "Millions and millions of leaves."

"Hungry leaves," Lupe said.

"Don't say that," Faye said. "Should I wish for my flashlight back?"

Before anyone could answer, there was a sound of breaking glass and metal being stressed and bent. The mound that had taken the flashlight flexed and shuddered and the remains of the flashlight flew out to land at Faye's feet.

"I guess not."

~ ~ ~

Lupe took the lead as they started walking on the trail. The bare middle of the trail was only wide enough for them to walk in single file. Faye came behind Lupe, with Brenna bringing up the rear so she could make sure Faye, who could neither see in the dark nor smell the vines, did not trip.

The trail split after the first turn north, with one trail going northwest and the other southeast.

"Which way?" Faye asked behind her.

Lupe sniffed the air, then led them to the left.

"Are you sure?" Faye asked. "Isn't this going the wrong way?"

"This is the way *it* went," Lupe said. "The Spring Hag."

"Can you smell Flub?"

Lupe shook her head, then realized Faye had not seen that. "No," she said. "Not here."

The trail continued to turn and split and sometimes trails would come back together. They walked along the trail between mounds of all sizes. Some were large enough to be houses, but there was no way to be sure what they had been before the vines took them over.

Except for the leaves, and the disturbing way they rippled as the girls walked past, the whole thing reminded Lupe of a maze of hay bales, like the one she and Steven had walked through last Halloween. Except then the spooks had just been other kids in costumes.

"Dang it," Faye said at the same time that Brenna said, "Watch out!" Faye tripped and fell into Lupe, pushing her forward so she tripped over a vine that had stretched taut in front of her.

Lupe fell to her knees with Faye on top of her. She held her right hand, the one with the knife out to the side to avoid cutting herself or Faye.

Too far out to the side.

She felt the combination of rough vine and smooth leaf wrapping around her wrist before she could pull the arm back.

"It's got me!" she shouted.

"Where?" Faye asked, still trying to get off her and stand again.

"My arm," Lupe said. She and the vine were having a tug-of-war for her arm. She shifted to get a better position, and lost ground as she slid a few inches. "It's pulling me! Get it off!"

"You've got the knife," Faye said, then added, "I wish I had a hedge trimmer– Fudge!"

The sound of leather tearing preceded something heavy and smelling of dust and machine oil bouncing on the ground near Lupe. Lupe stared at the Black & Decker electric hedge trimmer as vines wrapped around it and pulled it into the mound. At the sound of metal and plastic bending and breaking she spun on her bottom and dug her heels in to get more leverage against the vine pulling on her wrist.

She almost cried out when Brenna's arms wrapped around her waist, before she realized what was happening. The two of them pulled. Lupe hoped the vine would give out before her shoulder did.

Behind them, Faye was still talking. Lupe could hear the stress in her voice, the growing panic. Much like her own. "I wish I had ... Oh ... I don't know what they're called ... Yes!"

There was another sound of tearing leather, then Lupe heard two metallic snips, one after the other. Faye stepped in front of her with a large pair of hedge clippers. It took Faye three tries to hack through the vine.

Lupe and Brenna fell backward.

Brenna grunted, then screamed in Lupe's ear. Lupe felt a creeper push itself between Brenna's chest and her back. Lupe twisted around in Brenna's arm and reached around the other girl. The knife–her extra tooth–seemed to find the vine as if it had eyes of its own. The blade cut the vine easily.

Faye helped Lupe to her feet and she pulled Brenna up. The three of them stood in the middle of the trail, back to back to back. Lupe had her knife in front of her and her teeth bared. Faye held the hedge clippers in both hands, breathing hard. Around them, the leaves trembled without a breeze, but no more vines reached out for them.

"Do you have another pair of those?" Brenna asked.

"No," Faye said. "This is the only pair we have."

"You can't wish for another one?"

"I don't know," Faye said. "I tore the pouch with Dad's hedge trimmers, then destroyed it getting these out. We have some, I don't know what they're called. Loppers? But I'm not sure it's safe to keep wishing."

"Then give me the clippers," Brenna said.

"Why?"

"Because I can see in the dark. I can cut the vines that are trying to trip us."

While the other two girls came to an agreement, Lupe kept watch around them. They set off again with Brenna in the lead, carrying the big hedge clippers in front of her. Faye walked behind Brenna, her right hand holding Brenna's cloak because seeing Brenna in the dark was almost impossible. Lupe brought up the tail. She kept looking over her shoulders, first left, then right. She could not smell any new threats, but she did not trust the vines. She hoped she did not have to come back this way.

"Help!"

"Flub!" Faye cried, and pushed past Brenna.

"No!" Lupe shouted. "That's not–" But Faye was already running around the next turn in the trail. "Come on," she said, and she ran past Brenna too. The voice had sounded like a little boy's, had even sounded a little like Faye's brother, but Lupe could tell it was not him. She gripped the knife even tighter and hoped she would be able to use it against whatever they were about to face. Brenna followed her.

Ahead of her, she heard Faye stop. "Edward?" Confusion was in Faye's voice.

Lupe smelled Faye before she saw the girl, but still almost ran into her. Faye was squatting in front of a bundle of vines. The white oval of a face protruded from one end of the bundle. Lupe could not make out the face, but she recognized the scent of the little man she had seen that morning in North Park Other.

"Miss Faye, I am so happy to see you," Edward said. His voice no longer sounded so much like Faye's little brother. He sounded jangling and tinkling, like he had this morning, but now she could understand him. She could hear his words through the noise of his voice. And she could smell his oddly metallic sweat and fear when the wind shifted.

"Who is Edward?" Brenna asked, coming up behind Lupe.

"He's a fairy," Faye said. The confusion in Faye's voice had taken on an edge.

Brenna stepped beside Lupe. "Oh, it's him. What happened?"

"Yes, Edward," Faye said, "tell us what happened."

"I am trapped," the little man said. "The vines have me wrapped. Will you not cut me loose, Miss Faye? Please?"

"The last time I cut something loose for you," Faye said, "the Spring Hag took my brother."

"I had to do that," Edward said. He sounded scared now,

like a wind chime in the breeze that blew in Lupe's face. She could smell traces of the Spring Hag on him, just as she had detected in her backyard while washing dishes. She could even smell traces of Faye's brother. "She made me do it," Edward whined. "I did not wish to, but she made me. I had to trick you. I am so sorry."

"Is he saying something?" Brenna asked. "All I hear is a low buzzing."

"Shh," Lupe said. The combination of the little man's high-pitched, jangling voice and the constant rustle of the leaves in the wind made it hard to hear what he was saying.

"Why?" Faye asked. "Why did you have to do that?"

"The Spring Hag," Edward said, his words becoming a tinny clamor of whimpering, "she said if I did–if I did not–trick you–she would–she would–" The vines wrapped around him shifted, becoming tighter as they jerked him further into the mound. "You must help me!" he cried out.

Faye said nothing, and moved no closer.

Lupe's right hand twitched, the knife in her grip wanting to cut more vines. But something she could hear in the little man's voice did not sound right.

"Aren't we going to help him?" Brenna asked.

"You're lying," Faye said.

"What do you mean he's lying?"

Edward gasped and sobbed as the vines became even tighter. "She tricked me," he said, tears running down his face. "She always tricks me, kicks me, tricks me, kicks me."

"We can't just let the vines take him," Brenna said. "Faye, he's crying."

"Faye," Lupe said. "Brenna's right."

"How did you get caught in the vines, Edward?" Faye asked.

"She tricked me," Edward said.

"You did what she said," Faye went on, "so why did she give you to the vines?"

Edward's metallic scent changed, and Lupe could sense even more fear from him. She could smell little else, she realized, other than Edward and the honeysuckle-like sweetness of the vines. The breeze, which had been gusting from the east and southeast as they walked through the vine-covered maze had been blowing steadily from the west for the last few minutes. Not gusting. Just a constant breeze in her face, from a constant direction.

"Ah–!" Edward shouted as the vines finally pulled him into the mound, out of sight.

"Edward!" Faye shouted and leaped forward to grab him. Her hands disappeared into the shadows of the mound. Lupe could not see if Faye had managed to get hold of Edward, but she saw several vines wrap themselves around Faye's outstretched arms.

Lupe and Brenna moved to help Faye at the same time. Brenna grabbed Faye around the waist as Lupe tried to bring her knife to bear.

The wind stepped up as if it were trying to push Lupe back. The noise of the vine leaves became a white noise that drowned out almost everything. Lupe sliced through the vines around Faye's right arm. More vines came out to replace them, and still more vines flailed at Lupe's wrist, trying to grab her. She felt a vine wrap around her left ankle. She bent to cut at that one.

Bright, white light exploded out of the center of the mound and burned away Lupe's night vision. Brenna cried out in pain and fell back.

Faye lurched forward and would have been pulled headfirst into the mound had Lupe not managed to get her left arm around Faye's waist.

The white light winked out.

Lupe wanted to lash out with her knife, but all she could see was still a churning green darkness. She did not want to risk cutting Faye. Leaves brushed across her face. She growled as she bit down on a vine, trying to tear it with her teeth. She tasted bitter sap, but the fibers of the vine did not separate. All she could smell now was vine sap and Faye. She thought she heard Brenna scream, but she could not be sure. The wind had become a roar. It might have been Faye yelling in her ear for all she knew. She tried to pull Faye back, but there were too many vines on both of them now.

Another vine hit her left leg and wrapped around, then Lupe's leg came out from under her. She did not fall, though. The vines pulled both her and Faye into the darkness of the mound before either of them could hit the ground.

PART 4
THE CAVE OF THE HAG

~ 18 ~
BRENNA
BEFORE MIDNIGHT

HANGING UPSIDE DOWN in a cage, Brenna turned her head as much as she could to the right, trying to hide her face in the hood of her cloak. She squeezed her eyes closed so she could not see the pain on Faye's face or the tears of frustration in Faye's eyes. She could not stop her ears, though.

"I wish–" Faye started. Her voice was tight, and muffled by her clenched teeth. Then she let out a gasp of pain.

She and Faye were in a cave. Faye was across the cave from her, shackled to the worn, stone wall with her thin arms pulled wide. Faye had been manacled there when Brenna awoke.

Brenna had been disoriented, at first, thinking that Faye had been chained to the wall upside down. She had even asked, her voice hoarse, hardly a whisper, "What are you doing like that?" Then she had realized it was her, not Faye, who was upside down. She hung from her ankles, which were held in iron manacles attached to the top bars of a narrow gibbet cage. Her arms were bound behind her, but in the tight confines of the gibbet, she did not think she could have moved her arms anyway. Her skirt had fallen to her chest, exposing her legs to the chill air of the cave. She still wore the cloak Mrs. Lipscomb had given her fastened about her neck, so the cloak hung from her chin and created a pool of rumpled darkness on the bottom of the gibbet, below her head. She had no idea what had happened to Norv, nor could she see Lupe.

Brenna's eyes still stung from the blinding blast of light that had struck her full in the face back in the vines. Her lungs still felt as if they had been attacked with sandpaper. And her head pounded and ached from being hung upside down. All she remembered after the light was falling back–she must have lost her grip on Faye–being grabbed by large, rough, clawed hands, then struggling to breathe as a foul, fetid stench was blown into her mouth and nose. She had no idea how long she had been unconscious.

She risked opening her eyes again. Faye hung limply from the manacles, which were bolted to the wall. The girl was obviously in pain. Her face and the skin of her arms and legs were shiny with sweat. Something about the iron in the manacles on her wrists was hurting her. Like the iron bars of the gate back in North Park Other that had burned her hands.

From what Brenna could see, the cave was not a big one. All that separated her from Faye was about twelve feet. And the manacles on her ankles. And the iron bars of the gibbet. She used to think that gibbets were cool, fun even. But that was before she had been hung upside down in one.

The cave seemed to have been carved by water, then expanded with a hammer and chisel. She could see a narrow exit tunnel to her right. On the other side of that tunnel, before the wall curved around to where Faye was bound, metal pegs had been driven into the stone. From most of the pegs hung woven sacks, some of them sprouting dried flowers and other plants. On one peg, though, hung an old-fashioned key on a ring. It was the only key visible in the cave, and Brenna's eyes kept coming back to it.

In the opposite "corner" of the cage from Brenna, not far from Faye, Faye's little brother, Finn, lay on the dirt floor of the cave next to a basin of dirty water, surrounded by six skeletons of what had to have been children. The skeletons were too small to have been adults, even short adults. Two of the skeletons were smaller than Finn. All the skeletons were intact, their bones held together by twisted rawhide strips. Around the neck of each skeleton was a hinged manacle like the ones holding Faye's wrists and Brenna's ankles, the two iron semicircles locked shut with rusty padlocks that hung beneath the smiling skulls. The skeletons had all been posed as if they were playing together in a circle around Finn, their heads tilted back and their jaws separated in silent laughter. One of the skeletons wore a faded baseball cap. Beyond the skeletal children, the cave narrowed and might lead to another exit, or maybe that was where the Spring had originally carved its way through the rock.

The last corner of the cave, to Brenna's left, she tried to never look. The dark, nightmare shape of the Spring Hag moved about there, leaning over a crude table. The top of the table was scattered with ceramic pots of various sizes and small, carved rocks and the dried bones of what Brenna hoped were animals and not people. Also on the table was a hammer and a large, antique hourglass full of black sand that drizzled and twirled in a steady stream. She did not know what the hourglass was counting down to, but the Spring Hag keep looking at it, occasionally tapping it with a clawed finger. More iron pegs had been driven into the wall behind the table. Tools were suspended on these pegs.

The ceiling of the cave extended up twenty feet or more. Hanging from a chain bolted to the ceiling was a pair of what looked like dragonfly wings, except that they were about two feet across from tip to tip, and encrusted with layers of tiny coins. The coins were stacked thick along the center line of the wings, getting thinner toward the tips. The coins in the center were also the most discolored and obscured by oxidation and corrosion. Only a few coins nearest the tips of the wings still gleamed. The chain wrapped around the center of the wings, which hung lopsided. Edward, the little man Faye had called a fairy, sat in a nook carved in the wall near the ceiling, staring sullenly at the wings.

The Spring Hag let out a bubbling, gurgling laugh at Faye's pain. "Do not stop there, little fairy."

The Spring Hag dominated the cave. *Its* cave. Brenna refused to think of it as a she. It might have been a woman once, but those days were long past. It might still sound like an old woman, like any aging grandmother Brenna had ever met, but whatever humanity the Spring Hag might once have had, there was nothing of that left now. Every breath it took moved the air of the cave and burned in Brenna's lungs like that first, suffocating breath that had rendered her unconscious. The Hag was stooped, but still as large as a bear, and it moved fast, shifting from one part of the cave to another with the speed of a shadow.

The Spring Hag moved back to loom over Faye, blocking Brenna's view. "You should always finish your wish," it said. "To the last drip, drop, drip. Isn't that right, Edward?"

If Edward said anything, Brenna did not hear it.

"I wish," Faye said again, "that you would—" Her voice was tight with suppressed pain. "—let us go!"

Brenna felt—*something*—pulse through the rock of the cave, then the Spring Hag laughed again.

"But I will let you go, little fairy, and your friends too. But not until you are all old and gray and very nearly as beautiful as me. We will be girlfriends, all of us, for years and years and years while the Spring drips and drops and drips." It laughed. "Now, wish again, little fairy. This is fun and fun and fun."

"I wish—"

"Stop it!" Brenna said, her anguish at seeing Faye hurting herself making her shout. "Faye, stop it," she added in a softer voice. "It just wants to see you in pain."

"Hush, little bat," the Spring Hag said without turning around. "Little bats should learn not to squeak until they are squoken to. Edward," it snapped, "take away her words."

The wings hanging from the ceiling pulsed like a low-power camera flash, then Edward pushed out of his nook and floated down to the table. His expression was resigned and sullen. He picked up a small pot, and dumped its contents of dried herbs on the table. He peered into the mouth of the pot, then blew in it.

"I-wish-Edward-had-his-wings-back," Faye shouted in one, long breath, then cried out in agony.

Brenna watched Edward freeze, then jerk around to stare at Faye and the Spring Hag. His eyes darted to the wings above him, then back. His breathing came in short, shallow breaths.

The Spring Hag cackled and burbled. Its whole body shook and the air of the cave became rank as it laughed.

Edward's expression fell, and he sighed.

"So does Edward, little fairy," the Spring Hag said, still laughing. "So does Edward." She glanced back at Edward. "Yes, he does, the little scamp." It chuckled some more. "But you see, little fairy," it went on, pointing at Edward, who was standing still on the table, "Edward does not have wings anymore. He gave them to me. See?" It gestured up at the ceiling where the wings pulsed again. "They are pretty, don't you think? All those pennies." It stopped laughing. "Your wings are pretty too, little fairy." The gloating was gone from its voice now, replaced with greed. "Give me your wings, little fairy, and I will take the shackles off your wrists."

"No!" Brenna shouted.

Faster than Brenna could see, the Spring Hag turned around and leaned its huge, misshapen face close to the bars of the gibbet. It grabbed the cage and turned it so one large eye had a clear view of Brenna. Brenna tried to draw back, away from it, but there was nowhere to go.

"Edward," the Spring Hag said, "this little bat still has her words."

Brenna coughed, then struggled to breathe. The Spring Hag's breath stank worse than a school cafeteria garbage can. Coughing made her pull against the bands on her ankles, jarring them painfully. She felt a thousand little needles piercing the soles of her feet as some circulation was restored.

Edward might have said something, but it was just a low buzz in Brenna's ears. He disappeared from the table and reappeared at the feet of the Spring Hag, his face level with hers. He held the small pot in both hands.

"Well?" the Spring Hag said.

Edward's lips moved and she heard the low buzz-buzz again. No clear words, but what he wanted her to do was clear enough. *Speak, please.*

Brenna closed her mouth and pursed her lips. She shook her head. She focused on the pain in her feet to distract her.

"Stupid fairy," the Spring Hag said and batted Edward away with one clawed hand. Edward struck the cave wall next to Brenna's cage. He cried out in pain, but still cushioned the pot against his stomach and did not let it drop. "You will never get her trained if you say it like that. Give me the pot." It took the pot from Edward, then looked at Brenna again. "Speak," it said, the tone of its voice lower, harsher than Brenna had heard. *Do what I say.* The words of command were not spoken, but Brenna could feel the compulsion. "Speak, little bat."

She squeezed her eyes close and tried to resist.

"Speak!"

"No!" Brenna shouted, then realized what had happened. She had not meant to speak. She had only meant to shake her head. Then she felt lightheaded as all the air in her lungs was squeezed out of her by an unseen force that wrapped around her chest. She tried to breathe and could not. Her chest would not expand.

"Perfect," the Spring Hag said with a nod. "That will be the last time I ever have to hear you say 'no'." She handed the pot to Edward. "Put this with the frog croaks." She turned her back on Brenna as Edward disappeared with the pot.

~ ~ ~

The air came back into Brenna's lungs at a rush, bringing with it the reek of the Spring Hag, making her cough again. The coughing brought a fresh wave of pain in her ankles and feet and shoulders. She had to fight the urge to choke and gag from the stench. She did not want to vomit while hanging upside down.

"Now, little fairy," the Spring Hag said to Faye. "Give me your wings."

"What did you do to Brenna?" Faye asked.

"I'm OK–" Brenna started to say, then closed her mouth. Her voice had not come out when she spoke. Instead, there had been only screeching. "What did you do to me?" Her question also came out as a series of screes and screeches.

"That is not your concern," the Spring Hag said to Faye. "Give me your wings. It's easy, little fairy. You just tell me–"

"I don't have any wings!" Faye shouted.

Brenna jerked her head left and right, looking for Edward. He had returned to his nook near the ceiling. "What did you do to me?" she asked. Or tried to ask. She could hear the words in her mind, but she could not say them. She could only squeak. Like Norv. If Edward understood her question, he gave no sign.

"Every time a fairy denies she has wings," the Spring Hag said, its voice rising with each word, "it makes me *very angry*. And when I get angry, I go out and whip my new dog. You don't want that, do you, little fairy?"

"Why don't you just ... make me say it," Faye asked. "You made Brenna talk."

"You must give me your wings of your own free will," the Spring Hag said. "And you will. I will leave you hanging there until you do."

"Huge One?" said a small voice below her. "Brenna?"

Brenna twisted her neck looking back and forth. "Norv?" Her voice sounded like Norv's now. "How long have you been down there?"

The rat peeked out from under a fold in the cloak on the bottom of the cage. "You sound like a bat."

Brenna sneaked a look at Edward and the Spring Hag. Both were focused on Faye. "You can understand me?" she asked. "What do you mean I sound like a bat?"

Norv pulled back into the shadows of the cloak, his whiskers twitching. "Yes?"

"Are you OK? Where have you been?"

"I'm unhurt," Norv said, brushing a paw across his nose. "But I did fall out of your pocket when the–the–the Big Big Black Dog–grabbed you. My legs aren't as long as yours." He extended one of his back legs and wiggled his toes. "See? So it took me longer to get here. Why is the Two-legged Dog tied up outside? I thought that only happened to normal dogs."

"Two-legged Dog? Lupe?" Brenna realized she was getting louder. She lowered her voice. "Lupe is outside?"

Norv's eyes flicked to the exit and his whiskers twitched. Then he looked back at Brenna. "Yes?"

"Did she see you?"

"She growled at me," Norv said. "I think it's a good thing she's tied up. We should have thought of that before. I wonder when she gets fed."

"How is she tied?"

"She has a collar." He pointed up at her feet. "Like the collars around your feet, but not metal. And there's a chain."

Brenna's eyes went to the key hanging on the wall. "Can you see that key?"

Norv twisted his head around to follow her gaze. "You want me to get the key? Can I eat it? I haven't had anything to eat–"

"No, you can't eat the key. Stop thinking about your stomach. Can you get the key off the wall?"

"Yes." He paused. "I would climb up the wall here, by your cage," he said, pointing. "It's rougher, easier to get a grip–"

"Then go get it," Brenna said. "Then take it to Lupe."

Norv stopped. "Are you sure about that? The Two-legged Dog? She *growled* at me."

"She's not going to hurt you. She's locked up."

"But if I take her the key," Norv said, looking at her sideways, "she *won't be* locked up."

"She won't eat you." Norv still looked dubious. "I promise. Just go get the key."

"OK, OK. I'll get the key."

Norv slipped out from under the cloak and through the bars of the gibbet. He tested one spot on the cave wall with his paws, then moved to his left, closer to the exit and tried again. He pulled himself up like a rock climber, then started reaching for the next pawhold.

Brenna realized that she had not heard either the Spring Hag nor Faye speak for a while. She twisted and looked around. Faye still hung from her shackles. Her head hung down as if she were staring at the floor. The Spring Hag was in the other corner, leaning over the table again. It had its back to both girls. Brenna heard the sound of bones rolling across wood and a low muttering. Brenna looked up at Edward–and her heart stopped.

Edward was looking at her. He met her eyes, then looked past her, to Norv scurrying up the wall of the cave. When he looked at her again, his gaze was impassive. A new bruise was forming on his right cheek where the Spring Hag had struck him.

Brenna's heart did not start beating again until he looked away from her. He looked up at his wings where they hung from the ceiling.

Brenna let out the breath she had not realized she had been holding. She hoped that Edward's antipathy toward the Spring Hag would hold out long enough as she twisted back to check Norv's progress.

Norv had crawled nearly to the ceiling to find a way over the exit tunnel. He crawled across to the other side, then made his way down to the pegs.

Out of the side of her eye, Brenna saw Faye shift. She turned and looked at the girl. Their eyes met. Burning pain was visible in Faye's eyes, and she was breathing hard. Brenna gestured with her head in Norv's direction. Faye looked confused, then looked to her left. She did a double-take when she noticed Norv swinging from one of the topmost pegs down to the one with the key on it. Norv hit the peg across his stomach and curled around the peg to keep from falling. Faye looked back at Brenna, then at the Spring Hag and Edward.

Both girls held their breath as Norv balanced on the peg and began pulling the key toward the tip. Once Norv had moved the key away from the wall, he shifted his position and began to push the key. He had both his front paws gripping the ring as it reached the tip of the peg. The key swung back and forth on the ring, but made no noise that Brenna could hear.

The key ring cleared the tip of the peg and the weight of the key pulled Norv forward, off balance. He fell against the peg, his back claws trying to find something to grab. There was a slight *clink* as the key rattled against the ring. Brenna clenched her jaws closed to avoid crying out. She heard a gasp from Faye.

Norv held on, but Brenna could see that the strain was pulling on him. Then it was too much. The key ring pulled out of his grasp and fell. Norv let go of the peg and fell after the key.

The key ring bounced between pouches and sacks, clanking and clinking all the way to the floor of the cave with Norv in its wake, still trying to grab it with his front paws.

The air in the cave moved with the Hag as it spun around. It looked at Brenna and Faye and Edward before locking on the key and Norv. Norv was getting back on his feet, shaky from the fall. He grabbed the key ring again.

"My little pet bat has a little pet rat," the Hag said. The Hag grabbed the straw broom propped against the table and rushed at Norv.

"No!" Faye shouted.

"Norv!" Brenna shout-squeaked. "Run!"

Norv let go of the key ring, darted to his right, toward Faye. He stopped and turned around just before the broom could strike the dirt floor in front of him. He ran straight for the exit this time and disappeared out of it before the Hag could take another swing.

The Spring Hag stood at the mouth of the exit tunnel shaking the broom. "I hate rats. Disgusting creatures. Even with salt." It spun and leaned over Brenna's cage again. "But I'll make an exception for you, little bat. I'll catch your pet and serve him fricassee. He looked fat and juicy. There should be at least a leg for all of us."

The Hag laughed as Brenna turned her face away.

The Hag stopped laughing. "Edward," it snapped, moving away from the gibbet. "Find the rat. Catch it and bring it back here. For dinner."

Edward pushed himself out of his nook and floated down to the floor of the cave. As he walked out of the cave, Brenna tried not to cry.

~ 19 ~
LUPE
BEFORE MIDNIGHT

LUPE SAT IN the dirt outside the mouth of the Spring Hag's cave. She looked over the vine-covered surface of Spring Pond Other and thought violent, frustrated thoughts. In the cave, Faye shouted painful, ungranted wishes and Brenna yelled at the Spring Hag. Every so often Lupe heard the jangle of Edward speaking or the sounds of bone or metal scraping on wood.

Lupe had her fists clenched in her lap to keep them still. She had to remind herself to relax her jaw. She could almost hear Grannie Litta telling her, *Don't grind your teeth, Lupeta.* Her hands wanted to be claws. Her teeth wanted to grip and tear. She had wanted to lunge at the rat she saw crawling into the cave, but the chain that hung from the collar around her neck was connected to a stake in the hard ground. She could do nothing. Only growl.

The ground was cold, but she resisted the urge to shift her position. Shifting would only make the leather collar around her neck chafe more, and would cause the metal clasps that held the collar together to touch the back of her neck. The metal clasps never seemed to get warm. Every time they touched her skin they were cold, and sent a chill down her spine. The heavy iron chain was cold too, so she sat far enough away from the stake that the chain did not touch her. Except where it was connected to the collar.

The leather of the collar was tougher than her fingernails. The metal of the clasps had been fixed to the leather with smooth staples that she could not get a grip on.

She had tried spinning the collar so the clasp with its bulky, antique padlock was under her chin, but then the weight of the clasp, the padlock and the chain seemed to be trying to drag her face down into the dirt. Plus the metal was colder against her throat, and the hard edges of the clasp poked against the soft area under her chin and her collarbone. Even worse, then she had to see the chain and the stake that held her.

Her hands wanted to become claws. She could see the claws in her mind. Those claws could pierce the leather and tear it away from her neck. The skin of her hands itched and the bones of her fingers ached, but they would not become claws. She was just a girl.

She had tried to pull up the stake. She had wrapped the chain around her arms and her waist and pulled. She had braced her legs against the ground and pushed. The skin of her palms and her elbows and around her waist showed red welts from her efforts, but she had not been able to budge the stake. She was just a girl.

She had been left outside the mouth of the cave, chained like a dog. The scent of the Spring Hag covered everything. Even her. Even the dirt she sat on stank of the Hag, so she could not use the dirt to scrub the smell off.

She had not seen the Hag, though, not since a vine around her neck had choked her into unconsciousness. She had only heard the Hag in the cave, taunting Faye and Brenna, laughing at them. Calling Lupe her "new dog" and Brenna her "little bat". Ordering Edward, the fairy, to do this, then do that.

Lupe had always thought of herself as a quiet girl. Easygoing. Peaceful. Sometimes prone to arguments–but only when she knew she was right.

The new, ripping violence of her thoughts scared her. She now knew what it meant to have blood in her eye. She now knew what it meant to want someone–no, some*thing*– dead.

She realized she had bared her teeth and forced her lips back over them. She flexed her jaw again to relax the muscles. She unclenched her fists but her fingers still wanted to curl into claws, so she balled her hands into fists once more.

The breeze shifted around her, testing the different points of the compass and teasing the leaves of the vines that covered everything in sight. Only the stone of the cave and the circle of dirt where Lupe was chained were free of the vines. Even the pond had not been spared. The level of the pond was lower than Lupe had ever seen it, and vines covered the surface with creepers and leaves and puckered flowers that smelled of honeysuckle and rot.

Sounds like a bat came out of the cave. Just one bat. Not a bat screeching for navigation in flight. More like a bat caught in a cage, unable to fly free. A bat that sounded a lot like Brenna. The Spring Hag cackled, then harangued Faye some more. Lupe could hear the words, but she did not listen anymore. She did not want words. She wanted action. She wanted violence.

The screeches of the bat resumed, but this time the screeches were answered by the squeaks of a rat.

Lupe's head came up. The chain moved, pulling against the collar. There was no doubt. The rat and the bat were talking. The bat still sounded, somehow, like Brenna.

What had the Spring Hag done to Brenna? Or could Brenna always talk like a bat? She seemed to be able to talk to that rat of hers.

Was the rat that sneaked into the cave Brenna's rat? Norm or Norv or whatever its name was?

It was so hard to think with the collar pulling against her throat.

Relative silence came from the cave now. Lupe turned to face the cave and focused her ears on the mouth of the cave. She could hear the Spring Hag breathing and moving about. She could hear Faye's labored breaths and Brenna's shallow, hushed breathing. She also thought she could hear tiny claws gripping stone, like a rat climbing a wall.

Something was happening. She could hear it in Brenna's breathing. She could also smell the girl's tension now.

Still facing the mouth of the cave, Lupe moved into a crouch. The chain would not let her reach the mouth of the cave, but if something came out, she would make a run at it. Maybe whatever it was would make the mistake of letting her get a grip.

Her muscles trembled as she waited, coiled, ready to spring. This time, she did not stop herself from baring her teeth.

The ringing, clanking sounds of metal on metal as something fell gave her a start, but she did not charge forward. She waited for a target.

"My little pet bat has a little pet rat," the Spring Hag said.

"No!" Faye shouted as a furor of bat-squeaks and rat-squeaks erupted.

Not even a second later, a rat came bounding out of the mouth of the cave. Lupe sprang. She pushed with her legs and flew forward, her hands stretched in front of her. The collar might be out of reach of her teeth, but the teeth of a rat could cut metal. She just needed to catch the rat before it could run away.

The rat saw her coming only an instant before her hands came together on it. She saw its eyes get big. Lupe felt the wind on her palms as it jumped straight up, evading her. Her hands came together in a loud clap as the chain pulled taut and yanked her back. She felt the warm body bounce off her right arm, but she could not twist around to grab at it again.

She lost sight of the rat as she choked and gagged. She scooted backward to release the tension on the chain and the collar. So she could breathe again.

"Stupid," she said, her voice tight and hoarse. "So stupid." She had no doubt now the rat was Brenna's, but she was also sure she had scared the poor thing so much it would never come back.

~ ~ ~

Lupe heard the Spring Hag talking again inside the cave but she ignored it. She had had one chance, and she had blown it.

The little man, the fairy, Edward, appeared out of the shadow of the cave mouth. He stood there, looking at her, until she looked back at him. She bared her teeth, then pursed her lips closed again. She saw he stood just outside the reach of her arms if the chain were fully extended, as if he were teasing her.

Except he was not teasing her. He was just looking at her with a sad, pained expression.

"What do you want?" Lupe asked, making no effort to keep the growl out of her voice.

"I want my–" Edward started in his tambourine voice, then pursed his lips together in a mirror of hers. He turned away and seemed to step into a shadow.

Lupe could not see the fairy, but she could hear his light footsteps and the sound of his skin against the vine leaves, and she could smell his metallic scent. She tracked him as he moved, always facing him, shifting in place to turn. She hoped she was unsettling him, scaring him. If she was, though, she could not smell it on him. Or maybe he was already so frightened of the Spring Hag, that her being there, wishing she could grab him and shake him back and forth, just did not make much difference.

She realized she could smell the rat now too. The rat was not moving. Lupe thought she could smell freshly turned dirt, as if the rat had dug itself a small hole to hide in.

She felt then heard Edward pounce. The fairy and the rat rolled around in the vines and the dirt in a tumult of tambourine jangling and outraged squeaking.

Edward appeared out of the shadows of a mound of vines holding the rat out before him. He held the squirming, squeaking rat with both hands, the rat facing away from him so it could not try for his eyes. Edward stood, Lupe noticed after a second, at the edge of her chain reach again.

She thought he would walk around her perimeter to reach the cave mouth, but he just stood there, holding the rat.

Holding the rat out. To her.

Lupe started to ask him what he was doing, but stopped herself when his eyes went wide and he shook his head. He looked scared. Now Lupe could smell fresh fear on him. The rat was also scared. Of both of them, Lupe realized.

She moved as slowly as she could to keep the chain from rattling and to reassure the rat. She expected Edward was teasing her, that he would pull back and run around her, but he did not move. When she reached the extent of the chain, she held out her hands.

The rat still squirmed, trying to get out of Edward's hands

and away from both of them. Lupe hoped she would be able to hold it long enough to calm it down.

Edward whispered something that sounded like tiny wind chimes tinkling in a breeze. Lupe could not understand him, but she saw surprise on the rat's face. Edward whispered something else. The rat twisted its head around to look back at the fairy. Edward gave a nod. Then he bent over and set the rat on the ground.

The rat twitched its whiskers and flicked its tail, but did not run away. Then it looked up at Lupe. She heard it take a deep breath, then it scampered to her and crawled on her shoe. She reached down with her right hand and the rat crawled into it.

"Growl at me," Edward whispered, this time in words she could understand. "Yell at me."

Lupe just looked at him. "What?"

A long stick appeared in Edward's hand. She heard it swish through the air just before it struck her leg.

"Hey!"

Another swish and her other leg stung.

"Stop it!" This time she growled.

The stick came at her again, higher this time. It struck her left shoulder. She scooted back, away from him, trying not to let go of the rat. The rat was squirming again, trying to get loose.

"Edward!" The Spring Hag's shout shook the air. "Stop playing with the dog and get in here."

Edward swung the stick one last time, but it went wide of her. As suddenly as it appeared, the stick was gone. "But I don't have the rat," he said.

"Then why are you playing with the dog? Hurry up and find the rat."

"Yes, Mistress," Edward said.

Lupe looked at him, trying to think what the fairy's game could be. She pulled back when he moved his hands, but no stick appeared this time. Instead, something glowed in the starlight with a familiar curve. Edward had her knife, her extra tooth, in his right hand. He also had something in his left hand that might have been a shorter stick. Edward stepped forward, well within the reach of the chain, and put both items on the ground. Then he turned and disappeared into a shadow.

Lupe lunged forward, dragging the chain noisily, and grabbed the knife. She held both knife and rat to her chest, listening. After a long minute, she whispered in the rat's ear, "Go help Brenna." The rat looked at her and its squeak seemed a question. "I don't know. Think of something. But squeak your head off if the Hag starts coming out."

She opened her hand. The rat squeaked, then jumped free. She watched it run to the mouth of the cave. She shifted her knife to her right hand, then noticed the other item Edward had left her. It was a short, straight branch from a holly bush. Three sprigs of holly leaves were still attached. Faye had been carrying a stick like that when Lupe first saw her.

She wondered if Faye wanted it back as she pulled the leather collar away from her neck and prepared to bite it with her extra tooth.

FAYE

MIDNIGHT

THE PAIN FROM the shackles on Faye's wrists had reduced from white-hot searing to merely red-hot burning since her last failed wish—

She diverted her thoughts from wishing as the heat of the metal against her skin started to rise again. She took deep breaths and tried to think of ... Anything. Anything except the pain. She failed.

She had smelled burning hair and flesh in the first agonizing minutes after the Spring Hag had held her to the wall with one huge hand and forced her wrists into the shackles with the other. The pain had felt the same as when she grabbed the bars of the gate in North Park Other, but in a tight band around her wrists. She had imagined the shackles burning through her wrists leaving only charred stumps. But none of that had happened. The pain was constant—she had never felt such pain—but it did not seem to be burning her flesh. Only her mind.

She was bound to the stone wall of the cave too high to stand or to slouch comfortably. If she stood normally, her hands were above her shoulders, straining them. If she relaxed her legs and leaned against the wall behind her, the shackles seemed to get tighter and she felt like her hands would be pulled out of her wrists joints. The only way to relieve the aching muscles of her arms and shoulders was to stand on her tiptoes. After the endless hours hanging there, though, she could only manage to do that for a few minutes at a time. Then she would have to ease herself back down.

The shackles did not look as tight as they felt. She had tried to pull her hands through the shackles. Dad always said she had tiny hands, like Mom, but there was no give in the metal. She doubted she had even moved her wrists in the shackles enough to chafe the skin. The shackles had her and they would not let her go.

From each shackle hung an antique padlock. Her struggles had not even been enough to cause the padlocks to swing. The old, rusty locks only hung there, motionless.

She had to lean forward as much as she could to see Flub. It hurt every time she did it. The shackles gripped tighter, the pain in her shoulders almost equaled the burning pain in her wrists, but she did it anyway. Flub lay almost as motionless as the skeletons of children posed around him. She had to wait painful seconds to see his chest rise as he breathed, but she would not relax back against the wall until she had seen him breathe at least once. Twice if she could stand the pain that long.

She was not sure she could stand the pain much longer.

Faye panted, struggling to breathe in the damp, dank air of the cave. The pain and the pressure on her shoulders made breathing difficult.

The only thing that did not seem to hurt was moving her eyes. She looked up at Edward's empty nook. He had only sat there, staring at his chained, penny-crusted wings, while the Hag taunted her, while the shackles burned her and burned her. She had seen him fingering small coins that gleamed in the dim light of the cave as he looked at the wings, as if he was choosing where he would place the coins in his collection. She had wondered if those were the pennies she had given him that morning.

Had it only been one day? How could all of this had happened in just one day?

His nook was empty now. He was still out looking for Brenna's rat, still doing what the Hag ordered him to do. She wondered if she would have a nook like that soon, where she would sit and stare at the wings she had never seen, waiting until the Hag told her what to do. Who to trick. Who to betray.

Edward had only met her eyes once since she had been shackled. Edward had noticed her looking at him–glaring at him–but his eyes had met hers for only a second. Then he had looked away. She had seen the shame in his face.

She let her eyes relax and looked down at the floor of the cave again.

After the first outrage and pain of being shackled to the wall, Faye had been more angry with Edward than she had ever been at anyone before. Even Flub. She had never really hated anyone in her life, but she had hated Edward. Because he had he tricked her. Because he had betrayed her and Brenna and Lupe. Because he had helped the Spring Hag kidnap Flub. And especially because he had given the Spring Hag his wings and made it so powerful. How could he have done any of that?

She was beginning to understand.

The Spring Hag had laughed and goaded Faye and Edward both as it had forced Faye into the shackles. "You're a bit bigger than the last fairy to wear these," it had said. "But I had Edward take your measurements and adjust their position on the wall. I do hope you're comfortable," it had added, then cackled at its own joke.

"I wish–" had been the first words Faye had said, and the last for many minutes. Because it had felt as she had been touched by a red-hot branding iron. It had taken her three gasping tries to get her first useless, pointless wish through her lips. "I wish ... that you would ... let us go." She had only *thought* the shackles were burning her before. The completed wish had wrapped the shackles around her wrists tight enough to grind the bones while the iron tried to burn off the flesh.

Brenna had been hanging unconscious in the gibbet cage until then. Fayes screams woke the other girl.

"Little Edward wished the same thing, didn't you, you little scamp?" the Hag had said, then laughed again. "Go on, wish again, little fairy. I enjoy the sound of your screams."

She had wished again, the same wish. The burning got worse. By the third wish, though, by the time Faye saw Brenna try to hide her face, the pain had peaked. The agony had reached a point past which it could not go any further. She could not hurt any more than she already hurt.

By then, she had stopped blaming Edward. She had stopped hating him. She understood now. She wondered how much more pain she could take before she did the same thing he had done.

That was when she had wished Edward had his wings back. That wish had not hurt any more than the previous wishes. But it had not hurt any less, either. And it had been just as wasted.

Even after Edward helped the Hag take away Brenna's words and leave her squeaking like her rat, Faye could not hate him. Edward had been unlucky. Just like her and Brenna and Lupe. The Spring Hag, on the other hand, she could hate. It was the Hag that had done this to both her and Edward, and had put Brenna in a cage and chained Lupe outside.

After Brenna's rat had been chased out of the cave, the Spring Hag had seemed to lose interest in Faye. It had moved the hourglass with the black sand so it rested on the floor of the cave beside Flub, opposite the basin of water, then returned to its table and picked up an unfinished leather collar. Faye had stared at the humped back of the Hag, hoping the Hag could feel her anger, her hate. The Hag muttered as it poked and pounded at the collar using crude leatherworking tools and a heavy hammer, but did not seem to notice her at all.

Faye watched the Hag hold a rivet in the flame of a candle using short tongs. The tone of its voice changed. Above them all, near the ceiling of the cave, Edward's wings flickered, then the rivet began to glow a dull red. The Hag used the tongs to push the rivet through the metal clasp and a hole in the collar, then it grabbed the hammer and struck the rivet. A single bright spark flew away from the impact and made Faye blink.

Faye heard a familiar snuffling and a whimper. She let go of the hate and anger and leaned forward, straining past the ache in her shoulders to look at Flub. He still lay in the center of the ring of child skeletons but he had rolled over. She could no longer see his dirt-streaked face, but she could hear him crying. She pulled against the shackles, gritting her teeth against the pain. She wanted nothing more than to go to him and comfort him. He was her little brother. And he was in this bad place because of her. But the shackles held her. She was helpless.

Warm, wet tears flowed down her face as she cried. She could not stop the tears, but she refused to sob. She did not want the Hag to hear her.

"Sleep, my child," the Hag said in a whisper that hung in the air like smoke. "Sleep. It is not time yet for you to wake up and play with your brothers."

Faye yanked at the shackles, then sniffed and said, "He's not your child. He's my brother."

The Hag did not turn around. It only chuckled and went back to muttering.

Flub's whimpers continued, but he did not wake up.

Gritting her teeth, Faye settled back into the least uncomfortable position she had managed to find. She tried not to cry but the tears came again. The Hag continued to heat rivets and pound them into place, muttering all the while. Brenna hung in her cage, arms bound behind her, silent now after all the pitiful squeaking earlier. Brenna's eyes were closed as if she were asleep or unconscious. Faye wished she could cry herself to sleep.

She heard a soft rasp of metal on metal near the entrance to the cave, among the pegs and the hanging sacks of dried weeds. She saw Brenna open her eyes, then both of them looked at the peg with the key.

Brenna's rat, Norv, was back, trying again to get the key.

Faye resisted the urge to hold her breath as she watched. She did not want the Hag to notice her doing anything different. Her tears dried on her cheeks as she watched Norv struggle with the key ring. She wondered how he was going to keep it from falling this time.

When the ring reached the end of the peg, Norv let go of the ring and grabbed the peg with all four feet. Then he relaxed his grip and rolled to his right until he was hanging from the peg. He thrust his head through the key ring, then used his neck to pull the ring the rest of the way off the peg.

Faye realized she was holding her breath as Norv hung there, upside down, with the key ring around his neck. She let the breath out slowly. She wondered what he was waiting for.

The Hag brought the hammer down on another rivet.

Norv let go.

As Norv fell he twisted his body around within the key ring and grabbed for the key itself. He managed to catch the key with his front paws and pull it to his body–or his body to it–as he fell. Then both rat and key fell through the opening of a burlap sack of weeds hanging from a lower peg with only the slightest clink of metal on metal.

Faye glanced at Brenna and saw the other girl shaking her head.

Faye tried not to wish Norv would be able to get out of the sack, but the thought formed before she could stop it. The burning pain in her wrists flared and peaked. She gasped at the pain.

"Have you been wishing again, little fairy?" the Hag asked. It brought the hammer down loud, as if punctuating the question. "You don't have to wish I had your wings. You just need to give them to me."

"You can have my wings," Faye said through clenched teeth.

The Hag paused with the hammer over its head. It looked over its shoulder at Faye with one black, gleaming eye.

"Let my brother go," Faye went on, "and they're yours."

The Hag cackled then turned back to its work. "I think I will hold out for both," it said, and struck a rivet with the hammer. "And he's not your brother anymore." She struck the rivet again.

"Yes, he is."

The Hag cackled, then started muttering again.

Faye saw Brenna trying to get her attention. She followed Brenna's gaze back to the sack where Norv had fallen with the key. Norv's nose was poking out of a hole in the bottom of the sack. A hole that was getting bigger.

"Where is that pest, Edward?" the Hag asked.

Faye turned to look at the Hag and hoped it had not noticed the missing key or Norv's little pink nose.

The Spring Hag still stood by the table, but it had turned around. In its right hand it held the finished collar. Faye saw the Hag look at the hourglass on the floor next to Flub. There was very little black sand left in the top of the glass.

Faye felt the Hag staring at her and made herself look it in the eye.

"I hope you can manage that pesky boy better than I can," the Hag said. It smiled and showed black, jagged teeth. "Once I have your wings."

"Flub?" Faye asked. "I'm not going to—"

"Of course not! Your once-brother will be another of my perfect children."

Faye looked at Flub, lying there defenseless and sad. "He's still my brother." She faced the Hag again. "I wish you were *dead!*" she said, her voice getting louder with each word until the last was a raw shout that hurt her throat. The shackles burned her again, but this time the fire seemed less, as if the hate growing inside her had protected her. She hoped the hate showed in her eyes as she glared at the Hag. If her mouth was not so dry, she would have spat.

The Hag's smile grew into a huge, hungry grin. Then it threw back its head and laughed at her.

"Say it again, little fairy. I dare you."

Faye did, shouting the whole wish, and felt the hate become stronger, the burn of the shackles weaker. She began to feel weakness in the iron of the shackles, cracks that she could push against to break them.

"Good, little fairy. That's very good."

Brenna squeaked something.

"Be silent, little bat," the Hag snapped and Brenna's mouth closed with a loud, painful sound of teeth on teeth. The Hag focused on Faye again. "Give in to the hate, little fairy, give in to those wishes. Then you won't have to give me your wings. You will be my apprentice, and you will be the perfect master for that pest, Edward."

The Hag's words hit her like a blow. Faye had taken a breath to shout again, but she let it out as if she had been struck. She wanted to hate the Hag. It had taken her brother. It was going to turn her brother into another of its skeletal children. It had hurt her and taunted her. It had hurt Brenna and Lupe. Hating it was easy. Nothing had ever been so easy in Faye's eleven years of life. But she did not want to do anything it wanted her to do. She fought the urge to hate it more, to wish for its death. She pulled against the shackles to distract herself. She panted from the pain and the effort to not hate.

The Hag cackled. "So close, little fairy, so close. But there's time yet. Imagine how you'll feel when I put this collar on your brother and set him to dancing with his new brothers? Oh, just imagine. I bet you'll wish me dead then. You might even wish for that hard enough to break free and hurt me." The Hag's expression lost all semblance of mirth as it looked around the cave again, then up at the ceiling. "Where is that pest Edward? How long does it take to find a rat?" It threw the collar down on the table and strode to the entrance of the cave.

Faye froze. So did Brenna. Faye saw Norv, with the ring still around his neck, had made it as far Brenna's cage. She almost started crying again. She had hoped Norv was coming to help her. The pain was so bad–

"EDWARD!" the Hag bellowed through the tunnel to the outside. The fairy's name echoed around the cave. Flub moaned and rolled back over. The Hag drew a deep breath, then shouted again, longer and even louder this time. *"EDWARD!"*

Faye watched Norv take advantage of the Hag's shout to drag the key into Brenna's cage. He scrambled up the cloak that still hung from her neck, then up her back and out of sight.

The Hag waited, listening, for at least a minute, then turned to look at Faye. "When you're my apprentice later," it said, "I want you to think of some particularly nasty way to punish him."

Faye shook her head. She wanted to hate the Hag. She wanted it so, so much. But all she said was, "It won't happen."

The Hag shrugged. "You'll like being an apprentice better than being a slave. But it's your eternity of servitude." It went back to the table in the far corner of the cave.

Brenna squeaked something that sounded a lot like, "Oww!"

"I told you to hush, little bat," the Hag said without turning around.

Movement at the entrance to the cave drew Faye's attention. She stared at Lupe as the girl crouched in the tunnel close against one wall. Lupe's skin was scratched and her teal tanktop was so dirty that the peace sign was no longer legible. Lupe no longer had on her sandals. In her right hand, Lupe held the knife that Mrs. Lipscomb had given her. Lupe met Faye's gaze, then held a finger to her lips.

Faye pulled against the shackles, then said, "I wish–" The pain from the shackles tried to stop her, but she went on, "–someone would–save my brother–"

Lupe stared at her in response and put the finger to her lips again with more intensity this time.

"Back to that again, are we, little fairy?" the Hag asked from its corner.

Brenna squeaked in alarm, then slumped in her cage, her feet no longer bound but still confined by the narrow gibbet. She was able to get her arms from behind her in time not to land on her head. The gibbet shook on its chain but the cage did not open. Three small, heavy objects fell and landed in front of Brenna's face and bounced around on the cloak. One of the objects, a padlock, hit Brenna's cheek and she let out a squeak of pain. Faye thought she saw Norv racing up the chain toward the ceiling, but she could not be sure.

The Hag turned around. "What are you doing, little bat? How did you–?"

"Faye? Faye?" Flub's voice interrupted the Hag and pulled both its and Faye's attention from Brenna's cage. Flub had sat up in the circle of skeletons. He was rubbing his eyes. Beside Flub on the floor, the last of the black sand in the hourglass settled into the bottom half. "What's going on, Faye?" Flub asked. "Where are we? Where's Edward?"

"Run, Finn!" Faye shouted. "Run!"

The Hag's expression showed grim triumph as it moved toward Flub.

"Faye!" Flub cried out as the Hag loomed over him. He shrank back into the corner of the cave.

"Stay away from him!" Faye screamed. She heard Lupe shouting the same thing.

The Hag ignored all of them. It reached down and picked up Flub with one large hand. "It's time for you to join my family, little boy."

Faye screamed something even she did not understand and pulled against the shackles hard enough to wrench her shoulders. Lupe ran and jumped on the back of the Hag, the hand with the knife trying to reach over the humped back to its throat.

"Bad dog!" the Hag said. It held Flub with one hand while it reached with its other hand in a way no normal person could have to strike at Lupe. The clawed hand struck Lupe and the girl flew backward, striking Brenna's cage before falling to the floor. The front half of the gibbet swung open and Brenna fell out on to Lupe.

"The first step to joining my family, little boy," the Hag said, "is a sort of baptism." It shifted its grip on Flub and used both hands to push his face into the dirty water of the basin. Flub struggled and tried to shout, but the Hag held him fast. His shout was only an eruption of bubbles from the water. "What do you think of this, little fairy?" it said, twisting its face around to look at Faye. "Don't you hate me even more? Don't you wish me dead?"

The light of the cave swung back and forth.

Faye hardly noticed as she screamed again. She pulled against the shackles so hard that she felt her left shoulder pull out of socket. This was a new pain, but it did not stop her from still trying to pull free.

The light became much brighter and spun, throwing the shadows of the Hag and everything else against the walls in a circle. A light breeze smelling of old pennies and fresh cedar shavings followed the shadows around the cave.

Faye watched the Hag look up in surprise. It let go of Flub and turn around. Faye followed the Hag's gaze and saw Edward's wings glowing bright and hovering near the ceiling of the cave. The chains that had held the wings hung loose, empty. Both the light and the breeze came from the wings as they beat faster than the eye could see.

"Give those *back!*" the Hag shouted and jumped. "They are *mine!*" It moved fast and jumped higher than Faye expected for something so big and heavy. The Hag swatted at the wings midleap, but the wings swooped, leaving a trail of coppery sparkles, and the Hag's hand missed. The Hag landed with a crash against the wall by the table. If the landing hurt the Hag, it did not slow it down. It spun around. "Edward!" the Hag shouted. "Get back in here this instant!"

The Hag leaped again. The wings eluded the Hag once more, leaving it grasping at sparkles that fizzled into nothing when touched by its hand. This time Faye spotted Brenna's rat, Norv, clinging to the spine at the center of the wings, looking at the Hag with huge, scared eyes as it pulled first left, then right to avoid the Hag's hands.

Brenna squeaked something that sounded encouraging. Then she was standing in front of Faye with the iron key. Faye started crying in relief even before Brenna had the key in the first padlock.

"I can't believe you fell on me," Lupe said as she rushed past Brenna and Faye to Flub.

Behind Brenna, the Spring Hag had climbed on the table. The Hag had the hammer in one hand, swinging it at Norv and the wings.

"Edward! Edward! Those are *my* wings! Edward!"

Brenna twisted the key and the padlock popped open. The shackle became loose on Faye's wrist and she tried to pull her left hand free. Her dislocated shoulder refused to cooperate, but her hand slipped out anyway and her arm fell limp at her side as she cried out in pain. Brenna moved to the other shackle.

"Stay back!" Flub shouted from the corner of the cave. He had retreated beyond the circle of skeletons into shadows where Faye could not see him. "Stay back! Faye!"

"Come on, kid," Lupe said. Faye could see her in the circle of the skeletons, leaning forward, one hand held out toward a pool of shadows. "I'm here to save you."

226 / DAVID MICHAEL

"It's ... it's OK, Finn," Faye said, half sobbing.

Brenna put the key in the second padlock and gave it a twist.

"No!" the Spring Hag shouted as Faye pulled her right hand free. The Hag still stood on the table, glaring down at them. It pointed the hammer at Lupe. "Stop her, my children!" it said, then swung the hammer again at Norv and the wings.

Faye fell to her knees. The rush of release from the pain of the shackles overwhelmed her. She wanted to laugh but it came out as a gasping sob. She managed to grab Brenna's skirt with her right hand before she fell on her face.

"Crap!" Lupe said.

Faye heard the sounds of dried rawhide and old bones popping and rubbing against each other before she saw the first of the skeletons move.

Four of the six skeletons converged on Lupe. The other two skeletons went out of Faye's line of sight, into the corner where Flub was hiding. Lupe growled and struck with her knife but the blade only scraped against bone. She kicked at the chest of one of the skeletons. Three ribs broke from the impact and the pieces of bone flew out the back of the skeleton. Her next kick went wild as she tripped over the stone basin and dumped its contents. One skeleton managed to get its bony fingers around Lupe's left arm.

"Just get the boy and run," Lupe said. "Go. I'll hold them here."

The Spring Hag laughed, then growled as it swung at Norv and the wings again. Norv tried to bank right, but the wings brushed against the wall of the cave and flipped over. Norv hung from the wings as they spiraled down toward the ground. The Hag laughed again and jumped down from the table as Norv and the wings crashed against the cage where Brenna had been held.

Faye pulled against Brenna and tried to stand, to go help Flub. Her legs did not want to hold her up any longer. She lost her grip on Brenna and fell forward. The dirt of the cave floor was cool against her skin, with a hint of moisture, but stank of the Hag. She rolled over and looked up at Brenna.

Brenna stared at the collared skeletons with a terrified expression. She looked wound tight, as if she were about to run away. Or fall apart. The knuckles of her right had gone white from clutching the iron key. Faye knew how she felt.

"Come back here, you rat," the Hag said, reaching around the cage to get at Norv. "Give me my wings."

"Brenna," Faye said. "Help them. I wish ..."

The sound of her voice, or maybe her unfinished wish, spurred Brenna into action. Brenna still looked terrified, but she took a step forward. She held the key in front of her like a weapon.

Flub's cries preceded him as two skeletons pulled him by his arms and shoulders out of the shadows. His arms flailed and his legs kicked, but he could not stop the dragging.

Brenna whispered a series of squeaks, then squeaked again, louder. Faye could not see her face. She had no idea what the girl was trying to say.

Lupe, both of her arms and one leg held by skeletons, looked at Brenna as if she were crazy. She tried to kick against the skeleton that held her leg and stumbled.

Brenna squeaked again. This time the skeletons all stopped. The four who had grabbed Lupe let her go. Lupe fell to her hands and knees in the mud churned on the dirt floor. The other two released Flub. All of them turned to look at Brenna. No, Faye realized. They turned to look at the key.

Faye saw Lupe about to attack the skeletons again. "No, Lupe," she said. "Wait."

"No!" the Hag shouted. It had picked up the gibbet in its left hand and was reaching into a cranny in the wall. It withdrew its hand as it turned around. "They're my children. Mine!" It rushed at Brenna.

Faye lunged forward on her belly and reached with her right hand, trying to trip the Hag. She missed.

Lupe scrambled between the skeletons, readied her knife, and leaped. Faye watched as the girl leaped past Brenna and collided with the Spring Hag. Hag and girl crashed together then rolled across the dirt floor in a snarl of growls and grunts. Lupe snapped with her teeth and tried to bring her knife to bear, but the Hag held her off.

When Faye looked back, she saw Flub crawling into the corner shadows again.

One of the skeletons, its bones the color of polished ivory, its rawhide straps black and falling apart with extreme age, stepped forward. Brenna took a deep breath and stepped up to meet the skeleton. She had to stoop to fit the key into the rusty lock. She could not turn the key, though. Not even with both hands.

Brenna made a frustrated squeak. She stopped when the skeleton grabbed her hands. Brenna let go of the key and stepped back.

The skeleton gripped the key. The squeal of rusted metal hurt Faye's ears and caused Lupe and the Hag to stop and stare as the padlock opened, then fell off the collar and clanked on the floor. The iron key fell out of the padlock.

"No!" screamed the Hag. It managed to push Lupe off and tried to stand. Lupe caught its legs from behind and it fell down again. The Hag grabbed at the dirt floor with both hands and started to pull itself forward.

Faye did the same thing, pulling herself forward with her good hand, trying to reach the Hag and help Lupe hold it back.

Brenna stooped to pick up the key, but one of the other skeletons grabbed it first. The skeleton did not straighten before it had the key in the padlock and twisted it with another painful, high-pitched protest of rusty metal.

The first skeleton pulled apart the metal clasps of its collars as the padlock fell off the second. Then a third skeleton picked up the key as the second removed its collar.

The first skeleton fell apart with the sound of breaking twigs.

The Hag shrieked and pulled free of Lupe.

"Brenna!" Lupe called out.

Brenna dropped to the floor of the cave, arms covering her head. The Hag ignored Brenna, reaching for the bones of the first skeleton.

"My son!" it sobbed. "My son! Stop this! Stop this, all of you!" The second skeleton fell apart just as the Hag's hands grabbed it. The third skeleton had already removed its padlock and the fourth had picked up the key. "STOP!"

The Hag's voice had become more shrill. The Hag looked smaller now. Much smaller. As Faye watched, as the third skeleton fell apart, the Hag diminished in size.

Lupe grabbed the Hag from behind and pulled her back. Both of them tripped over Brenna who was still curled on the floor. Brenna squeaked in protest as Lupe shouted, "Crap!"

Faye pushed herself to her hand and knees, and from there to her feet. She managed to get past Brenna and Lupe and the still struggling Hag, past the skeletons as the fourth one went to pieces and the sixth one, the one with the faded baseball cap, put the key into the lock on its collar.

"Faye," Flub whimpered as she collapsed beside him. She could only get one arm around him, but he got both of his around her and buried his face in her neck. Whatever he said next she had no idea, as he was sobbing and talking at the same time.

"It's OK," she said. "It's OK."

He pulled his face back and looked up at her. Muddy tears streaked his cheeks. "You came back for me."

"Of course, you moron. You're my brother."

He shook his head. "No I'm not. You wished–"

Faye let out a frustrated sigh. "Fine. I wish–" A sob stopped her throat. She swallowed it and went on. "I wish you were my brother, Finn Reilly Woods." Then she hugged him to her as tight as she could with just one arm.

In front of her, the last of the skeletons fell apart. The padlock with the key, the opened collar, the shredded strips of rawhide, the bones, and the baseball cap fell one after the other into the mud as the terrifying face of the Spring Hag became that of a grief-stricken old woman.

The Hag was no longer huge. It now appeared to be nothing more than an old woman. Her skin was darker than Lupe's, and mottled and wrinkled. One eye was swollen closed. The other was open, showing yellow where the whites should be and black irises. It fixed its eye on Faye. The grief in the ancient face morphed into fury and the Hag again tried to pull itself forward. Lupe held it back with no visible effort.

Lupe continued to hold the Hag as she got to her feet, then flung the wizened body away from her, toward the table. When the Hag only curled up on the floor, pulling its arms and legs up to its body and did not seem about to attack again, Lupe moved to help Brenna. Brenna squeaked something that Faye could not understand.

The cave wall behind Faye shifted and the ground shook. The sound of water bubbling over rocks followed the shaking.

"What was that?" Lupe asked.

Over by the table, the Hag wheezed then cackled.

The cave wall shifted again and cold water drenched Faye

from behind.

The Hag's cackled became a retching cough. "You wished me ... dead ... little fairy," it managed to say between hacks. "You will die with me."

The ground shook. A piece of the ceiling fell free and smashed onto the mud and bones in front of Faye. Cold, brown water flowed over and around her from behind.

"Let's get out of here!" Lupe shouted. She pushed Brenna in the direction of the exit tunnel, then came to help Faye and Flub. She held one arm over her head, and reached with the other.

"Take Flub," Faye said. "I'll follow you." She tried to push Flub one-handed, but he did not let go of her. He held on tighter.

Lupe bent over got her free around Faye's shoulders. "Come on," she yelled in Faye's ear. "Stand up!"

With Lupe's help, and the sudden increase in the pressure of the water against her back, Faye managed to stand. The water pushed against both her and Lupe as they stumbled through the cave and to the exit tunnel. The ground shook and the walls moved. Faye would have fallen under the weight of Flub and the uncertain footing, but Lupe held her up. As she regained her balance, Faye saw strips of rawhide floating on the water, then the ballcap, spinning in the current.

The Spring Hag was still laughing as they made it out of the tunnel. Brenna was there, and she helped pull Faye and Flub clear as the ground shook once more. Just above Brenna, Norv hovered and lit the darkness with Edward's wings.

Behind them, the rock hill cracked and fell together. Then there was a whoosh and a roar as brown water erupted from the remains of the tunnel and through the new cracks and poured into the pond.

~ 21 ~
FAYE
AFTER MIDNIGHT

FAYE WATCHED AS the rush and roar of the water receded to a gentle stream and the brown color became a blue-black under the stars. The smell of the water improved too, but did little to counter the stench of rotten mud that arose from the refilling pond. Faye managed a chuckle as Lupe held her nose.

Suddenly she felt very tired, and Flub seemed to weigh a ton. "Finn," she said, "Finn. You need to get down." Her legs gave out slowly, at least, so she did not collapse. And Brenna and Lupe helped too. Flub still did not want to let go. She whispered in his ear until he finally released her and moved to sit next to her, his knees pulled up his chest.

Her left arm still hung useless. She tested moving her fingers, and they seemed to work, if with a lot of pain. "I need a sling for my arm. Or something."

"Lie down," Lupe said. "I can do this."

"Do what?" Faye asked.

"Just lie down," Lupe said. "On your back."

"How about I just wish–?"

"No!" Lupe said. "I can do this."

Brenna squeaked something.

"Can I at least wish Brenna could talk again?" Faye asked.

"There is no need," said Edward. He stood away from the girls, just outside a vine-covered mound. He held a clay pot.

Lupe growled and Brenna squeaked. Flub caught his breath.

"What are you doing here?" Faye asked.

"Here," Edward said, and put the pot down. "It's her words." He nodded at Brenna. "I am sorry."

"He must be sorry," Faye said. "He's not rhyming."

Edward turned his face away and said nothing.

Brenna picked up the pot. She squeaked a question, then rolled her eyes and shook her head. She held up the pot to her face and sniffed it. She scowled and said, "Whoa. Is that what my breath smells–?" She stopped. She looked at Faye and Lupe. "I talked. I can talk!" She shook the clay pot over her head, causing her cloak to billow in the breeze.

"Great," Lupe muttered. "I was just getting to like the squeaking." She pushed against Faye's right shoulder. "You need to lie back. And you need to relax."

Faye lay back and looked up at the black disk of the new Moon right above her. Norv still hovered over them with Edward's wings humming. The light from the wings, though, did not obscure the clouds, even as it lit the area around her and the girls. She gasped as Lupe started kneading the muscles of her left shoulder.

"Sorry," Lupe said. "This is going to hurt. You need to relax."

"How," Faye asked, trying to ignore the pain, "are we ... going to get ... back–Oww!"

"Sorry. I can retrace our steps–"

"No," said Brenna, interrupting Lupe. She shook her head. Her face looked pale. "No no no. I'm not walking through the cemetery again."

"But we already ... paid the trolls," Faye said. "The bridge won't be ... a problem."

"It's not the bridge," Brenna said. "It's ... no. We can't go back that way. Not tonight."

"You do not have to," Edward said. "You can fly."

"How?" Brenna asked. "I don't have wings."

"What kind of bat would be that without wings?" Edward asked.

"You mean the cloak?" When Brenna held her arms wide, spreading the cloak, Faye thought they did look like wings.

Edward nodded.

"It did look like you flew before," Faye said. "Back by the bridge."

"You were flapping your wings like a chicken," Lupe added. "But it seemed to be working." She lifted Faye's arm, keeping the elbow straight. "This is probably going to hurt," she said to Faye. "Unless it doesn't work."

"Hey!" Faye said, then, "Oww!" She felt her shoulder slip back into place. The muscles, the bones, everything still hurt, but she was able to jerk her arm out of Lupe's grasp. She sat up and rubbed her shoulder with her right hand. "What do you mean? 'Unless it doesn't work'?"

Lupe shrugged. "Sometimes it works better than others. My brother, Steven, has dislocated his shoulder a few times. It gets easier, by the way, the more you do that."

"I don't want to do that ever again."

"How do I fly?" Brenna asked.

"Jump and flap your arms," Lupe said.

Flub laughed.

"It is good to hear you laugh again, Finn Reilly Woods," Edward said.

"You don't get to talk to him," Faye said, standing. She

ignored Brenna leaping into the air. She leaned over Edward, who seemed to shrink away from her. He did not look away, though. She took a breath to start yelling at him. Blaming him. But she just let the breath out in a sigh.

"Wow," Lupe said. "OK. I guess you don't need to flap your arms."

Faye looked up and saw Brenna hovering in the air, her arms stretched out but not flapping. As she watched, Brenna moved her right hand and rotated to the right. Then she moved her left hand and rotated to the left. Brenna was smiling, then laughing. Norv fluttered over to Brenna and flew around her, surrounding her in shiny, copper glitter trails.

Faye shook her head. "And all I got was a leather pouch. And that ripped."

"Oh, yeah," Lupe said. "I got your wand back." She held out the holly branch.

Faye took the branch. The three sprigs of holly leaves still looked fresh.

"Faye Ellen Woods," Edward said, pulling her attention back to the fairy. "Did you mean it? What you said? What you wished?"

Faye nodded. "Yes—"

"You do not have to, Faye Ellen Woods. You defeated the Spring Hag, who had me bound. Edward Pennyfeathers can be yours to command."

"You mean we could have our own fairy?" Lupe asked.

"What did he say?" Brenna asked. "I still can't understand him."

"Hush," Faye said, meaning all of them. "Yes, Edward Pennyfeather, I wish you had your wings back." She twisted her wrist around and gave the wand a flick, like a fairy godmother.

Norv squeaked as the wings disappeared from under him. Brenna spun and caught him with both hands.

The wings appeared to sprout from Edward's back. They shone bright with the yellow-green light of the sparkles. Edward spun around, twisting his neck to see. Faye laughed because he looked like a puppy chasing its tail.

"Thank you, Faye Ellen Woods!" Suddenly Edward was a full-sized man. He picked her up with his hands on her waist and kissed her on the cheek before she react. She was still trying to react–and trying not to blush–when he was two feet tall again and shooting into the air like a winged comet. "A new Moon is a good Moon, Faye Ellen Woods. I am in your debt," he added, coming back to hover near her face. "You know my name. If Edward Pennyfeather can aid you, all you need to do is face the sunrise and say my name."

"Great," Lupe said. "Faye gets to fly too?"

"You're flying, Few!" Flub shouted. "You have wings like Edward's. And you're flying!"

Faye looked down and realized that she floated in the air where the oversized Edward had let go of her, about a foot off the dirt. Then she felt the thrumming in her back, between her shoulder blades, and heard a low humming. She looked over right shoulder and saw her wings for the first time. She could not see them clearly. They were like a hummingbird's wings, or a dragonfly's, moving too fast to be seen.

Edward laughed his tinkling laugh and shot straight up into the night sky. He left a sparkling trail as he went, connecting the Earth to the new Moon above them. Then he shot to the east, in the direction of the sunrise, and disappeared into the distance.

"Can I fly, Few? Can I? Wait for me!"

Faye looked down and saw that she had risen farther while

watching Edward. Her muddy tennis shoes were as high as Lupe's head now. Flub was standing almost directly under her. He jumped and caught her right foot.

"Wait!" she said, startled. She pulled–somehow–against his weight as he started to bear her down.

"I'm flying, Few! I'm flying!" Flub swung from her leg like a pendulum.

Brenna swooped around them in the dark, looking less like a bat, Faye thought, than a huge raven. "Isn't this wonderful?" Brenna asked in her fly-by. Faye heard Norv squeaking.

"I said wait. Hang on, Finn." Faye tried to think how they would get back down. She did not want Flub to fall. The thought was the descent.

"Ah, Few," Flub said as his feet touched the ground again. "It was just getting fun." He let go of her foot as she kept coming down until her own feet were on the ground.

"OK, so you can carry him," Lupe said. "Brenna! Get back down here and see if you can carry me."

"Can you fly with me on your back?" Flub asked and jumped on Faye's back.

"Oww!" Faye said. "Fudge, Flub. My shoulder– Get down!"

~ ~ ~

Faye flew carrying Flub in front of her, her arms wrapped around him, his arms flailing about as if he were on a carnival ride at the state fair, screaming happily in her ear. Brenna held Lupe's left hand as the two of them soared along beside Faye and Flub. Lupe's expression alternated between terror and delight as they flew.

Faye could not help but wonder when she was going to wake from this dream.

The Other Side was dark below them, but they could make out the gray glow of the cemetery and the clear space that was North Park Other. Their landings in the tall grass of the park were far less graceful than their flights had been. Brenna and Lupe rolled free of each other as Faye stumbled under the renewed weight of Flub.

"Again!" Flub shouted, laughing. "Again! We have to do that again!"

"Not tonight," Faye said. "We need to get home."

"I can't believe you dropped me," Lupe said, standing. She offered her hand to Brenna.

"I didn't drop you," Brenna said, taking the offered hand. She pulled herself to her feet, then brushed off the cloak. "You let go." She turned to Faye. "You go first," she said, "with Finn."

Lupe nodded. "We'll guard your back."

"Will your wings fit?" Flub asked. "Oh, they're gone."

"No, they're not gone," Faye said. She could feel them. "Come on, Finn."

Faye went first, doing a three-legged crawl because her left shoulder still did not want to take any weight.

The dark, quiet night of North Park Other fell away behind her as she came out of the hole in the fence. It was still dark in Spring Hollow, darker than when they had left, but the darkness felt different. There were fewer stars in the sky. The smells of road construction assaulted her nose as the distant sounds of traffic grated against her ears. She stood.

She found herself rubbing her wrists, first her left wrist, then her right, as Flub came through the hole. The memory of the pain from the shackles was still there even if she could not feel any scratches or scarring.

Brenna came through, then Lupe.

Faye heard someone walking slowly toward them. She

turned and saw Mrs. Lipscomb picking her way around the debris of the holly bushes. The old woman carried a basket on her left arm.

"So this is the little boy," Mrs. Lipscomb said. "I'm so happy to see you, young man. I'm so happy to see all of you. A bit scuffed, are we?"

Flub moved to stand behind Faye, his arms around her waist. He peeked out at Mrs. Lipscomb.

"Here's your knife back," Lupe said, holding out the knife hilt first.

Brenna unfastened the cloak from around her neck and took it off her shoulders with a flourish. "And here's your cloak."

"Sorry about the pouch," Faye said.

Mrs. Lipscomb smiled but made no move to take either the knife or the cloak. "At least you found your wand, dear, that's much better than the pouch." She stepped through the girls to the hole in the fence. "If you want, though, I can make you a new one. I made that one for Tink. No, you keep the cloak, Brenna, dear, and you keep the knife, Lupe." She put the basket down on the ground. "I suspect you'll be able to make more use of them than I will."

"What?" Faye asked.

Mrs. Lipscomb bent over and took a spool of ribbon out of the basket. She started humming as she pulled out a length of ribbon.

"I want to go home," Flub said, pulling on Faye.

"I guess I should go home with you," Lupe said to Brenna. "That's where I said I was spending the night."

"My mom's probably left a hundred messages on my phone," Brenna said.

"Mmm-hmm," Mrs. Lipscomb said as she paused in her work. She took a small purse out of the basket and handed it to

Brenna. "Your phone's been chirping in your purse on my coffee table." A chime sounded in the purse as Brenna took it. "Just like that."

"I better call her," Brenna said. "She's probably freaking out."

"No, wait," Faye said. She was grounded. She had no idea what she would tell Mom and Dad in the morning. But she did not want to be alone. Not tonight. "Brenna, Lupe, just come up to my room. You can call from there. We'll figure out what to tell my parents–all of our parents–in the morning. Maybe we'll get up early enough to sort everything out."

"Get up?" asked Brenna. "I'm not ... I'm not going to be able to sleep tonight."

"Me either," Lupe said.

"Then come on over. We can all not sleep on my balcony."

Mrs. Lipscomb straightened and made a satisfied noise. "That should hold this time," she said. She looked at Faye. "Assuming no one cuts it loose ... ?"

"It won't be me," Faye said.

"You never know," Mrs. Lipscomb said. "Good night, girls, and you too, young man." She picked up her basket and walked away.

Faye watched the old woman walk away, then said, "Come on, Flub."

Brenna called her mom while she and Lupe and Faye and Flub crossed the street to Hawk Briar. Faye let them in. She paused to look in the living room. Mom and Dad still slept on the loveseat. An infomercial was playing on the TV.

"Should we wake them up?" Flub asked.

"No," Faye said. She went to the TV and turned it off. "Let them sleep."

"Can I sleep in your room tonight?" Flub asked.

"No–" Faye started, then stopped. "OK. But just for tonight. You can sleep on the floor."

Lupe and Brenna waited for them at the bottom of the stairs. "You know what I wish?" Lupe said as she followed Faye and Brenna up the stairs. "I wish I had brought a change of clothes."

"Me too," Brenna said.

Faye managed a tight smile and twirled the wand in her fingers. "I'll see what I can do."

THE END

of

New Fairy Moon

About the Author

Most days, David Michael is a software developer and a writer. Some days, he's a writer and a software developer. Other days, he's an amateur photographer. Because, really, who is the same person *every day?*

David lives with his wife and kids in Tulsa, Oklahoma.

David blogs about writing at Guns & Magic: **www.gunsandmagic.com**

About the Cover

Cover painting, *New Fairy Moon*, by Don Michael, Jr., inspired by an original image by Serene Michael.

See more of Don's artwork on his Web page: **www.donmichaeljr.com**

"Lupe, Faye, Brenna & Norv" by Serene Michael.

DavidRM Software's The Journal
http://www.davidrm.com/thejournal/

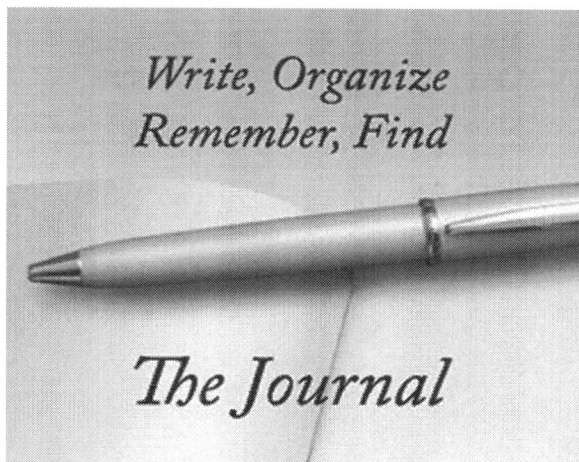

Keep a journal on your computer!
Whatever your journaling or writing needs, The Journal gives you unmatched convenience, flexibility, and security. The Journal is always available when you need it, and lets you make entries with text, images, and just about anything else.

DavidRM Software's The Journal
http://www.davidrm.com/thejournal/

Special Discount! Enter this coupon code on The Journal's Web page to receive 20% off the list price:

TJFictionCoupon

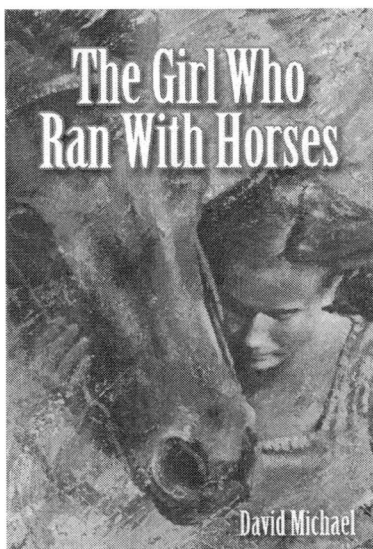

12641552R00144

Made in the USA
Charleston, SC
18 May 2012